Dr. Theophrastus Campl[...] with his twin brother, bu[...] for obscure languages [...] University students to conjugate Latin. Everything in his world is just as it should be; restrained, understated, boring. He would give anything to break away. In all his daydreams of adventure, Theo never expected it to arrive in the form of an outrageously attractive Outlier covered in intriguing tattoos. And Theo never thought the price he might pay for adventure would be his own freedom.

Captain Park Jun-Seo leads a dangerous life, running a Crew of misfits through Restricted space as he desperately searches for the key to completing his parents' work. Work that could mean the difference between life and death for countless others. In all of his frantic searching, Jun never expected to find the key in the form of a beautiful professor with more brilliance than good sense. And he never thought the price he might pay for knowledge would be his own heart.

Stoic Jun and irrepressible Theo must work together to break the code before their time is up. Falling into bed together is effortless, but their growing connection wasn't in the plan. Theo charms his way beneath Jun's skin with every nonsensical move he makes. Jun must decide if he can make room in his harsh, goal-driven life for the unpredictable force of love. Theo begins their journey as a lighthearted adventure—until he cracks Jun's tough facade to reveal the hero within. Theo must decide if he can risk his battered heart when Jun is risking everything.

In the lawless depths of space, can two captive hearts set each other free?

CAPTIVATED

The Verge, Book Two

A.C. Thomas

A NineStar Press Publication

www.ninestarpress.com

Captivated

© 2021 A.C. Thomas
Cover Art © 2021 Natasha Snow
Edited by Elizabetta McKay

This is a work of fiction. Names, characters, places, and incidents are either the product of the author's imagination or are used fictitiously. Any resemblance to actual persons living or dead, business establishments, events, or locales is entirely coincidental.

All rights reserved. No part of this publication may be reproduced in any material form, whether by printing, photocopying, scanning or otherwise without the written permission of the publisher. To request permission and all other inquiries, contact NineStar Press at the physical or web addresses above or at Contact@ninestarpress.com.

Printed in the USA

ISBN: 978-1-64890-267-3

First Edition, April, 2021

Also available in eBook, ISBN: 978-1-64890-266-6

CONTENT WARNING:

This book contains sexually explicit content, which is only suitable for mature readers. Warnings for abduction of a main character, discussion of sex trafficking.

*For my friends, who bring light into my life.
Enjoy the filth.*

Chapter One

Ding. Ding. Donk.

Theo held his index finger up at the uneven chime of the ancient bell over the door—yet another harried university student bustling into his office after hours. It was practically midnight, hardly the time to ask for an extension.

Honestly, students were the worst part of teaching. Theo didn't know why he had taken the TA position in the first place.

Okay, yes, he did. But, to be fair, Professor Gladwell looked amazing in his spectacles and fitted waistcoats, and who could blame Theo for going a little glassy-eyed whenever they had private meetings?

Well, Professor Gladwell's wife, for one, probably.

Theo finished his note and dropped his pen into the onyx holder on his desk, preparing to give the student his full attention.

Some of his attention.

Whatever was left over while Theo drifted off on thoughts of the strain Professor Gladwell's buttons were under on a daily basis as they tried to contain all that athleticism. Those poor, poor buttons.

He lifted his head with the bored expectation of finding another skinny, pasty academic struggling to hold armfuls of paper with desperation written all over their ink-smudged face.

In other words, someone like Theo.

This person was holding a sheaf of papers, and there the resemblance ended to every expectation Theo had.

Perhaps it was time to expand his expectations.

"I'm looking for Dr. Campbell." The stranger's voice curled around Theo's ears like smoke.

Theo smiled up at him, admiring the way the lamplight glinted off of his black hair and deep bronze skin. Stars, but he was a handsome specimen.

With a flip of his hair back over his shoulder, Theo marked his place in his notebook by closing a finger in the pages. "Well, you're certainly in the right place for it! Though I suppose that depends on which Dr. Campbell you are looking for. There are three of us in my immediate family alone. Although, Campbell isn't a terribly uncommon name, so there could easily be many more Dr. Campbells that I'm entirely unaware of."

The stranger looked like he very much regretted initiating this conversation. Theo was, unfortunately, familiar with the expression being directed his way.

The stranger shook his head slightly, as though Theo's chatter were water in his ears. Something else Theo was extremely familiar with.

He leaned in slightly, casting a wide shadow across Theo's cluttered desk when his bulk blocked out the light beside the door. "Dr. Campbell. Where is he?"

Theo traced the impressive line of the stranger's shoulders underneath his unusual many-layered black leather coat before offering his free hand to shake. "I am

Dr. Campbell. Pleased to meet you! My brother is also Dr. Campbell, and my father is Dr. Campbell as well, though they would be less pleased to meet you. Nothing against you, personally, they just aren't terribly fond of interacting with strangers. Or people in general, to be honest. Sometimes I think they can barely tolerate me!"

The stranger winced as if he could relate to the sentiment and quietly responded, "Dr. Campbell has been described as a thin male with green eyes, red hair, and pale skin."

His deep voice sank into Theo's bones like the pleasant rumble of a hovercoach over cobblestones.

Dark, hooded eyes skipped over Theo as his visitor described each feature, as though checking off a list in his head, ignoring Theo's offered hand.

Theo dropped it to the desk with a shrug; the slight couldn't hamper his enjoyment of this diversion from his research. "I'm afraid that doesn't narrow it down even the slightest bit. My brother and I are identical twins, and we definitely favor our father, to the eternal dismay of our poor mother. My dismay as well, to be honest. It would have been ever so nice to have her chestnut hair rather than this glaring beacon I've got atop my head. I tend to stick out like a redheaded thumb."

The stranger sucked in a breath through clenched teeth, square jaw held tight as his broad shoulders rose and fell in a long, measured sigh.

Theo felt like sighing himself at the sight. The man really was uncommonly beautiful.

He could happily watch those shoulders move for hours. He even had some suggestions regarding the nature of the movement.

His attention was brought to the desk when the stranger slapped a battered manuscript on top of his notebook—an older heatbound copy, of all things. The stranger's fingers were marked with ink, tattooed on the metacarpals between each knuckle with Hangul letters in beautiful calligraphy. Theo had never seen the like.

The stranger put pressure on the hand he held splayed across the document, pinching the finger Theo had left inside his notebook. He yanked it out hastily as the stranger growled at him. "*This* Dr. Campbell."

Absently shaking his pinched finger, Theo scanned the manuscript. The simulated parchment was stained and rumpled. It appeared to have been dog-eared at the corners over and over again, and the pages bristled with assorted tabs. All signs of a book well loved.

He tried to read the cover page, lifting the stranger's long fingers distractedly with his thumb and forefinger until he was hit by a jolt of recognition, filled to the brim with unexpected delight. "Wherever did you get this? I wrote this years ago during my graduate studies! I'm honestly surprised that anyone outside my thesis committee has even read it. It's such an obscure topic, after all. I had the most terrible time just—"

The stranger's palm slammed back down on top of the document, missing Theo's hand by a hair. "You are this Dr. Campbell?"

It appeared as though he already knew the answer and was dreading it as he squinted dubiously in Theo's direction. There was a slight tremble in the man's fingers as they pressed hard against the sheaf of papers.

The stranger's eyes remained shadowed by his strong brow, but his gaze washed over Theo—a wave of heat, laser-focused and far more intense than the conversation warranted.

A frisson of caution tried to nip at Theo's mind, sounding an awful lot like his brother hissing in his ear about good sense. He shook it off the way he usually did and leaned his chin on his hand to peer up at the stranger through his lashes. "Why, yes, I am. To whom do I have the pleasure of speaking?"

The stranger lifted the manuscript, his fingers unmistakably trembling as he flipped through pages with a dry rustle of sim-parchment. He held the document open to a passage of translation Theo had featured in his study of long-dead languages and shook it rather rudely in his face. "This. You can read this?"

Theo launched into a recitation of the passage, finishing with a flourishing roll of the tongue. It was rare to find a fellow enthusiast on the topic, particularly one so pleasing to the eye. The stranger seemed unusually passionate about the subject, his breath quickening audibly as Theo rattled off the words of a people long gone.

Theo cocked his head to the side and reached for his pen as he opened his notebook. "If you have an interest in the topic, I keep one of my sources here in my office. Just there, on that shelf." He gestured off to the side where his cluttered bookcase leaned heavily against the wall for much-needed support. "It's titled *An Annotated Glossary of Dead Languages* by Dr. Fernsby."

The stranger folded his sheaf of papers into his coat and walked to the bookcase in two decisive strides. Theo took the opportunity to study him further, pen hovering above his open notebook.

Quickly skipping past a few dozen sketches of Professor Gladwell standing at his lectern, he found an empty page.

As the stranger turned to face the bookcase, Theo caught a glimpse of black ink trailing up his neck to frame his sharp jawline in an odd geometric pattern of thin parallel lines intersected with tiny circles. He attempted to sketch the tattoos onto his paper.

Even more ink snaked out of the cuffs of his coat, wrapping around his wrists and stamping all the way down to his fingers with that lovely calligraphy scribed across his knuckles. Theo wrote down the characters and translated them to Core Standard in the margins.

Honor on one hand and Valor on the other. Fascinating.

Closer examination revealed a design of clustered hexagonal shapes running up the wrist of his left hand. Theo had just begun to sketch them when the stranger turned back toward him, book clutched in his fist.

Theo had never seen anyone remotely resembling the man; nothing about him said "Core," from his sprawling ink to the look in his eye. He gave the impression of someone midway over a rickety rope bridge, unsure of every step but determined to get across.

Theo couldn't help but find his appearance a little bit dangerous as he took in his severely handsome face framed by unevenly shaved black hair, all of it underscored by the dramatic sweep of his coat.

The impression was cemented when the man tucked the book away inside his coat and pulled his hand back out with a ray gun pointed in Theo's direction.

Theo's pen dropped a blot of ink onto his notebook as the man stepped closer.

The stranger's eyes were so dark his pupils disappeared into the black of his iris. His unrelenting stare sent shivers down Theo's spine that could not be attributed entirely to fear. "Come with me. Now."

Theo chewed on his lip for a moment, considering, and then he turned the page of his notebook to jot down a short list of words.

When Theo's attention fell to his notebook, the man repeated himself at an increased volume. His vowels were clipped, initial consonants rounded, almost like a citizen of the Core world Goryeo but significantly sharper. His words had a cutting edge to them Theo had never heard before.

A heavy boot kicked Theo's desk, and the man's handsome face twisted in anger. Theo glanced down at the chunks of mud littering his carpet.

"Your accent is absolutely fascinating. I need you to repeat these words back to me, if you please."

Pen poised to take down the man's answers, Theo rattled off his list of words expectantly.

The stranger's scowl slid from his face, his eyes widening in Theo's direction in the manner people often did when he caught them off guard.

It seemed to happen fairly frequently.

"I have a gun," the man said, returning to his original volume if not his original vehemence.

Theo sighed, scribbling on his pad with a shake of his head that had his hair falling in his face. "No, no, that doesn't help at all; that would take me ages to decipher. Repeat the list, if you please."

The stranger gestured with his ray gun, raising it level with Theo's head. His fingers had finally stopped trembling.

"I have. A gun."

Theo used his pen to shove the tapered barrel of it away from his face in irritation. "No, you mustn't obscure your lips that way. I need to see the movements. Now, the list, if you please."

The stranger's face did something decidedly odd and incredibly diverting where his features couldn't seem to decide what direction they wanted to go, so they never went anywhere at all.

To Theo's absolute delight, he actually repeated the first three words on the list before giving his head an emphatic shake, gesturing with the gun once more. "I don't think you understand. This is an abduction, Dr. Campbell. You're coming with me."

Theo didn't turn away from his notebook, busily adding to his notes. He sketched out the pattern the man had shaved into his close-cropped hair on the right side: three intersecting triangles. Theo directed his answer to his notebook, pen flying across the page. "Or else you intend to shoot me, I suppose, is meant to be the implication with the gun?"

A large muscle began ticking in the stranger's clenched jaw.

"Yes," he gritted out between even, white teeth.

Theo beamed at him, tucking his hair behind his ear with an excited wriggle. "How thrilling! Just give me a moment to jot off a quick letter for my brother, and we can be off. I must say, this coincides nicely with the due date for that stack of term papers I've been putting off marking. Well done, you."

The stranger gave the aforementioned stack of papers a baffled glance as Theo turned to another page to leave a short note for his twin brother, Ari.

He was bound to be perturbed if Theo did not make it home in time for tea tomorrow after all.

Ari didn't like it when Theo diverged from their schedule, which was a constant source of conflict as Theo was appallingly bad at keeping to a schedule. The dear thing spent most of their lives nudging Theo back on track—

"Enough."

The dark snarl of the stranger's voice, crackling in the space between them like a bolt of lightning, startled Theo into dropping his pen.

The stranger tugged up a hood of soft gray material attached to his black leather coat, casting his face in shadow. He reached across Theo's desk, plucked him from his seat one-handed, and lifted him effortlessly across his desk, scattering clutter all over the floor.

One muscular arm curled around Theo's midsection, holding his back tightly against the man's firm chest.

Theo ran his hands over the corded muscle of the man's tense forearm with an appreciative hum as they started to move across the floor.

He was quite tall indeed for Theo's coltish legs to dangle midair. It made Theo want to turn and wrap those legs around his waist. It was evident he'd have no trouble supporting Theo's weight.

Altogether, an absolutely delicious thought. And here Theo had thought he was in for yet another lonely, boring Thursday night.

The stranger considered the door for a moment, then reached out with his gun hand to yank at the figured brass handle, prompting Theo into action.

"Oh, I almost forgot!"

He stomped down on his captor's boot, showering the carpet with another layer of caked-on mud and debris. The arm across his stomach tightened uncomfortably as the man hissed through his teeth.

The ray gun prodded Theo's side menacingly, but he just turned his head with an apologetic smile. "So sorry about that; I assure you it was quite necessary!"

With a noise reminiscent of a lion with a thorn in its paw, the stranger carried Theo out the door and into the cold night air.

Chapter Two

"Get in."

Theo cast a dubious eye on the heavily dented ship and attempted to back up a step until the hard edge of a gun prodding at his kidneys urged him forward.

"Hardly seems spaceworthy," he sniffed as he gingerly climbed the rust-bitten ramp into the ramshackle craft.

The stranger followed him closely. Once on board, he raised the ramp with a horrendous howl of abused hinges. A large metal door screamed shut behind them, closing them in.

The silence that immediately followed landed like a weight on Theo's chest. He strived to fill it while the stranger latched the door.

"So, effectively, I'm your prisoner."

His captor made no response as he flung his coat onto a scratched-up emergency seat bolted to the side, revealing a gray knit shirt straining to contain his shoulders beneath the black leather straps of his holster.

More tattoos decorated every inch of skin exposed, the meandering lines on his neck disappearing beneath the low collar of his shirt. Theo contemplated the possibility of following those lines to find out where they might go.

With his tongue, preferably.

The man shoved past Theo to enter the open door of the cockpit and fiddle with the flight controls.

Theo leaned against the wall in what he hoped was a fetching pose, allowing the lace at his cuff to fall away from his wrist in a move that had twice proven effective in turning a man's head. "Shouldn't you have tied me up or something by now? What if I overpower you and make a daring escape?"

This time, he received a response in the form of a skeptically raised eyebrow and what Theo personally considered to be an offensive lack of concern.

"I could do it. I assure you I have unexpected depths."

He took the silent flex of rippling back muscles as reply.

"Am I technically your prisoner if there is no prison? 'Captive' would be a more accurate descriptor, one would think."

The man inclined his head toward the battered copilot seat. "Strap in."

He waited until Theo had clumsily buckled the harness before reaching over to yank on the straps to tighten them. Theo's heart went into double time as he manipulated the straps over his hips with a firm hand.

Theo had always been partial to a firm hand.

Never before had he encountered one that was so charmingly decorated. Theo had also always been partial to calligraphy.

His captor strapped into his own seat and initiated takeoff. The ship lifted from the dock, leaned distinctly sideways, then righted itself with a wobble and fell directly back onto the dock in a worrisome shriek of metal.

A colorful and culturally diverse selection of cursing filled the cockpit as the stranger banged his fist against the dash. He then lifted the ship from the dock again, this time without the sideways lean.

There was still a significant wobble though.

Muttered cursing underscored the creaking, rattling symphony of their wobbling ascent into the darkness of space.

Theo used what he liked to consider covert techniques to observe his captor, who focused on controlling the ship with knuckles white beneath his tattoos.

The hexagonal designs on his wrists wrapped around strong forearms, also accented by the odd botanical element, which jarred against the severe geometric patterns.

One of the botanical elements draped down across the back of his Honor hand; its lush greenery, caged by wandering geometric lines, spilled from under the pushed-back cuff of his thermal knit shirt. More calligraphy kissed the nape of his neck, framed by the parallel lines snaking down below his collar.

Theo leaned closer to try to interpret the letters and earned a quelling glance. The man's lips tightened into a line of disapproval. Lips that were molded into smooth, lush curves. Theo pondered how they might feel caught delicately between his teeth.

Or indelicately, for that matter.

The stranger relaxed his grip on the controls as he peered at the projections across his screen, then let go to sit back in his chair.

Theo released his harness to tilt forward, wrists draped over his crossed knees. "What should I call you?"

The stranger kept his attention on the view screen. "My name is unimportant."

Fiendish delight curled through Theo as he lifted his hands to fuss with his cuff in a flourish. "Unimportant, is it? That's a strange name. Maybe not where you come from, but certainly where I live. Cultural naming practices are absolutely fascinating, don't you agree? It is a pleasure to meet you, Unimportant!"

The stranger slowly turned to Theo, his face stricken in a very familiar "did he just" grimace. He shook his head, brows scrunching at Theo before turning away. "No. My name is not relevant. You don't need to know it."

Theo flung his arms in the air, fingers spread as irritation won out. "Well, I can't just call you 'stranger' forever!"

The stranger considered him with growing concern, as though he was just now considering the possibility that Theo may be slightly unbalanced.

It usually didn't take people quite this long.

"You have never called me 'stranger.'"

Theo churned his hands through the air emphatically. "In my head, obviously! I need something to refer to you by, if only in my thoughts!"

The stranger's expression grew less concerned and more contemplative. "You have been thinking about me."

The problem was that when Theo blushed, it was both hideously and violently as if someone had dumped a bucket of red paint over his head and let it run down his body. He fidgeted in his seat, tucking his elbows in tightly. "Well, there isn't really anyone else here, is there? Of course I have been thinking about you! In a strictly socially acceptable, non-creepy way."

The stranger said nothing, but the way his chest rose and fell with a deep, extended breath seemed judgmental to Theo.

"I'm sorry," Theo said, "that sounded creepy. Not that I should worry about what you think of me, considering you're my abductor. If anyone is creepy here, it is clearly you."

"Park."

Theo took a deep breath of his own, thankful for the interruption as he could feel himself building up to an absolute mountain of babble. "Pardon?"

The stranger turned to the view screen, but Theo could tell he was keeping him in his peripheral. "My name. Captain Jun Park."

Straightening in his seat excitedly, Theo extended his hand once more. "Absolutely smashing to meet you, Jun! You may call me—"

Jun winced at Theo's use of his name, his body language already suffused with regret. He frowned as he interrupted Theo's introduction. "I know your name."

Theo used his extended hand to toss his hair back over his shoulder, then swirled one lock around his index finger. "Well, yes, you did come searching for Dr. Campbell, but my given name is—"

"Theophrastus."

Theo's ears perked up at the accurate, if accented, pronunciation. He tilted forward in his seat, perched at full attention. "However did you know that?"

Jun twitched his head in the direction of his coat, one shoulder lifting in a quarter of a shrug. "Your paper."

Humming thoughtfully, Theo laced his fingers together over one knee as he swung his foot. "Of course. I had quite forgotten you were a fellow linguistics enthusiast. I only use my full name on academic documents. My friends call me Theo. Well, perhaps 'friends' is an overstatement. My associates and Ari call me Theo anyway."

Theo firmly stomped down on the familiar prick of pain at the reminder that he had no one but his brother to call a friend. People didn't tend to spend time with Theo on purpose, not for any length of it anyway.

No point in dwelling on such dreary matters. Every day a new opportunity. One never knew when a handsome stranger might carry one off into the sunset, after all. The fact that there had been no sunset and, instead, a depressing fog did nothing to dim Theo's delight with the possibilities.

"I really must insist that you call me Theo rather than trying to muddle through Theophrastus." Theo slanted a sly glance up through his eyelashes. "I've been told I'm quite a mouthful."

Jun made an odd choking noise, face drifting out of his frown for a few stunned, glorious seconds.

Now, that was fascinating. Theo needed to see more of that.

Jun released the controls to run a hand through the longer strip of hair on the top of his head, gripping it by the roots as he turned a glare on Theo. "Do you ever stop talking?"

Theo considered this, head tilted to the side as his foot continued to swing. "Generally, no. Not unless my mouth is otherwise occupied."

Jun's gaze fell to his lips at that before darting away to the view screen.

A blush crept up Theo's neck to settle warm against his cheeks as he scrambled to elaborate. "With food, I meant. Or something similarly innocuous. Although I suppose the same could be true of more inappropriate applications. In fact, there was one incident during my final year of undergraduate studies where a particular companion of mine made ingenious use of a—"

He cut off as he finally heard himself, snapping his mouth shut in the face of Jun's naked fascination. The man observed him exactly as one would a carriage accident in progress, with a potent mixture of horror and rapt attention.

Theo cleared his throat, his fingers busy with picking imaginary dust off the knee of his trousers. "My apologies. I do tend to chatter when I am nervous. This is my first abduction, you see. Not that one tends to experience multiple abductions, in the general course of things. Though I suppose this is very much out of the general course of things. I've certainly never met someone like you before, and—"

Theo dropped wide eyes to the tattooed hand covering his mouth. Jun's calloused palm rasped against the sensitive skin of his lips.

It was decidedly not unpleasant.

Jun's quiet voice boomed in the silent cockpit, his face sharp with warning. "I will gag you if you will not. Cease. Speaking."

Theo's eyes attempted to go even wider but met their limit. Jun removed his hand with a fleeting glance at Theo's lips and curled it into a fist by his side as he settled back into his chair.

Theo sucked in a noisy breath, lips tilting up with shocked glee. "Will you really? Goodness, I've read some rather fascinating stories where that happens, to various effect. Some much more pleasant than others. Though I suppose this isn't that kind of story."

Theo got the distinct impression that if Jun had been a cat, he would have hissed.

A strobing light brought Theo's attention to the dash, half again as big and twice as complicated as the one on his and Ari's little ship.

A clear dome with an open padlock covered a large red button just left of center. Theo stood, moved toward it, and lifted the dome. "What does this button do? It's ever so tantalizing, isn't it, under the little cloche? Shall I press it?"

Jun leapt from his seat and wrapped his hands around both of Theo's wrists. "No! Sit down. Touch nothing."

Huffing, Theo blew his hair out of his face. "What a nonsensical request. I can hardly 'touch nothing,' can I? For instance, my boots are touching the floor as we speak. Were I to sit in the chair, my derrière would be touching the seat. And, just now—" He turned his hand to brush against the bony protuberance of Jun's wrist. "—I am touching you."

Jun let go of him as though burned, eyes narrowed to dark, angry slits. His voice dipped into a lower register, sending lovely shivers down Theo's spine. "Sit down and shut up."

Theo cocked his head to the side and lazily stretched his arm out to hit one of the buttons on the dash.

Chapter Three

The tape was unexpected.

Theo had always pictured rope when he imagined this particular scenario. And considerably less in the way of clothing.

He pulled against the tape binding his arms to the chair, twisting his wrist in a thoughtless effort to fidget.

Sitting still and being quiet were not amongst Theo's strengths. Or even amongst his capabilities, to be brutally honest about the matter.

Jun's lips twitched as Theo jerked against the tape again. A shadow of a smile crossed his face like an errant cloud.

Well, at least one of them was enjoying themselves.

Theo kicked his feet against the base of his chair, delighting as Jun's shoulders tensed at the noise. He kicked harder. "It might interest you to know"—he raised his voice to be heard over the boisterous clank of his spats hitting the dented metal—"that while you are certainly not the first to threaten to adhere me to my chair, you are the first to actually follow through."

Jun smirked, just a little, the lines beside his mouth deepening on one side with a glint of amusement. He said nothing in response, only continued to adjust the flight controls by tiny increments. Theo could not help but notice it did nothing to correct the wobble.

Theo shook a tangled lock of hair out of his eyes and tugged his wrists against the tape with the compulsion to tuck it behind his ear. "Oddly enough, most people grow irritated with me in a surprisingly short amount of time."

"I find that difficult to believe," Jun muttered.

Theo sparked with joy, biting his lip against a happy curve. While he was fully capable and willing to carry the entire weight of a conversation, he derived much more satisfaction from eliciting a response. "Right? I think the problem is that people are never open to experiencing refreshing—"

Jun cut him off with a scowl as he swiveled his seat to grace Theo with the full-frontal view of his tightly crossed arms, which caused the thin leather straps of his holster to cut into the muscle of his shoulders.

The open vee of his worn-thin shirt fell away to one side, revealing the tantalizing curve of his strong chest and a continuation of the designs flowing down his neck.

Theo had to drag his gaze away to focus on his face as Jun spoke.

"No. I find it difficult to believe"—his deep voice rumbled through Theo until he felt as wobbly as the ship—"that there is any amount of time in which people do not find you irritating."

Theo deflated, sagging back into his chair. His feet shuffled to an awkward stop against the floor. "Oh."

The lock of hair fell back into his eyes, but Theo couldn't muster up the will to blow it away again. He tucked his chin to study the bony knobs of his knees outlined by the fine brown velvet of his trousers.

Yet another social interaction up in flames due to his inability to be quiet. Why had he ever thought Jun might be willing to put up with him?

There was something about the thrill of being wanted, the idea that this unknown, handsome man had actually sought out Theo of his own volition. It made Theo lose his already tenuous grip on good sense.

He tossed his head halfheartedly, the lock of hair stubbornly clinging to the crest of his cheek beneath his left eye. Theo sighed and closed his eyes in defeat, hands falling limp in their binding.

The unexpected brush of tattooed fingers across his forehead sang through his senses like an aria, the lock of hair tucked neatly behind his ear.

He peeked up at Jun to find him determinedly turned away, profile blank as his hand lowered back to his crossed arms and folded tightly beneath as if to keep it in place.

Theo couldn't contain his smile; a happy glow started across his forehead and ran down his body like warm water. He leaned closer, the new angle bending his wrists uncomfortably. "I don't suppose it would make a difference if I asked you nicely to let me go?"

Jun swiveled farther away, arms still crossed as he pondered the dash as though it had recently punched him in the face.

Theo marveled at Jun's ability to sit in silence as the minutes ticked away—until Theo's fidgeting began to grow necessary. He cleared his throat, noticing Jun's jaw clench while he refused to acknowledge him.

Theo jiggled his legs, pressing his knees together tightly. There was a screw loose somewhere in his seat that rattled with the movement. Jun's eyes shot over to him, face forbidding.

Theo jiggled more insistently. "Presuming that you intend to keep me captive for any significant amount of time, is there any way you could release the tape? I have a need of the facilities, and I'm afraid matters may grow somewhat urgent in the very near future."

Theo turned his attention to the tangled mess of exposed wiring hanging out of an open panel just above the floor. "The last thing you want is a flood in the cockpit."

Jun's gaze dropped to his crotch for a split second, then moved on to the tape with a thoughtful frown.

Theo was thankful the urgency of his full bladder prevented any noticeable movement in the area. Any further attention from Jun was likely to have resulted in an uprising in the lower ranks, if one wanted to be coy about it. "In your own time, of course, but quite quickly please."

Jun didn't move except to swivel his chair once more, scrutinizing Theo closely. Theo tried to convey his urgency, to glorious success if the alarmed expression on Jun's face was anything to go by.

As he reached into his trouser pocket, Jun lifted his hips in order to fit his hand inside the tight fabric. Theo's teeth caught his lower lip at the motion, holding back a sound that would have been, at best, unfortunate.

Jun retrieved a knife and flicked it open in a practiced motion that had Theo's blood racing for all the wrong reasons. That really should not have been as attractive as it was.

He stood and approached Theo's chair, knife held out at his side as if Theo might yet break the bindings and lunge for it. Theo found his caution surprisingly flattering.

Jun stopped in front of his chair, knife at the ready. "If I remove the tape, will you stop pressing buttons?"

Reluctant to prevaricate, Theo seesawed his head. He tried to make his eyes as big and pleading as possible, holding them open to achieve a watery effect.

Jun sighed, his free hand pinching the low bridge of his nose in a move Theo had watched his brother perform countless times. And his father. And his academic advisor. And his housekeeper, come to think of it.

"Will you promise not to press random buttons that might kill us?"

Theo nodded in what he hoped was a trustworthy manner as Jun squinted at him doubtfully. "I promise to do my level best." The button hadn't even done anything particularly interesting, as far as he could tell. Not so much as an activated light on the dash.

Jun's reaction had been more interesting by far. It had been worth pushing any number of buttons just to have his undivided attention.

Jun appeared to hold little faith in Theo's best efforts, huffing out a muttered curse as he braced Theo's wrist, knife still held away from them.

He went still, eyes locking on Theo's. "If I tell you not to do something"—his voice low with command—"you will listen. I am the captain, and my orders must be obeyed."

Oh.

Well, that was interesting. Theo was learning something new about himself every day. Today, he learned that all it took was a commanding voice and a pair of beautiful dark eyes, and his internal organs could be rendered entirely liquid.

Fascinating, if inconvenient.

Jun didn't move, unblinkingly trained on Theo's face as he struggled to nod, having somehow lost all control of his neck muscles.

With his finger hooked under the binding, keeping it between the blade and Theo's skin, Jun cut through the thick utility tape.

The other wrist took even less time. Theo worked it free and shook the feeling of idleness from his fingers while Jun tore the remaining tape from the arms of the chair. Strips of plastic upholstery came off with the tape, the damage merely adding to the patina of wear along the uneven surface.

Theo examined his jacket cuff to find that the tape had marred the velvet, pulling delicate fibers free of the weave in chunks. He rubbed his wrist as he clambered to his feet, grateful that Jun had refrained from putting the harsh adhesive directly on his bare skin. "I suppose I should consider myself fortunate you decided not to gag me after all."

They were standing far too close to each other, crowded together between the chairs. Jun studied him with an intensity that had Theo squirming in place, heat curling low in his abdomen.

"Not yet," Jun said, catching and keeping Theo's gaze. He then turned and walked out of the cockpit.

Theo stood frozen in place until his body reminded him of his priorities, and he rushed to follow. Jun led him through a narrow corridor to an open doorway, which he gestured to with a sharp slash of his hand.

"The head's through there. I'll wait outside."

Theo took advantage of the facilities, astonished to find them spotless if a little cramped. He stepped back out under Jun's watchful glare. The captain had remained standing at attention just where Theo had left him.

Theo's mother would approve of his posture, if nothing else. He'd wager Jun could sit still and straight-backed in her parlor for absolute ages. Unlike Theo, whose record for sitting still had just been broken by a judicious application of tape.

Jun didn't move except to point back into the room with his chin.

"What?" Theo asked, glancing over his shoulder in bewilderment. He'd definitely washed his hands and could not imagine what else he might have missed.

Jun repeated the motion with his chin, jaw set. "There's the bed. It's late. Go to sleep."

Theo surveyed the small chamber, almost entirely taken up by a single thin mattress set into a metal platform. This appeared to be the only habitable room besides the cockpit. As far as he could tell, the rest of the ship was composed of storage rooms stuffed to the gills with large metal crates. Which led to a pertinent question.

"Where will you sleep?"

Jun's gaze slid from Theo down to the bed and back, a frown settling onto his face like it was getting cozy before the fire, comfortable and familiar there. "Doesn't matter."

He leaned back against the wall and hit the light panel, sending them into the dark of the night cycle, the cabin now lit only by the soft glow of the emergency lights lining the hallway.

In the deepened shadows, Jun's cheekbones looked sharp enough to cut oneself on.

Theo would certainly enjoy trying anyway.

A blanket—a soft pile of well-worn material—lay draped across the foot of the bed. Of an indeterminate gray color, and clearly homemade in an uneven open knit, it gave the cold, dark room a softening flair of personalization.

Theo picked it up, rubbed the chunky yarn between his fingers.

It smelled faintly of leather and ozone and clean man. The same fragrance that had burned itself into Theo's mind when those tattooed fingers had pressed over his mouth.

It smelled like Jun.

Theo stifled the impulse to bury his face in the blanket and roll around on the mattress like a pig in mud. That would likely be frowned upon.

He perched on the edge of the mattress, smoothing the blanket as he swung his feet. "This is your bed, isn't it?"

Jun shifted against the wall and slid down to sit with one leg stretched out in front of him, the other bent at the knee. The light from the hallway caught his face just enough for Theo to know he was being observed.

Curling his legs under himself, Theo leaned on one wrist while he wrapped the other hand around his ankle. Ari would have been horrified to see him put his shoes on the bed. He held back a private grin at the small taste of rebellion. "Not much of a conversationalist, are you? That's alright; neither is my brother. I've learned to adapt so that I can talk enough for the both of us."

Jun didn't say anything, but his boot scuffed against the floor. Theo took that as confirmation that he should continue.

"Where are we going? Will we get there by morning? Do you suppose we'll have time to stop for coffee? Ari likes to fuss about caffeine, but I've never noticed much of a difference. It doesn't seem to have an effect on me, but I like the ritual of it in the mornings. Are you a morning person? I adore a nice crisp sunrise more than anything except perhaps a good book. Do you have any books in your crates? There are so many on your ship. If it were my ship, most of them would have books inside."

Jun's head hit the wall behind him with a *thunk*, eyelids squeezing shut as he pressed one hand to his forehead. "Tell me you do not talk in your sleep."

Theo considered, stretching his neck as he leaned further back against the bed. "I'm not entirely sure. I've never had complaints from Ari, but then again, he sleeps like a petrified log. I'm not sure he would have noticed even if I managed a song and dance in my sleep."

Jun's head raised up at the word "he." His eyes traced over Theo's face before turning to stare at the wall, his hand rolled into a fist on top of his bent knee. "Shut your mouth and go to sleep."

Theo sat up with a thoughtful hum and crossed his legs into a pretzel. "No, thank you. I'm not particularly tired. It has been a rather exciting evening; I am far too wound up for sleep, I'm afraid."

Jun groaned softly, sending Theo's brain spiraling straight into the gutter. "Just lie down and be quiet."

Theo sat quietly for a moment, and then two, and he made it all the way to three before he had to move. He started by humming and ended with clapping his hands against his folded knees and singing a bawdy Verge shanty about a widow and her pair of ducks.

Jun sat up from the wall, jaw tight and shoulders tense. "Stop that."

Theo sang louder, bouncing against the mattress just a little, in time with the melody, delighting in having gained Jun's full attention.

Jun pushed to stand with a growl, baring his teeth. Something low in Theo's belly quivered at the sight. "Stop singing. Go to sleep."

Theo started the first verse over again gleefully as Jun stomped closer with such single-minded determination that he tripped against the edge of the mattress just as he reached out his hand to cover Theo's mouth.

They fell together in a tangled heap, Theo's second verse breaking off under Jun's rough fingers.

Jun's hand was hard against his lips as he pinned him to the bed with a forearm across his collarbone and a muscled thigh over his hips.

Theo froze, ice running through his veins.

When this had happened before, it had been thrilling, adventurous. This felt different. Simply by virtue of being horizontal upon a bed.

The darker implications could no longer be ignored.

Jun's hips shifted minutely, an unmistakable hard line pressing against Theo's thigh, and Theo slammed his eyes shut, breathing noisily against Jun's fingers as he started to tremble.

Rearing back, Jun fell off of the bed in his haste to release him.

Theo covered his own mouth against the awful sobbing noises erupting from his chest, fingertips numb with shock.

As Jun jumped to his feet, he shook his head over and over again, eyes wide on Theo's tear-stained face. "No. I wouldn't. I would never."

Theo curled into a ball, crying harder at the sound of his voice, deep and harsh and overloud in the tiny chamber.

Jun's footsteps were heavy as he backed out of the room. He left the door open behind him, and Theo could hear him pacing in the narrow hallway.

He buried his face in the blanket, then kicked it away as the scent of Jun flooded his senses.

The familiar sense that he'd made an error in judgement settled all around him.

Theo wanted Ari here to talk things through. To help make sense of things. To lend a shoulder to cry on like he always did.

He needed his twin.

A horrible thought pushed to the forefront of his mind—that Theo wasn't going to see his brother. Not today. Not tomorrow. Possibly not ever again.

Perhaps another, more forward-thinking person would have considered this right away, but Theo was not that person.

Theo had been equipped at birth with an external impulse-control unit named Aristotle. "Considering the consequences" had always been Ari's job. Theo had been more than happy to outsource those thoughts. He preferred to focus on other things. Ari kept him from making mistakes like this, usually.

He had never been so far away from him before.

Whatever was he going to do?

Chapter Four

"Sorry. For scaring you."

Jun hovered in the doorway, reluctant to breach the threshold as he waited for Theo to get up. He had done enough breaching, already. Felt like the worst kind of brute. Considering that he used to get paid for roughing up his boss's enemies, he should know how a brute felt.

Exhaustion molded the steel in his spine into brittle lines as he crossed his arms in an attempt to hold himself more tightly together.

Hold it together, Park.

He felt as if he was falling apart, like some Raider junk ship, razor-edged pieces flying off in all directions. Crumbling from within beneath pressure he wasn't built to withstand.

Theo sat up on the bed, eyes wide with alarm and blazing red hair flying in every direction. He swiftly buttoned his jacket and felt around for something among the sheets without ever looking away from Jun.

Jun kept his gaze respectfully above Theo's open collar, ignoring the slender throat on display. He had not earned the privilege of seeing things usually kept hidden.

An Outlier he might be, but he was no stranger to Core conventions.

With sharp, quick movements, Theo righted his clothing and tied his cravat around his neck, freeing Jun's gaze to wander as he spat out his response, emerald eyes on fire. "To which occasion do you refer? You do seem to expend an awful lot of energy on intimidation tactics. I would be hard-pressed to pinpoint exactly which you feel the need to apologize for."

Oh, he knew exactly what Jun was referring to. The little shit.

Stars. He was magnificent.

Jun had not been this blindsided since he was fourteen, joining up with his first Crew only to discover they were a bunch of bloodthirsty bullies with no moral compass.

The feeling of self-betrayal was the same, even if the circumstances couldn't be more different.

Jun didn't have time for admiration, for the possibility of it developing into anything more. He didn't have room in his life for more. Not now.

Certainly not with someone he had wronged so severely.

He kept his gaze steady and contrite, dragging each word out by sheer force of will, harsh and staccato and still only half as awkward as he felt. "Last night, on the bed. I didn't mean to imply that I would—" He couldn't even say the word, internally cursing himself for a coward. "—do that. I won't. So. You don't need to worry. About that."

Great.

Very clear, well done, Captain. So commanding. That definitely made up for throwing an innocent man on the bed and pinning him down with your inappropriately invested dick.

He fought the urge to bury his face in his hands, maintaining his authoritative stance by a hair. The back of his neck burned with shame and humiliation he hoped his less-than-willing guest couldn't see.

Theo scoffed as he yanked the lace at his collar and cuffs into place, his harsh movements against the delicate material only serving to underscore Jun's guilt at his rough treatment the night before.

Although, Dr. Campbell was already proving to be significantly more substantial than he appeared at first glance. Partially because, at first glance, all Jun had found was astonishing beauty.

It wasn't fair for him to be so gorgeous. Why couldn't he have been a doddering old man with whiskers down to his elbows? It was nothing short of the universe punishing Jun for his misdeeds that Theo was made in the exact, bratty shape of his most embarrassing dreams.

Theo gave a disdainful sniff, every inch of him screaming his upper-crust Core background. Jun would know, having endured the same affectation from his Core-born parents for most of his life.

"I suppose," Theo continued, "I ought to thank you for your chivalry, is that it? You want to assure me that while you are perfectly willing to hurt me, and you wish for me to remain in fear of you, my virtue shall remain intact. How magnanimous of you. Truly, sir, you are a gentleman of the highest order. My knight in shining armor."

The gun at Jun's side weighed more heavily in his holster beneath Theo's accusing gaze. Jun struggled to come up with the words to reassure him that he would not come to harm at Jun's hands. It was with the full, exhausting knowledge that it was too little, too late, that he finally responded, soft and low. "I won't hurt you."

"Really? Excellent." Theo's voice had gained an edge that left Jun metaphorically bleeding all over the grungy metal floor. "So I'll just leave, then, shall I? Whenever I want?"

Panic surged, toppling Jun's good intentions like a flimsy tower of sticks as he stepped into the room, resisting the urge to reach out and hold Theo in place. "No. You can't leave."

Jun had only just found him. Dr. Campbell, the key to the brick wall of code he'd been slamming his head against for over a year. He couldn't allow him to slip through his guilty, bloodstained fingers, now.

In true, magnificent form, Theo pushed off the bed and stood facing Jun, arms akimbo.

Throughout his career, Jun had stared down heavily armed men twice Theo's size who weren't half as fearless. He tried to dampen the fire in his heart that Theo's snappish tone had set ablaze.

"And precisely how do you intend to enforce my captivity without hurting me?" Theo demanded. "Tape me to another chair? Glue my shoes to the floor like the villain of a children's story?"

In different circumstances, Jun would have him against the wall with his slender wrists pinned above his head, where he could show Dr. Campbell exactly what his insolence would earn him. Probably twice, before he was done for the night.

But the inestimable Dr. Theo Campbell was Jun's captive, not his...anything else. He was a crucial component in Jun's plans. Thousands of lives hinged upon his cooperation. Any attraction Jun might feel, however intense and unexpected, was a distraction he couldn't afford. In these circumstances, Jun had to think with his head, not with his—

Circumstances being what they were, he kept a respectful distance, meeting Theo's glare with one of his own, an expression that usually cowed all but the toughest members of his Crew. "I'll do what I have to do."

Bare, pink toes curled against the cold metal floor as Theo stalked closer, not in the least intimidated by Jun's carefully cultivated scowl. "Yes, that's just what a villain would say, isn't it? Now, can you do an evil laugh for effect? I'd like to get the full experience."

Three times. Twice, against the wall, and then once on the bed after Dr. Campbell was all wrung-out and needy.

Under different, less shitty circumstances.

But Jun didn't have time for thoughts of long red hair and fiery eyes when every ounce of his exhausted focus must remain on his goal.

Or else, what was the point of all this? All of the sacrifice and loss, the compromised ethics, the kidnapping of an innocent academic. And all the other things that kept him awake during his rest cycle.

He had to remain firm, speak honestly and quietly, try not to intimidate while retaining his authority. "I have no intention of hurting you."

Theo stepped a little closer, lifting his chin, elegant spine rigid with defiance. "I suppose you know what they say about good intentions? You will or you won't; your intentions mean nothing. Either way, I'm leaving at the next opportunity, so I imagine you'll have to decide."

There was fear in the back of his eyes. Fear matched by the dread in Jun's chest at the notion of losing him when Jun was finally so close to getting the answers he needed.

Jun fought against pleading. "No. You can't." He winced internally as panic echoed in his voice, low and sharp.

Theo strode purposefully toward the doorway Jun was blocking as if he had any idea where he was going. "I suppose we shall just have to wait and see precisely what I can and cannot do."

Pressing one hand flat to Theo's warm chest, Jun held him at arm's length, palm sweaty against the lace of his cravat. In his exhaustion, Jun finally lost control, panic breaking through as he rasped, "People will die."

It was painfully obvious Theo was not prepared for that. He froze midstep, knee bent as he leaned into Jun's restraining hand. "What do you mean by that?" Righteous anger leaked out of his voice until only confusion was left behind.

The space between them shrank by slow inches as Jun let Theo fall forward into the step he had been meaning to take. From this distance, he could see the hint of stubble on Theo's chin, like tiny dots of sunlight caught within the dismal confines of the ship.

"If you don't help me"—Jun put every ounce of determination into his words, each one weighed and measured—"if you leave now, people are going to die."

Theo took a sharp breath, and Jun removed his hand, reminded of what a terrifically bad idea it had been to touch him in the first place. Intelligent eyes searched his face as if scanning a complicated document. "What? Which people?"

It was an exceptionally Core thing for him to say, and it sent a flash of rage through Jun like a power surge.

No different than the Quorum, the corrupt Core governing body that blithely ignored the tragedies of those with the misfortune of existing beyond the chosen few planets. Verge settlers and Outliers from the Restricted Sector, who scraped and clawed their way through life outside Core protection, were considered less-than. It made Jun's blood boil.

Jun clenched and unclenched his hand beside his hip, trying to erase the phantom warmth of Theo from his fingertips. "Does it matter?" His control slipped further, venom dripping. "Would you refuse if they were Outliers like me?"

Theo pushed his hair back behind his ears, face creased with confusion. "No, of course not. It's just that you aren't making any sense. What are you talking about? If there is some imminent danger, why didn't you tell me immediately?"

A sliver of sadness embedded itself in the anger, cracking it open to reveal even more sorrow at the core. Jun had lost all chance of artifice, shrugging helplessly as he could tell nothing but the truth, worn down to bare honesty. "I didn't think you would come with me."

Without further warning or, apparently, an ounce of good sense, Theo wrapped soft hands around Jun's biceps. Jun froze, barely breathing, tense and quiet in the gentle grip. Theo squeezed lightly as he tipped his sweet face up in sincerity, hammering that sliver of weakness all the way through like a wedge splitting Jun open. "I would have, if I had known. I would have offered my assistance willingly, Captain Park. If matters are indeed dire, then I suggest you tell me everything right now."

The fire Jun had tried to stamp out spread unchecked, warming parts of him that had long gone cold in the merciless depths of space. He drew in a ragged breath and stepped back so quickly he bumped his shoulder against the metal rim of the doorjamb, wrenching himself from Theo's grip.

It was unimaginable that a Core-born academic with no knowledge of the harsh realities surrounding his comfortable life would willingly place himself in danger to save those considered beneath the notice of the Quorum.

Not once had it crossed Jun's mind to ask for his cooperation. It was as absurd a notion as, well, everything else about Dr. Campbell, really.

He blinked brightly up at Jun, completely unaware of the danger ahead of them, the danger Jun had dragged him into because he wasn't smart enough to think of a better solution.

Jun fitted his frown back into place and straightened into his command posture. "No. The less you know, the better. I don't want you to get involved any more than you have to."

There was a chance Jun could keep him out of the spotlight, out of harm's way and far removed from the target Jun was painting on his own back. He just had to keep his distance, create narrow boundaries and uphold them. Keep Theo confined to his one necessary task and otherwise uninvolved in Jun's reckless mission to dismantle the unjust machinations of powers greater than either of them could conceive.

It was a slim chance, but Jun had survived on slimmer. He retreated farther into the doorway as Theo advanced with eyes narrowed in consideration, raking over Jun from head to toe as if answers might be spelled out in the shuffle of his boots. "But you are saying that I need to be involved, somehow? Me, specifically?"

Jun stopped retreating the moment he realized he was doing it, heat creeping across the back of his neck once more. He crossed his arms, face and body slamming shut on Theo's curiosity. "Yes."

They entered a staring contest in which neither was willing to admit defeat, Theo's eyes wide with interest and Jun's carefully blank.

Theo stepped back with a thoughtful hum. "Intriguing. Now I require you to turn around, please." He waved his hands in a graceful circular motion.

Jun blinked, losing the staring contest along with the last shreds of his dignity in his confusion. "What?"

Theo repeated the motion expectantly. "I have no intentions of offering a free show, Captain. If you are half the gentleman you claim to be, you will turn around at once so that I may adjust my stockings before my feet turn into elegantly sculpted icicles."

Stockings.

Jun's overtaxed mind shorted out for a brief moment as he considered the image of such an intimate garment sliding up Theo's long legs.

He knew that Core clothing involved many layers, with rigid rules pertaining to each one. His own mother had never embraced Outlier fashion and had stubbornly insisted upon dressing as if she were to attend a meeting of the Quorum each day. As though they might welcome her back with open arms, if only she dressed refined enough.

There, that was a bucket of ice water on his incredibly unwelcome interest in Theo's clothing.

Next, he would have to think about the time he'd taken his Crew to the beach, and his pilot had worn something that could only be described as a neon windsock, and nothing else.

Yup. Interest gone.

Without waiting for Jun to leave, Theo bent forward and began to work on the fastenings of his trousers, silky hair swinging across his face.

Jun spun around so rapidly he banged the other side of the same shoulder against the door jamb. With a hiss, he stood stock-still as he stared into the hallway.

The soft rustling sounds of Theo donning his layers hit Jun like a sledgehammer, raising his heart rate as he desperately tried to recall the horrors of the windsock instead.

"All clear, Captain. I am decent once more, everything in its place and accounted for."

After a deep, steadying breath, Jun turned around. He did his best to avoid staring at Theo's thighs, wondering what color his garters might be. Much the same as many of Jun's best efforts to be a better man, he failed abysmally.

Theo stood and stretched with a wide yawn, leaving Jun to suppress a yawn of his own as his sleep deprivation pressed insistently at the back of his mind.

Green eyes blinked up at him, and Jun couldn't resist. He swayed closer, met that gaze with a smirk. "You do, by the way."

Theo lifted inquisitive brows as he pulled his waistcoat back down into place after his stretch. "What is it that I do, precisely?"

It was impossible to look away. Theo was a spatial anomaly, and Jun was caught in his pull. His voice rasped low as if they'd actually made it to that wall he kept thinking about. "Talk. In your sleep."

Theo blushed furiously, as pink as a sunset over Britannia, and Jun was in a galaxy of trouble.

Chapter Five

The crunch of Theo's slightly stale protein bar echoed loudly in the quiet of the cockpit. He wondered just how long it had been in Jun's pocket before he'd retrieved it to fling at Theo's head with grunted instructions to eat.

Judging by the taste, at least three months.

Jun peered down at the flight projections as he perched on the edge of the pilot's seat with the rigid posture Theo was coming to expect from him. He made occasional disgruntled noises, muttering to himself in three languages thus far by Theo's count.

None of it had been complimentary to either Theo or the ship.

Theo struggled to swallow his last dry mouthful of crumbling protein mix, loath to speak with his mouth full. He was just beginning to wish for a cup of tea when Jun held out a dented metal canteen, pushing it into Theo's chest without turning away from his projections.

Theo opened it with a cautious sniff but was unable to discern any aroma. Mouth still as dry as the sands of Tunis Prime, he threw back the bottle with a shrug.

It was water, flavored only with the slight metallic tang of a magnetic filter. He gulped greedily, then passed it back to Jun, who rectified the misthreaded cap and stashed it beneath the dash.

He went back to the flight screen while Theo explored all the different ways he could drape himself across the copilot's seat, particularly enjoying the configuration where he let his head dangle from the seat while he hooked his knees over the backrest, ankles crossed for security.

Jun leaned back in his chair with a low sound, digging the heels of his hands into his eye sockets.

Theo watched him, amazed to find that he was just as handsome when viewed upside-down. Although the deep shadows of exhaustion were perhaps even more pronounced at this angle.

"Have you slept? At all? I got a refreshing eight hours. I know I inspire confidence in my capabilities, but surely you did not expect me to engineer my escape whilst unconscious?"

Jun's habitual scowl had twitched into a grimace at the first sound of Theo's voice. Now, his head lolled back against his chair, his posture slumping into disarray. He took in Theo's unorthodox position without comment, although his expression lightened incrementally in a way that wouldn't have been noticeable on anyone else but, on him, seemed to indicate amusement. Theo considered that a win.

He swung himself up to sit cross-legged in the chair. Jun's eyes widened slightly as he removed his legs from the backrest in a shameless display of flexibility. Theo knew how to play to his strengths.

He tapped his fingers on his knees, tone tilting up into disbelief. "You're just not going to sleep? For the rest of the journey? Admittedly, I have no idea where we are going, but it is giving every appearance of taking days."

Jun lifted heavy-lidded eyes to stare silently at Theo from beneath thick black lashes. He shook his head once to each side and rested his hands upon the arms of his chair.

Theo cocked his head, nestling his chin into the palm of his hand as he balanced his elbow on his own armrest. "Well, that doesn't seem like a very good plan. It isn't terribly sustainable, is it? Never going to sleep? Do you know, I read once about a man who was so determined to complete his life's work that he stayed awake for days and days until his body finally revolted and dropped him dead right there on the spot. I'm not entirely certain whether he had finished his work before his untimely demise, but he certainly would have if he'd just had the good sense to take a nap now and again."

Jun shut his eyes for a moment, shoved the palm of each hand into his temples, and pressed as though he might squeeze the sound of Theo's voice from his brain.

"You are unbelievable," he said, hands still pressing into his skull.

His voice came out as tired as he looked, raspy with sleep and bringing to mind all kinds of delicious imagery of rumpled sheets and pillow talk. Admittedly, even Theo had a difficult time imagining pillow talk with Jun. He seemed more a man of action than words. Theo had absolutely no difficulty imagining Jun in action...

But, at those words, Theo sat up straighter in affront, prepared to defend his research abilities. "No, I'm fairly certain I read that from a reputable source, actually."

Jun's eyes opened to pin him to his chair, hands falling carelessly into his lap. Theo struggled not to follow them with his gaze. It was a near miss. "No. You. You are unbelievable. Like, as a person. How are you a real person?"

Theo would have been offended if not for the edge of hysteria flavoring Jun's voice. He leaned closer in concern. "I think you may be growing delirious in your exhaustion. I've never heard you talk so much of your own volition."

Jun laughed low and hard and long enough that Theo's concern deepened exponentially.

Theo risked placing a hand on the closest of Jun's abandoned armrests, edging into the space between them. "What is so very amusing?"

Jun melted back into his chair; his shoulders dropped heavily as his feet slid out along the floor. "You. You think I talk too much."

Theo nodded and sat back in his own chair as he considered his options. A moment later, he launched into a recitation of his least favorite works of poetry in the low, droning tone he usually reserved for particularly irritating undergraduate lectures.

Jun's brow furrowed in confused irritation. He rubbed his eyes, then left them closed as his hand fell back into his lap.

Theo continued to drone until the lines on Jun's face smoothed miraculously away, underscored by soft snoring.

Thankful for his hours of practice sending undergrads to sleep at their desks, Theo stood and began to examine Jun's holster.

*

It really was a shame how stunningly beautiful Captain Jun Park's face was in repose, and how terrifyingly furious it was in wakefulness.

"Give it to me. Now."

Theo pursed his lips in mock contemplation as he trained the gun on Jun's wide chest. He took a step back into the main cabin beneath the force of Jun's rage from his seat in the cockpit. "Hmm, no. I think I'd rather not. I have loads of questions I'd like answers to, first."

Jun's glare, sharp and calculating, measured the distance across the floor between them. He pushed to stand, all traces of exhaustion gone even though he had only slept for an hour.

Theo clicked the wheel on the side of the gun until it made a low buzzing sound that vibrated in the bones of his hand.

Jun went very still very quickly, focus trained on Theo's restless fingers hovering over the trigger.

"Yes. Now you're going to answer my questions, Captain Jun Park. I did warn you that I had unexpected depths."

Jun swallowed hard, his Adam's apple bobbing down his throat as his attention never faltered from the gun.

Theo set his jaw with determination, widening his stance as he held the gun with both hands. "What is your favorite color? No, food. No, animal. Actually, I'd like to know all three, please."

Jun's focus finally left the gun, flying to Theo's face with an expression that could only be described as flabbergasted. "Are you serious?"

Theo attempted the stern expression his brother liked to use while lecturing him on the importance of proper desk organization. "I do appear to be the man with the gun, yes. All three, and be quick about it."

Jun's face really was incredibly handsome without his habitual scowl in place. He looked confused and tired and shockingly young. His expression lines disappeared into smooth bronze skin stretched tight across the most beautiful bone structure Theo had ever seen.

His mouth moved silently before he spit out a rapid-fire answer. "Black. Bibimbap. I don't like animals."

Theo heaved a disappointed sigh, clucked his tongue as he held the gun steady. "Black is hardly a color. I suspect that's a decoy answer to conceal your true love of some color you find undignified for whatever reason. Bibimbap is an excellent choice. Pick an animal anyway."

"Cat," Jun said, exactly as though a cat had once murdered his entire family.

Theo dropped the stern expression like an unwanted rag, his face shining with delight. "My favorites are blue, profiteroles, and hedgehogs. See, isn't this nice? We're getting to know each other! Things really are much better when I have the gun. We ought to do this more often."

Jun tracked Theo's hand as he gestured between them with the barrel. He pointed it back at Jun, fingertips tapping the stock as he considered his next question. "Butter or jam? On your toast."

Some of the tension in the hard line of Jun's shoulders began to dissolve. He took a small step closer to Theo, voice quiet. "Butter."

Theo hummed, unsurprised. Jun had that buttered-toast look about him. "I like both, with some sugar sprinkled on top for crunch. Ari thinks that's disgusting, but he never could appreciate my genius in the kitchen."

Jun's face tightened at Ari's name. He took another step toward Theo, this one slightly larger than the first.

Adjusting his grip on the gun, Theo resisted the urge to back away. Even without the gun, Jun's shoulder holster lent him an air of danger that pressed in on Theo like an electric charge in the room. Or perhaps that was just Jun himself, bringing the promise of a storm wherever he went.

Theo had always enjoyed stormy weather.

He scanned Jun's face and forced himself not to linger on those full lips as Jun licked them nervously. They really were quite distracting.

Now, pointing the gun at him as if it were a stick of chalk and he was calling upon a student in his lecture hall, Theo asked, "How old are you?"

Jun's nose scrunched with irritation in a manner that Theo didn't hesitate to label adorable. "What does it matter?"

His arms grew tired from holding out the gun, and Theo shifted with discomfort. Jun gave no sign of answering, so Theo gave his answer first in encouragement. "I'm nearly twenty-four. My brother and I completed our degrees in acceleration. I've been reliably informed that we're remarkably intelligent, though I have provided a staggering amount of evidence to the contrary."

Jun's hands twitched at his side as he stepped closer, boots gliding silently across the metal floor. "Twenty-eight." He started to lift his arm from his side, feet planted, knees bending.

With a sharp inhale, Theo sensed an electric storm approaching, building across his skin until he buzzed with it. "Alright, fine. I suppose I should ask more relevant questions as well. Why did you take me? What kind of help do you need from me?"

Jun paused, then slid one leg in front of him, still bent slightly at the knee. He was definitely measuring the distance between them, adjusting his stance. His voice dropped even lower, just above a mumble. "I need you to translate something."

A smile lit up Theo's face, transfixing Jun in the bright burst of happiness. "I would be delighted! I adore a good translation project. But, why didn't you just bring it with you? I likely could have translated it there at my desk. You could even have enjoyed waving your gun about. I'm beginning to see why you like it so." Theo brandished the weapon in demonstration, bringing the muzzle near his own head.

Jun's shoulders jerked as he followed the movement. "I couldn't risk bringing it across the Verge," he said. "It's too important."

The low buzz of the charge made Theo's fingers ache, so he switched hands on the trigger. Jun jolted at the motion and pressed his lips into a tight line. "Intriguing indeed," Theo said. "Now, what else did I want to know? I think it's fairly obvious you aren't a morning person. Oh! Do you have any hidden talents? Art, music"—he scanned down Jun's well-defined muscular body thoughtfully—"dancing?"

Jun's scowl developed an edge of petulance that Theo struggled not to find charming. He resembled nothing so much as a cranky little boy being asked to sit for tea. Who could also snap a man in half if he wanted to.

Theo was definitely charmed.

"No. And if you're not going to stop asking stupid questions, I'd honestly rather you shoot me."

Theo tried to school his features into something half as serious as Jun's solemn face, reining in his wild curiosity to focus on gaining pertinent information. "Where are you taking me?"

It seemed Jun would refuse to answer, but he appeared more comfortable with questions regarding Theo's abduction than his own personal details. He answered quickly and quietly, "To my ship." His mouth barely moved as he tracked every minute movement of the gun and continued to inch forward.

Theo's arm drooped, his shoulders sagging with befuddlement. "But we're already aboard your ship."

"This isn't my ship; this is just the dinghy." Jun moved dangerously close, hands out and ready at his sides.

Theo scooted backward until he bumped up against the bulkhead, gun raised but not in the least ready. "I'm afraid I'm not familiar with the term."

Jun didn't slow his approach, stalking Theo with the hard eyes of a single-minded predator. Theo felt a slight tinge of concern for his own mental state that he found it so devastatingly attractive. His survival instincts really were appalling.

Jun's voice was clipped with the sharp edge to his accent that had originally fascinated Theo. He wanted to analyze every soft phoneme and clipped consonant until he could pin it down.

Until he could pin Jun down.

"It's a single-person craft for making short trips planetside," Jun said.

The space between Jun's chest and Theo's gun was closing rapidly.

"Oh." Theo's voice was small as his hands began to shake.

Only a few feet between them now. Jun bit his lip as he stared at the gun, every muscle tense and his words almost too low to hear, dropping into a growl. "That, and it's dingy as fuck."

Theo jumped, knocking his head against the wall as Jun snatched the gun away and continued to move closer until he pressed Theo into the bulkhead with the entire length of his body.

His eyes held Theo's for an endless moment, his breathing so harsh that his chest brushed against Theo's lapels on every exhalation. Theo refused to turn away despite his trembling, fear and arousal sending his body into a tailspin of hormones until he was drunk on them. Jun's gaze fell to Theo's quivering lips just before he stepped back with a dissatisfied grunt.

"I shouldn't have released you from the rusted tape."

Chapter Six

Jun shoved away from Theo to stomp across the length of the cabin and slam his hand against a security panel. The upper half of the wall slid away after a series of beeps.

Hidden behind the wall was an impressive collection of weaponry, neatly displayed and ranging from items as small as Theo's little finger to launchers he suspected he would not be able to lift.

He dared to walk closer, stopping a few feet away at Jun's baleful glance. "You had all of these other weapons at your disposal? I can't imagine why you were so concerned when I took one little ray gun. You could have simply outgunned me at any point. It appears to me you made a fuss for nothing. Bit of a tempest in a teapot, really."

Jun snapped the gun he had taken back from Theo into the wall. He considered for a second before choosing a larger pistol, equipped with bio-locks, which he quickly set to his hand, then muttered his answer, "Wouldn't you be concerned if an orangutan picked up a gun?"

With a gasp, Theo pressed a hand to his chest, knocked back a step by the force of his offense. "I beg your pardon. Are you comparing me to an orangutan?"

The lock clicked shut on the panel as Jun closed it. Then he secured the new pistol in his holster as he aimed a pointed look at Theo's hair.

Theo hastened to brush through the tangled mess with his fingers, longing for a mirror and comb and bemoaning his unusual coloring. He and Ari had certainly endured more than their share of schoolyard taunts about their red hair, but orangutan was a new one.

Jun's lips twitched up as he watched Theo's frantic efforts. He pitched his voice low and dry as he walked past Theo toward the cockpit. "I would have felt safer with the monkey."

Theo remembered the small, cracked mirror over the sink in the washroom and made his way there to remedy his hair. Jun didn't seem in a hurry to produce more tape, and Theo didn't feel inclined to press his luck.

He groaned darkly when he caught sight of the mess on his head, setting it to rights with little more than his fingertips and a judicious application of muttered threats. It was almost lying correctly when he was startled by the sound of metal smashing in the cockpit.

Hair forgotten, Theo scrambled his way to the cockpit to be greeted by the sight of Jun destroying a small section of the dash with his fist, cursing loudly all the while.

Theo slid into the copilot's seat, being careful to give Jun a wide berth. "Are we experiencing technical difficulties?"

Jun declined to answer. Instead, he buried his fist into the ruined section with a roar of fury, pulled out a handful of busted wiring, and tossed it to the floor at his feet.

Clucking his tongue, Theo tucked his own feet underneath himself on the chair to avoid the sparking wires spilling from the ragged hole in the dash. "Well, if we weren't before, we certainly are now."

Jun turned to him with clenched teeth and bloody knuckles, stormy face daring Theo to say another word.

Theo never could resist a dare.

"Does that usually work for you? This type of extreme percussive maintenance? It certainly seems an imprecise method at best. I can't imagine that it has ever proven to be effective. Whatever was the problem in the first place?"

Jun turned back to the dash, running the fingers of his uninjured hand through his hair. He sat abruptly in the pilot's chair, shoulders slumped. "Navigational error. Can't make the jump without new coordinates."

Theo put one foot on the floor to swivel his chair and leaned out to grab hold of Jun's injured hand. Blood ran down around the letters spelling "Honor" in a way that might have seemed metaphorical had Theo been in the mood for such nonsense.

He examined the cuts, then retrieved his pristine monogrammed handkerchief and blotted away the blood, Jun's regard heavy on his bent head all the while. "And the solution to this is for you to split your hand open by losing a round of fisticuffs with several tons of steel?"

Jun let out a low noise as Theo wrapped his knuckles tightly in the handkerchief. A picture of exhausted misery, Jun shook his head and pulled his hand back to examine the makeshift bandage. He ran a finger across the delicate lace edging and embroidered initials. "No. The solution is much worse than that."

Theo scoffed with a gesture to his ruined handkerchief. "What could be so much worse than beating yourself bloody?"

Jun's sigh contained an entire crateload of reluctance as he pulled up the flight screen and tapped in a new location. His voice dragged down with the force of his dread and revulsion.

"Contact with the locals."

*

Jun halted Theo's progress with a firm hand around his arm, jerking him to a stop on the red dirt road just outside a decrepit saloon.

Constructed of little more than discarded metal and a dash of misplaced hope, the squat building stood smack in the middle of the worn-down Verge settlement Jun had decided upon.

He released Theo, then pulled his hood down lower on his head as he considered the dilapidated entrance. "I'll do the talking."

Theo giggled, then failed at suppressing an exuberant and very undignified snort as Jun's offended face glowered down at him from within the shadows of his hood. "Oh. You were serious? I honestly thought you were in jest, making reference to your taciturn nature. You know, something like saying I was going to do the heavy lifting when, clearly, I am unsuitable. Not that I wish to imply that you are unsuitable for speaking. More that I mean to emphasize your apparent distaste for the endeavor. Conversation and the like."

Jun tightened his jaw and pointed his index finger rather rudely in Theo's face. "Just. Be. Quiet."

Theo turned his fingers in front of his lips in imitation of a key, applauding himself for his silent agreement. Jun watched the gesture stone-faced. He then turned back toward the entrance and stalked through the door with a put-upon sigh quickly overshadowed by the screech of rusted hinges.

Which was just as quickly overshadowed by the overwhelming stench of the place.

Theo mourned the loss of his handkerchief, desperate for the scent of lavender sachets even as he was aware there was no refreshing scent powerful enough to undo the horrors being wrought upon his olfactory senses.

Judging by Jun's expression, he was in wholehearted agreement.

Every eye in the saloon, thirteen by Theo's count, turned to stare at them as they paused just inside the doorway, the smell having affected them like a blow to the head.

Jun emitted a subvocal growl at the attention that reminded Theo of nothing so much as the buzzing of a charged ray gun.

Squaring his shoulders, Theo approached the metal bar, which was decorated with naught but a deeply embedded pattern of rust stains and grime.

In fact, Theo challenged himself to describe the establishment without using the word "grimy" and came up short.

After swinging up onto the nearest barstool, he lifted a finger to gain the attention of the elderly bartender.

Jun pressed up against his back, hissing in his ear, "What are you doing?"

Theo tossed a smile over his shoulder, nodding at a gentleman at a nearby table who seemed to consider him an exotic animal exhibit. "This is a bar; I am ordering drinks so that we may better blend in with the clientele."

Jun's answering snarl was cut off by the approach of the bartender, whose fluffy white eyebrows raised as far as they would go beneath an undulating sea of wrinkled skin.

"What can I get you fellas?"

Theo could hear Jun's teeth grinding directly behind his head as he aimed a friendly smile at the man. "Hello! What a lovely little place you have here; I was just admiring the decor."

The man's wrinkles rearranged into a pattern that might have denoted confusion. He turned and spat behind him, almost hitting the large brass spittoon sitting between barrels of ale.

Theo's smile slipped as he stared down at the dark puddle of spittle soaking into the concrete floor.

He folded his hands on the bar top, marveling at the variety of textures that could all best be described as sticky. "I'll have a brandy spritz, if you don't mind."

"What," the man replied, in such a way that the word was not a question so much as a statement of incredulity.

Jun tossed a handful of credit chips onto the bar, the clattering noise swiftly gaining every last ounce of attention in the building. "Two whiskeys. Straight."

Theo turned to place a hand on Jun's arm. "Oh, I don't drink whiskey. I'm afraid I ca—"

"Shut. Up."

The last remnants of Theo's smile fell away entirely in the face of Jun's fury. Every impressive muscle practically vibrated beneath his coat, his arm like steel under Theo's hand.

The bartender dropped two cloudy glasses onto the bar top and slopped an indiscriminate amount of whiskey into each one, easily spilling half the amount onto the bar.

Jun's head turned like a hawk, snapping to a table set into the back corner. "There. Go."

Theo aimed a soft thank-you at the bartender, who'd already turned away to laugh uproariously with a man who gestured at Theo with a whisper.

After gathering the glasses, Theo led the way to the table, keeping his expression pleasantly neutral as every eye in the place followed his movements. Jun followed so close at his back that he nearly trod on Theo's heel.

A lone man sat at the indicated table, watching them over the rim of his glass. He set it down into a drying puddle of beer foam as they approached.

"Good day, sir!" Theo nodded at the empty chairs. "Would you mind if we joined you?"

The man leaned back in his chair with a growing smile as he let his eyes run from the tips of Theo's spats up to the length of his hair. A puff of dust filled the air when he slapped one of his thighs. "Sure thing." He slid down in his seat, spreading his thighs. "Got just the place for you right here. Your frownin' man's gonna have to split though. I don't like to share."

His smile dropped when Jun kicked out one of the chairs. A firm hand on Theo's shoulder pressed him into it. Jun turned the next chair the wrong way around and straddled it, arms crossed on top.

Theo set their drinks on the table, the clink of glass muffled by the thick layer of grunge coating the surface. He studiously ignored the flutter of heat trying to start a fire in his belly at the sight of Jun's confidently spread legs.

The man rested a hand on the holster at his hip while he scoped out the visible edges of Jun's tattoos. Theo leaned forward to gain his attention as tension crackled across the table. "I'm terribly sorry to approach without a proper introduction, but needs must. I'm Theo, and my companion is—"

"In a hurry." Jun shot a poisonous glance Theo's way.

The man managed to smile warmly at Theo while keeping a hard eye on Jun. "Some folks call me Sam. Pleased to meet you, Theo. Pretty little thing, ain't you?"

Jun stiffened at Theo's side, hostility radiating from him like rising clouds of steam. The man's smile only grew wider.

Theo leaned in closer to Sam, playing with the lace at his cuff as he angled a look up through his eyelashes. "Do you really think so? I wonder if perhaps you might be amenable to—"

Jun yanked Theo back by the collar of his jacket and ignored his strangled yelp. "We're looking for a"—he winced as he gritted the word out through his teeth—"singer. That's you. You give me the latest jump coordinates, and I give you credits. Then we"—he tilted his head meaningfully at Theo—"can get out of this shithole."

Theo raised his eyebrows, impressed with the length of the speech.

Sam appeared less impressed, squinting thoughtfully at Jun before turning back to Theo. "Look grown to me. I expect you can decide for yourself exactly what you'd like to do." He angled his head away from Jun as he lowered his voice. "And who you'd like to do it with."

Jun's growl was back, raising the hairs at the back of Theo's neck and stoking that heat in his belly.

Sam raised one of the whiskey glasses and brought the edge up to Theo's lips. "Have a drink. I'd sure love to wet your whistle."

Theo took a dutiful sip, only to choke back a cough at the harsh burn and aftertaste of vaporized fuel crystals.

Jun pulled out his pistol, knocking the glass away and spilling the potent golden liquid across Theo's jacket. He slammed the weapon onto the table on its side, his bandaged finger on the buzzing trigger, the barrel aimed at Sam's torso. "Cut the bullshit and give me the coordinates or I will shoot you. Still feel like singing?"

Theo rested his fingertips on Jun's tight wrist, a determined smile plastered on his face. He fluttered his lashes at a very unamused Sam who yanked his own ray gun out and aimed it at Jun. "What my associate means to say is that we are in a bit of a rush, and as much as I am enjoying your company, we really do need to put some bounce into our step. I would be ever so grateful if you could come to our rescue, Sam."

Theo let go of Jun's wrist to try the same approach with Sam, trailing his fingers up the outer seam of his trousers from knee to midthigh, finally getting the man to cut his eyes over to him instead of blazing a hole in Jun.

While the two men were glaring at each other, Theo had been biting and licking his lips until they were shiny and pink. He pouted them now in Sam's direction with his head tilted exactly so, his eyes appearing larger than they really were. "Truly, just, ever so very grateful, Sam."

He let his fingers trail back down to Sam's knee, then pulled his hand away to play with a lock of hair. Sam predictably followed the motion.

A spark of amusement lit Sam's face, transforming his unremarkable features until he was very nearly handsome. He gave Theo a broad wink. "All right, now. Watch out before you blow me across the room with those eyelashes. You tell Romeo over here to drop the gun, and we can talk credits."

Theo turned to Jun expectantly, holding his breath as several silent moments passed. At last, the buzzing clicked off, and Jun and Sam, staring into each other's eyes, holstered their weapons with slow, steady movements.

The amusement had fled Sam's face, leaving it hard and blank. "Sixty credits. I don't take Ident from Outliers, so you better have the chips." He tensed as Jun reached into his coat.

Jun pulled out a clinking pouch and dropped it on the table between them. "Eighty and you forget you ever saw us."

The pouch disappeared in a sleight of hand Theo would have loved to learn. Sam leaned forward and dropped his voice to blend in with the noise of the saloon. "Looks like we got a deal, fellas."

Chapter Seven

The loading ramp rattled beneath Jun's heavy boots as he boarded the ship behind Theo. Theo checked back over his shoulder at his approach, his breath quickening at the dark expression on his face.

Jun gave the impression he was trying to incinerate him with his thoughts, that Theo ought to just burst into flames from the concentrated heat of his fury. Theo couldn't decide whether to be thrilled by the attention or intimidated by the intensity.

Both. Evidently, he was both.

Sweat beaded along the back of his neck as Jun closed the bay doors, plunging them into the low lighting of the main cabin.

The yellowed interior bulbs gave off a feeble glow behind dingy covers, casting deep shadows and softening edges in an imitation of candlelight.

Theo shrugged out of his sodden jacket with a despairing sniff at the ruined material and reared back in disgust at the strong smell of cheap spirits.

Jun snatched it out of his hands, the velvet crumpling in his fist, and tossed it to the floor with a wet plop.

He captured Theo's eyes and held them as he pulled at the knotted handkerchief with his teeth, then yanked it off his hand and balled it up. Hauling back like he intended to throw it down, he shoved it into his coat pocket instead.

Theo was relieved to see that his hand had already started to heal nicely and resolved to locate some regeneration fluid before they took off. There had to be a med kit somewhere aboard the ship, tucked in amongst the maze of metal crates.

Jun stepped forward, crowding Theo against the wall as he struggled out of his coat. Succeeding, he threw it onto the emergency seat so hard that the slap of leather made the metal ring.

"I saw what you were doing," he snarled, continuing to push Theo back with the sheer force of his displeasure without ever lifting a hand to touch him.

Theo only halted his retreat because the press of steel at his back prevented further movement. He lifted his chin defiantly. "Did you? You saw the shocking way I ordered a drink at a bar and used every available resource to help you achieve your goals? How keenly observant of you."

Jun's upper lip lifted in a sneer that really ought not to have done anything for Theo's libido but undeniably did.

Several things, actually.

"What was your plan? Get down on your knees for some filthy Verge rat so he could help you escape?"

Theo scoffed. Beginning to feel overheated, he pulled his neck cloth loose and let it slither to the floor. "Don't be ridiculous. If that had been my plan, I'd have done a much better job of it. I certainly wouldn't be here with you if I had wanted to go home with someone else."

It was never getting someone to take him home that had been Theo's problem. It was getting them to let him stay until morning.

Jun's voice dipped deeper, and he bared his teeth. "You were flirting with him."

Theo licked his lips, fighting nerves as he squared his shoulders against the bulkhead. "Yes, I was, with excellent results. Well spotted; your powers of perception never cease to amaze. You really ought to consider applying to the Enforcer Academy Department of Intelligence. I understand they could use a man of your skills."

Jun's answering growl hit Theo right between his legs in a throbbing ache that had him pressing his knees together until they were shaking. "I do find that one catches more flies with honey"—a breathy tone ran through his voice that he was helpless to prevent—"than with threats of violence. Perhaps you should try it yourself, sometime?"

Jun didn't appear to be listening, his brow furrowing slightly as he stared at Theo's mouth like it had done something to offend him. He shook his head minutely as he said, quiet and rough in equal measures, "Try what?"

Theo shifted, daring a hand at his trouser front to adjust himself, then blushing hard as Jun followed the movement. His own voice came out as a whisper, bridging the short distance between his lips and Jun's ears.

"Honey."

It was possible Theo had imagined the brush of Jun's hand against his thigh, barely enough pressure to be felt but so hot he feared singe marks on the velvet.

Then again, it was possible he hadn't imagined it at all.

Theo reached out and hooked his fingers behind Jun's belt buckle so he could tug his hips closer.

Jun's hand slapped flat against the metal wall beside his head, his lips parted over a harsh exhalation, more breath than sound. His throat bobbed inches from Theo's nose, geometric lines undulating with the movement.

Theo yanked the belt from the buckle, opening it with a snap of leather that sent Jun into action.

Jun worked open the buttons of Theo's trousers, then knocked Theo's fumbling fingers away to unfasten his own trousers. Theo would have paid closer attention to the reveal if not for the glorious slide of Jun's hand down his aching cock.

He dropped his chin to his chest, gasping at the image of tattooed fingers working his flesh, then let out an embarrassing sound at the sight of Jun's cock. Thick and dark and even better than his highly imaginative dreams.

Theo's hand looked small and pale in comparison. It must have felt good, though, judging by the punched-out grunt Jun made at the first stroke.

Theo wanted to take his time exploring—exploring the heft and texture of him—but Jun set a pace that would end things sooner rather than later. Nerves sang as lightning arced from Jun's fingers to Theo's cock, and he bowed his back, throwing his head against the wall.

Jun let go when the air between them grew thick with Theo's desperate cries. Watching him with dark eyes, he spat into his palm and increased his pace, thrusting into Theo's grip with a low sound rumbling in his throat.

Theo pushed into Jun's frantic rhythm with his hips, reaching up for a kiss only to be pressed back against the wall with a firm hand against the junction of his collarbones.

Jun kept him there as his other hand worked steadily, and Theo made every effort to match him with his own blurring fist.

Jun's gaze pinned him to the wall as firmly as his palm, dark and beautiful and fierce with wanting. Theo keened as Jun leaned down to rest their foreheads together, his breath hot on Theo's cheek.

Theo dropped his mouth open. Jun's eyes darted down to Theo's lips, and then he squeezed them shut with a bitten off moan as Theo added a flick to the end of his wrist on every stroke.

Theo licked his lips fitfully, accidentally drawing the edge of his tongue along the length of Jun's red-bitten lower lip. At the contact, Jun's breath hitched in his throat, and his cock jerked in Theo's fist. His heavy lids shot open, sending a vicious glare that only pushed Theo closer to the edge.

He returned Jun's glare even as he repeated the motion, blatantly licking into Jun's mouth this time. Jun retaliated by turning his head with a sharp bite to Theo's neck, sending him flying over the edge in hot pulses over his fist.

Jun let go with a final squeeze, his messy hand covering Theo's as they worked to finish him together, their wet fingers tangling into a filthy knot. He opened his mouth over Theo's throat, teeth pressed to the thin skin there as he panted and groaned through his orgasm, adding to the mess of their hands.

Theo slumped back against the wall; their harsh breaths echoed through the cabin as they stared at each other, flushed and, for once, speechless.

Jun couldn't look away from Theo's lips, his mouth still hanging open as he caught his breath. Something flickered across his face that sent shivers down Theo's spine as he leaned over him, nudged a thumb between his lips, and hooked behind his teeth insistently with a low grunt.

"Lick it off," Jun said in a tone of command as natural as breathing.

He watched closely, broad chest heaving and jaw tight, as Theo cleaned his thumb with little kitten licks.

Theo finished with a nip to his thumb pad, breath hitching as Jun swayed closer. He brushed their cheeks together, then pushed away, rucking up his shirt to wipe his hands along the hem.

Theo struggled to roll his tongue back into his mouth at the sight of black ink climbing up the hard ridges of his abdomen like vines on a brick wall.

He endeavored to pretend he had not been ogling him as Jun grabbed his wrist and cleaned his hand on his shirt with all of his attention focused narrowly on his task.

Theo let out a nervous giggle as Jun spread his fingers to get every inch of him clean. "Well. That was certainly something, wasn't it? I don't know about you, but I could go for more of that. Preferably three times a day, at regular intervals. Possibly four, provided we make an effort to maintain proper hydration."

Jun's lips tilted up into his almost-smile before a scowl settled back into place. He stepped away and glared at the wall over Theo's head as he fastened his trousers in quick, angry movements. "It was a mistake. This can't happen again."

Despite his youth, Theo had found himself in similar situations more times than he would care to count, swept up into a passionate embrace only to have his partner pull away and express his regret just as Theo was imagining cuddles by the fire.

There was something about Theo that made men think of him as little more than a bad decision, immediately regretted and forgotten about at the first opportunity.

It was just as crushing to hear now as it had been when he was seventeen. "Oh. I see."

He examined the shiny toes of his spats as he buttoned his trousers, letting his hair swing in front of his face like a curtain. There was a small drop marring the toe of his left shoe that would require some attention in the very near future. Best to focus on that, for the moment.

It wouldn't do to dwell on anything else.

Jun's breath had finally evened out, the cabin now quiet enough that there was nowhere to hide Theo's discreet sniff as he attempted to force back the pressing weight of rejection.

A tentative brush of rough fingers across his forehead only increased the pressure as Jun carefully tucked his hair behind his ears. Theo refused to lift his face, painfully aware that he went all red and blotchy when he was holding back tears.

It was not exactly his best light in which to be seen.

Jun's boots shuffled against the floor grate as he moved closer and then immediately away in an awkward dance of indecision. "It's not you."

That brought Theo's chin up because, though he had heard his classmates complain of the "it's not you, it's me" speech, he had never actually received it. Likely because it was usually him, after all. Theo was the only common denominator in dozens of failed affairs. He knew it, and so did his partners.

Most often, he had been the recipient of the "I can't continue on with you because you're entirely too much…you" speech. Which was fair, if extremely hurtful. No one was more familiar with how difficult it was to remain close to Theo than Theo himself. Except perhaps his unfortunate twin, poor thing.

Jun's face was set with determination as he crossed and uncrossed his arms in the next step of his dance. His loaded holster swung with the movement, and the damp hem of his shirt hung out of his pants like a flag of surrender. Theo indulged in a burst of pride over how very undone he appeared after such a brief encounter.

"It's my fault. I shouldn't have—" Jun broke off with a low groan, gripping the top of his hair and twisting as he looked away and then back down into Theo's eyes. "I'll do better. This won't happen again."

Something in his face told Theo that, as much as Jun might want to believe everything he was saying, he wasn't any more convinced than Theo was.

They had broken something open against that wall, and it wasn't going to be a simple matter of slamming it closed again.

It was too late for that; it was out in the air between them, sizzling and sharp. Snapping electric in every shared breath.

Jun watched him like a trapped animal as Theo reached up to push a fall of silky black hair away from Jun's sweat-slick forehead, letting it run through his fingers in a moment of indulgence.

"Of course. Whatever you say, Captain."

Chapter Eight

"Do you have much confidence in the dinghy's ability to cross the Verge?" Theo asked as he surveyed the busted dash with a healthy amount of skepticism. "I'll admit, upon first viewing the vessel, I had my doubts of how spaceworthy it may be. Now that I have truly experienced the interior construction, however, I am entirely sure that it is not. Spaceworthy, that is. Something of a ramshackle death trap, more like. Probably best suited to completing the collection of a museum of mistakes in aeronautical engineering."

Jun didn't lift his head from his view screen as he entered the new coordinates, mouth set in a hard line of concentration. "I did it before."

Theo hid a small smile at the curt response. He had expected to continue his one-sided conversation all the way to the barrier of the Verge. It was a pleasant surprise to be acknowledged. He tried to rein in his delight, aiming for casual instead of jumping at the first real interaction Jun had allowed since they entered the cockpit. "That doesn't answer my question."

Jun huffed, sitting back in his chair as rapid-fire flight projections scrolled across his screen. He rubbed one hand over his head, his shoulders tense. The reflection from his screen emphasized the shadows clinging to the hollows of his face. "'Confidence' isn't the right word. It's going to work because I have to make it work."

Theo swiveled his chair back and forth with his toes on the floor. He played idly with the excess strap of his harness, letting it run through his fingers until he reached the frayed end, looping it around his palm, then releasing it to start all over again. "Well, you certainly do not suffer from a lack of determination; I'll grant you that. Perhaps you ought to add it to the lovely bit of calligraphy adorning your knuckles. Honor, Valor, and Determination. I say 'determination' because single-minded pigheadedness wouldn't fit in any language I know of."

Jun's head whipped around, his eyes comically wide. The tattooed knuckles in question gripped his armrests as he pressed forward into his harness, and then he jerked to a stop as if he'd forgotten it was there. "You can read Hangul?"

Theo couldn't determine whether to be insulted by Jun's obvious surprise. He decided that, ultimately, if he were to take offense every time a man underestimated him, he would spend his entire life in an unsustainable state of pique. Instead, he tilted his head to the side and pulled out a lock of hair from behind his ear. He began to braid it absently with a shrug. "Well, yes. Of course I can. Why? Can't you? I did assume you could, based on the amount of personal real estate you have allotted to it."

Jun's lips dropped into a frown, the rest of his face quickly following suit. "Yes. I can."

Theo considered for a moment, reading the tension in Jun's shoulders and the sharp question in his eyes that might have been hope if it weren't so ruthlessly stifled.

"*Do you speak Korean?*" Theo asked, voice lilting musically with the switch in languages.

Jun flinched, his face flickering from shock to joy to suspicion so quickly that Theo got emotional whiplash just from watching it. Jun leaned in as closely as his harness would allow, straps cutting into the solid wall of his chest as he flung out his words like an accusation.

"*Why do you know it?*"

Theo shifted in his seat as Jun's voice dipped even lower with the switch, hitting Theo somewhere deep below his navel. There was something about heirloom languages that made every word hit the ear like poetry, unlike the sterile, pragmatic flat tone of Standard.

"*I'm a linguist. I collect languages, especially heirlooms. Thirty-one, so far.*" He switched back to Standard, hoping to erase some of the suspicion from Jun's face. "I'm a hyperpolyglot."

The blank-faced rapid blinking was a fairly common, if somewhat disappointing, response to Theo's revelation. "You're a what?"

Theo bit back a sigh, more than accustomed to providing an explanation at this point. Accustomed, and entirely bored with it. "It means I'm multilingual. I understand, speak, read, and write in multiple languages. It's my only talent, I'm afraid. I've never been particularly good for anything else."

He wanted to add a cheeky "outside the bedroom," but Jun didn't seem receptive to bawdy humor, much less any reference to their previous encounter. He seemed to be making every effort to forget that it had ever happened, in fact.

Theo stomped down on a tiny twinge of hurt over it.

Jun nodded, his brow pinched thoughtfully together. "Makes sense."

Theo's chest clenched painfully at Jun's ready agreement that he wasn't good for much at all. As true as it was, it always hurt to have it so directly confirmed.

Though remaining aloof was not among his limited talents by any stretch of the imagination, Theo hoped to keep his tone light. He was afraid that an edge of the sharp band around his chest might creep in. "Why do you say that?"

Jun's smile was quick, there and gone in a flash. It left Theo with the impression he'd been stabbed through the heart with something beautiful and rare, yet he was too awed by the sight of it to mind the pain. "You talk too much for one language," Jun said.

His tone was teasing instead of disdainful. Just the slightest dash of fondness softening the insult. The combination of that and his toweringly rare smile left Theo reeling.

Jun's face was back to the usual mask of careful blankness and vague irritation, as though the smile had never been. But Theo knew the truth.

The moment was burned into his memory. He would do anything to see it again. Theo was capable of doing many, many things.

He drew breath to speak, only to choke it back, shocked when Jun started first, speaking without prompting.

"I haven't heard Korean spoken in a long time. Not since my parents—" Jun turned abruptly away to face the view screen. "Heirloom languages are rare out here. Everyone just speaks Standard, Patch, or Grunt."

Theo had heard of Patch and Grunt, usually spoken of in a derogatory manner in academic circles. They were the languages used by Outliers beyond the Verge. Raiders, in particular, were rumored to speak Grunt. Theo had always been fascinated by the possibility of learning more about them. Resources on both languages had been exceedingly scarce, even in the linguistics department.

There was no such thing as an uncivilized language, in his opinion. Only fools let their own ignorance and prejudice sway their minds away from new experiences.

Poetry existed in every language. As did expressions of love.

And, really, what could be more civilized than that?

Jun was still observing him cautiously, and Theo rushed to fill the silence. (Ari had always said that no silence was safe from Theo's interference, and he had always been correct. If slightly condescending.) "Gaelic was my first heirloom. My mother was bilingual; it was her parents' heirloom language. I only spoke Standard in school, of course. But I sought out other heirlooms, started collecting any I could find. On Britannia, it is still traditional to speak heirloom in the home and Standard in public areas. It was not especially hard to find a variety of languages to learn. Though my family did grow somewhat confounded when I began to speak them all at once."

Confounded, irritated, overwhelmed. Those terms rather defined most of his parents' reactions to Theo, actually.

Jun ran his fingers lightly over the buttons in front of him, his voice so soft it was almost shy. "Patch is like that. A whole bunch of heirlooms mixed up and stitched together into a hideous old quilt."

Theo grinned, the chair creaking ominously as he leaned forward with excitement. "That's what you've been cursing in all along, isn't it? I've caught bits and pieces of it, and it's only left me craving more. You'll have to teach me; everything I've heard so far was absolutely delightful."

Jun responded with something in Patch that definitely called into question Theo's standards for delight.

Theo threw back his head, laughter bubbling up and over like an overfull kettle on boil. "Oh, Ari will simply wilt with despair when he hears I've picked up a new language so diverting to curse in."

Jun gave Theo a solemn expression, all traces of amusement washed away. "You miss him. Your Ari."

Theo sighed, pulling his hair free from the braid and starting it over again just to give his fingers something to do. Something to calm the wailing tide of fear and longing that washed over him at the mention of his twin. "More than you can imagine. I've never been apart from him for so long. We do everything together. I hardly know who I am without him by my side."

A muscle jumped in Jun's jaw as he turned his attention to the view screen. "I'll bring you back."

Theo stood from his seat and clasped his hands together excitedly as he bounced on his heels. "Oh, would you? I fear it's been long enough now that he must be absolutely beside himself. He never was one to embrace a change in routine. Dedicated to his schedule, my Ari."

Jun shook his head once, firmly, gaze flicking to Theo before returning to his screen. "When you've finished the translation, I'll bring you back."

Theo deflated into his chair, pulling anxiously on the braided lock of hair and sprawling in every direction in a manner Ari considered uncouth. "I see. Yes, of course. I suppose I have not yet served my purpose, have I? I apologize, but sometimes I do forget that I remain your captive. It isn't always quite what one has been led to believe in books—captivity."

Jun didn't respond, tattooed fingers tapping on his screen with urgency for a matter of minutes while Theo braided and unbraided his hair. Jun finally lifted his hands from the screen. "It's time to prepare for the jump. Strap in tight."

He glanced over to check Theo's harness and sighed loudly when he saw that it was twisted and undone, shoved to the side so Theo could drape a leg over his armrest. After clicking out of his own seat with brisk efficiency, Jun walked over to grab Theo by the shoulders and righted him in his seat.

Theo swallowed hard as firm hands settled his hips into place, moving him as if he were as light as a feather.

Theo was an absolute sucker for manhandling.

Jun appeared to know how to handle a man such as Theo.

The penchant wasn't something Theo was proud of, but it was something that had him sucking in a sharp breath as Jun untangled the straps with a muttered Patch diatribe. A hard yank, securing Theo further in his seat, forced a noise out of him that should never have seen the light of day.

Jun's startled eyes met his as his fist clenched tight on the strap over Theo's chest. He released him, shoved away, and returned with half a stumble to his own seat. His ears, exposed by the close-shaven sides of his head, glowed red along the edges as he cleared his throat and strapped himself in.

Jun didn't say anything as they approached the Verge, his focus on the shimmering barrier of swirling colors and impenetrable energy filling their view screen.

Theo's breath caught at the sight; he had never been this close before, never seen it in person. The Verge was beautiful in the way that dangerous things could be beautiful sometimes, like standing at the edge of a cliff and staring down into the churning waters of the sea.

Theo never could resist edging closer to beautiful, dangerous things.

Energy crawled over his skin as they drew nearer and nearer, colored light twisting and snapping in lightning-hot flashes in every direction.

Every muscle in Jun's body tensed as he gripped a sturdy lever on the dash, his knuckles white beneath the ink.

He glanced over at Theo, then slammed the lever forward, sending the dinghy careening straight into the barrier. The ship shook so hard that the bolts holding Theo's chair to the floor rattled and whined beneath his feet.

Debris started to fall all around them. Small metal pieces pinged against the floor, and wires draped down from the ceiling as panels shimmied open.

Jun's teeth clenched over a low roar as he brought his fist down hard on the dash to force the lever the rest of the way. It fell into place with a quiet click, and then they were jerked back against their seats, energy crackling with a frequency Theo could feel in his teeth as the dinghy finally punched through.

Alarms shrieked overhead as the ship wobbled and somersaulted away from the barrier. Yelling out curses, Jun slapped blindly at switches and buttons until silence fell, and the ship was righted once more.

A silence that was immediately broken when Theo's chair teetered, tipped on its base, and crashed to the floor with a bang only surpassed in volume by Theo's undignified yelp.

The floor shook and juddered beneath his cheek where he lay pressed against the cold metal, wheezing a little as he gasped for the air that had been knocked out of him.

Jun's cursing took on an entirely different tone, softer and lower as he clicked out of his harness and dropped down to extricate Theo from his.

Strong arms wrapped around his back and hooked behind his knees. Theo's view tipped again as Jun lifted him with a quiet huff, placed him gently into the pilot's seat, and fastened the harness that required a great deal of tightening to fit down to Theo's leaner frame. "Are you hurt?" Jun asked, his words strained.

He ran his hands over the air surrounding Theo's body like he wanted to touch but was unsure of his welcome.

Theo tried to speak but only managed a cough as his lungs struggled to fill.

Cupping Theo's chin in his fingers, Jun turned his head to inspect the sore spot throbbing high on his cheek. Jun's face darkened at whatever he saw, and he brushed his thumb softly, just below the spot. He'd just parted his lips to speak when a static-slashed voice came over the ship's com.

"Can't believe you made it back here in that piece of shit, Captain. I was taking bets we'd be scraping both you and the dinghy off the Verge with a rusted spatula. You just lost me a stack of chips, you dick."

Jun's hand fell away from Theo as he leaned over the dash. He brought up his screen and tapped rapidly. "I'm sending you my location. Pickup in ten. My ship better be exactly the way I left it, Axel."

The voice laughed, a pleasing light tenor in distinct contrast with Jun's rumbling bass. "I think Marco's got her running even better than she was before you left. We all behaved ourselves while Daddy was gone; don't you worry."

Jun pressed a despairing hand to his face, muffling a groan. His ears glowed ever brighter over hunched shoulders as he growled his response. "If you ever call me that again, I will let Boom use your best arm for target practice."

He muted the com as Axel's voice started to come through again. Leaning over the dash with a deep breath, Jun turned to face Theo and frowned at his gleeful expression.

Theo tried not to laugh, but, like most efforts to contain himself, he failed miserably.

Jun stomped past him into the main cabin, grabbed his coat off the seat, and pulled it on. He returned to loom over Theo. "You'll meet the Crew when we rendezvous with my ship. They might be a miserable bunch of assholes, but I can personally guarantee your safety among them. While you are here, you are my responsibility. I take that very seriously."

Theo nodded, impressed with the speech and the intimidating figure Jun cut in his sweeping coat, with his forbidding scowl firmly in place.

He chewed on his lip, questions bursting from him in a shoulder-quaking fit of laughter.

"So, the Daddy thing—"

"Don't."

"Is it a universal ban or—"

"Stop."

"—is it up for negotiation?"

"I will flush you out of the airlock," Jun gritted behind clenched teeth, every line of his face a threat. Every line of his face a study in masculine beauty.

Theo held up both hands. "No, you won't, for several reasons." With a shark-toothed smile, he ticked items on his fingers as he listed them: "First, this ship isn't equipped for it. Second, you've already shown your hand, and I know you need me alive and well. Third, I think we both know you would miss me too much."

He added a flutter of lashes to the final point, causing Jun to snarl as he made his way back to the main cabin. From there, the sounds of panels opening and items crashing to the floor were underscored by dark muttering in Patch.

The dinghy jolted, caught in a loading beam, and Jun hit the wall with a shout as Theo rocked securely in his harness.

He didn't know whether to be frightened or thrilled over this next step into the unknown. Given his options, Theo decided to go with thrilled. Life was much better that way.

It took less than five minutes for Jun to load the dinghy onto the much larger ship and then lower the ramp down into a cavernous cargo bay stacked high with metal crates.

Three pairs of curious eyes peered up at them.

Chapter Nine

The first one to speak was a young man with spiked green hair and so many freckles scattered across his pale skin that he appeared to be made up of constellations. He gave Theo a once-over with a smirk, then turned to Jun, hands planted on his hips.

Well, one hand and one bright-blue bionic limb that attached just above the elbow on his left side. "A Doll? You went all that way just to bring back a rusted Doll? We could've dropped a line down the pipe and had one of those on the ship in an hour, Captain. Damn waste of time just to scratch an itch."

His voice was familiar, sharper without the static interference of the comlink. Jun ignored him, clomped down the ramp to shove past, knocking his shoulder belligerently against Axel's, which only earned him a bark of laughter.

"When you said you had to go pick up something in the Core to help us with the job," Axel continued, "we were thinking more along the lines of some kind of badass laser cannon. Not"—he gestured along the entirety of Theo's person disdainfully—"this."

Jun scowled, waving Theo down into the cargo bay as if he were directing a landing pod. "This is Dr. Campbell. He's going to help us."

Theo offered an abbreviated bow, trying not to gawk at the assembled Crew as he smoothed both hands down his wrinkled jacket and straightened his cravat. "Pleasure to make your acquaintances. I do apologize for my disheveled appearance; Jun abducted me directly from my office. I'm afraid I'm not at my best. It's lovely to meet you all, regardless of the unusual circumstances."

Axel's face lit up, pale-green eyebrows rising as he turned to Jun. "Oh. Sorry, Captain. You had me worried for a minute there. I thought you were getting us mixed up in the Doll trade. Turns out you were just abducting innocent, unsuspecting people directly from the Core for totally unrelated reasons. Cool."

Jun dropped down to focus on opening one of the cates surrounding the dinghy. He pressed his hand to the scuffed scanner panel and waited for the series of beeps. "You know I don't trade."

Axel assessed Theo again, tossing his words over his shoulder at Jun as he took Theo in like livestock. "Well, I also thought I knew you didn't kidnap adorable little redheads, but here we are."

Theo perked up at the compliment, flicking his cuffs into place as he smiled at Axel and moved slightly closer. "You truly think I'm adorable?"

Axel turned to Jun with a ringing laugh. Jun remained bent over the crate but stopped moving, shoulders hunched. Axel still seemed to be speaking to Theo, but aimed his words directly at Jun. "Sure I do, dollface, and I'm willing to bet I'm not the only one."

Jun yanked a surge launcher out of the crate and aimed it casually in Axel's direction, which only made him laugh harder before turning back to Theo. "The name's Axel, your resident handsome, sexy, hilarious ace pilot." Two voices snorted derisively at the description, one of them belonging to Jun. "I'd be happy to show you around. You must be dying for some conversation after being cooped up with Captain Chatty all the way here."

Jun continued to pile items on the lid of the crate without ever acknowledging his companions.

Theo considered his forbidding profile, then leaned in to Axel conspiratorially, pitching his voice to be heard over by the crates. "It wasn't all bad. Portions of the journey were particularly stimulating, I would say."

Jun's ears slowly tinted red as he dumped his assembled weaponry into a battered canvas duffel bag with a clatter, maintaining a pointed focus on his task.

The other two members of the crew waited in silence that grew somewhat ominous the longer it stretched on, both pairs of dark eyes trained on Theo. Axel gestured at them.

"These are the Valdez siblings, Marco and Boom. Marco's alright, but steer clear of Boom if you want to keep all your limbs intact, gingerbread."

Axel waved his bionic limb cheerfully as Theo stared at the siblings, who both shared the same clear olive skin tone and shiny black ringlets but were so different in build it was laughable.

Marco stood as tall and broad as Jun. His hopelessly stained shirt was missing the sleeves, leaving his arms, corded with muscle and streaked with engine grease, in full view. He noticed Theo's attention to them and flexed with a wink and a kiss, earning a glare from Jun that could have melted steel. His trousers had been cut off at midthigh as well, the hems frayed down to his knees. Well, knee. His right leg appeared to be composed entirely of dark, grease-stained metal.

Boom stood at least a head shorter than Theo, her petite figure barely contained by her extremely short garment. Comprised of thick, alternating strips of leather and mesh, it ended scant inches after her legs began. Only a small stretch of muscular thigh showed past the hem before disappearing beneath heavy-soled leather boots, the tops of which were folded down to expose a row of shiny blades tucked against her skin. Glowing augments adorned the backs of each of her small, elegant hands, with thin lines of metal embedded from wrists to the last knuckles.

Boom rolled her eyes and cocked one shapely hip to the side, her faintly glowing hands gesticulating lazily. "Oh shut up, Ax. You lost that arm before you even met me. Captain's gonna be pissed if you scare off his little Doll with your incessant bullshit."

Her clothing and demeanor were so far outside of the scope any woman Theo had ever met. It was fascinating.

Exciting.

Delightful.

He drew his hand slowly through the air between them, indicating her fantastic manner of dress. "Is that sort of ensemble *en vogue* in the Restricted Sector? How absolutely marvelous. You appear both completely terrifying and utterly magnificent, madam. I do so envy you your style. Monochromatic has never been so appealing, and I must say, you wear it well!"

Boom cast him a suspicious glare, then sneered over her shoulder at Jun. "Is he for real? He talks like he's in one of those historical vids my aunt used to watch."

Jun shrugged and dropped a double-barreled pistol into the duffel carelessly, heedless of the clatter it made. "You get used to it."

There was a tone to his sardonic voice that was very nearly fond, and it did something rather absurd to Theo's heart. So much so, he began to wonder if the fanciful organ had decided to take up jump rope.

Marco offered a shy smile. "I like it." He spoke in a soft tenor Theo would never have expected, considering his large build. "I think you sound nice."

Such a small, strange thing to send a lump to Theo's throat. He struggled against it in expressing his thanks to Marco, who accepted with a slight nod. People back home were not usually so friendly to Theo. So effortlessly kind.

His reputation usually preceded him.

Axel sidled closer with a comical leer. "Need me to show you to your bunk, Doc?" He spoke far too loudly to be addressing Theo, who was right beside him. "Get you tucked in for the night? Looks like the captain's busy, so I don't mind stepping in as a friendly gesture."

The duffel bag crashed to the ground behind Axel, which only made his face light up with glee.

Jun stalked over and grabbed Theo's upper arm in a firm but gentle grasp. He steered Theo away from the crew without a word of parting, weaving through the stacks of crates and out an open door into a wide corridor.

Theo stumbled along behind as they made their way through a makeshift dining hall and cluttered galley, past closed doorways, and down another corridor into a sparsely appointed bedchamber fitted with a bolted-down bed, a minuscule metal desk and chair, and little else.

Jun shut the door behind them with a flat palm against the panel, locking them in with a quiet beep.

That ever-present charge snapped and buzzed in the space between them, just as thick and inescapable here as it had been on the dinghy.

Theo was almost relieved by the constancy of it.

The reassurance that he had not imagined the intensity.

He took deep breaths to combat his racing heart as Jun waited silently, hands fisted at his sides. "Well, your crew seems lovely. I hope we can get to know one another better over the course of my work here. Develop a positive relationship as colleagues. Not that I've ever had a particularly positive relationship with my colleagues before, but it never hurts to make the effort."

Jun took a step toward him, the generously sized bunk growing smaller with the closing distance. Theo found himself backing up until the mattress pressed against the back of his knees.

Jun dragged his gaze in a scorching trail up Theo's body, landing on the pale sliver of throat exposed above his cravat. He took another step forward, and Theo's spats slid back until he scuffed his heel against the metal leg of the bunk. He would have spared a thought for the ruined polish if there had been a single thought to spare.

All of Theo's thoughts were much too busy screaming lewd suggestions.

He might as well have said them aloud, for the way Jun's expression darkened and burned.

"This is your bunk."

Theo didn't bother to check his surroundings. There wasn't much to see. Just a standard ship's bunk without a single shred of personality or decoration. Jun was by far the most fascinating thing in the room. Theo fiddled with his cravat as he tilted his head to give Jun his best angle, lashes lowered to a calculated degree. "How lovely of you to provide such charming accommodations. May I make one small request? Something that would improve the space markedly?"

It seemed Jun couldn't tear his gaze away from the movement as Theo loosened his neck cloth to a scandalous degree. "What do you want?"

Theo trailed his hand down his throat and across his chest. He popped open the buttons of his waistcoat. "I'd prefer a bit of company. I'm afraid I'm not used to living alone, and that bed appears exceedingly empty. Do you have any suggestions for how I might fill it?"

Inhaling sharply, Jun closed his eyes, his hands now rolled into restless fists at his side. His brow furrowed briefly before he pinned Theo with a gaze so hot it burned. The air between them crackled with energy. "Take it off."

His rich, deep voice stirred things hidden in Theo like pieces of a shipwreck breaking the surface of the water.

"Take what off, precisely?" Theo asked breathlessly, his fingers already returning to pull at the fabric wound around his neck.

Jun's face was stark with hunger, muscles tense. "All of it."

Theo's clothing practically melted away, tossed aside in careless heaps around the previously tidy room.

Tracking every piece as it was pulled away, Jun trailed his eyes over Theo's naked skin so heavily they might as well have been hands.

Jun shrugged out of his heavy coat and dropped it onto the bed, then stepped around Theo and sat on the edge of the mattress.

He reached out, snagged a small pillow, and tossed it to the floor between his splayed ankles. "On your knees."

Theo fell to kneel on the pillow as though his strings had been cut, his heart hammering in his chest and skin tingling with the charge between them.

Jun cupped his jaw, angling Theo's head to expose the bruise blooming along his cheekbone from his misadventure with the chair. Jun traced the edge of discoloration with careful fingertips, his face unreadable. "Do you want me?" His voice was unexpectedly, achingly gentle. "You're free to say no."

Theo pressed his cheek into Jun's rough palm with a helpless moan, shivering in the cold ship air. Tongue loose with desire. "Yes, I want you. Very much. More than I should, I'm sure. I so rarely do as I should anyway."

Jun released him to lean back. He opened his trousers and pulled out his cock. "Alright, then. Show me."

Tattooed fingers stroked from root to tip, foreskin pulling back on the downstroke to expose the dark-flushed head.

He was thick and long and everything Theo dreamed about in his loneliest moments. He was literally mouthwatering.

Theo swallowed the excess saliva, scrupulously keeping his mouth shut to avoid actually drooling over the sight. He swayed on his knees and leaned closer to watch Jun's hand move away from his cock and rest against his thigh.

The coarse fabric of Jun's trousers brushed Theo's naked shoulders, and he shivered again, looking up into Jun's face. One dark eyebrow lifted just enough to present a challenge, the fraction of a movement as good as a dare.

Theo could never resist a dare.

He threw himself face-first into Jun's lap and rubbed his cheek against the burning length of him as he buried his nose in the bunched-up fabric surrounding his jutting cock. He smelled deeper here, that same leather and ozone scent with an insidious underlayment of pure unfiltered lust.

Theo wanted to rub it all over his body.

He settled for nuzzling against him with every inch of his face. Jun's breath hitched as Theo's lips caught and parted against the underside of his cock, quickened as Theo's hair slid over the head.

Jun combed his fingers through Theo's hair. He fitted his palm to the back of Theo's skull, his hand heavy, perhaps with the effort of staying still and keeping himself in reserve.

Theo didn't want still and reserved. Theo wanted to crack Jun open and expose the source of that electric spark filling the air around them.

Pressing back into the cradle of Jun's hand, Theo extended his tongue just past his lower lip to rest the tip of Jun's cock there like a satin pillow.

Jun was leaking already, bitter and sharp against his tongue, the taste of him intensifying the ache between Theo's legs. He swirled his tongue as he reached down to cup himself, and Jun followed the movement with flared nostrils. His hand tightened and released in Theo's hair.

Theo fitted one hand around the base of Jun's cock, holding him in place as he opened his lips and sucked him down until he pressed against the back of Theo's throat. They both made a sound at that, Jun's low groan and Theo's muffled whimper synchronizing effortlessly.

Jun's other hand petted over Theo's shoulder and down his arm. Theo shuddered beneath his touch, every inch of his skin suddenly starving for contact.

He eased back only to shove down farther, still unable to meet his fist around the base. He pulled off completely, letting the flared head pop past his lips, then licked his hand and slid it down Jun's cock, squeezing the base in little pulses as he licked all around the head.

Theo took a deep breath and sucked him back down, found his limit, and pushed past it, opening his throat to take the hot length of him even farther. Jun made a glorious new sound as he slid down Theo's throat, a harsh, deep grunt of surprise that Theo silently vowed to hear again at the earliest opportunity.

He found a rhythm, breathing in through his nose and out through little stifled moans of satisfaction, reveling in the sensation of being filled. Of finally being so full that his racing thoughts had nowhere to run.

It was bliss.

Jun's fingers tightened in Theo's hair, his hips lifting sharply until Theo choked, then retreating back. Jun's hand fell away, and he held absolutely still, apart from his heaving chest, as apology dampened the heat in his eye.

Theo lifted Jun's hand and tangled it in his hair once more. He leaned down to drop an openmouthed kiss on the underside of Jun's cock as he peeked up at him through his lashes.

His voice was wrecked, whispering between them like shredded silk. "You can move. It's okay, I like it."

Jun fisted his hair, brought Theo's mouth up, and pressed the blunt tip of his cock past Theo's lips with a smooth roll of his hips.

Theo's eyes rolled back with a shivery moan at the loss of control.

Jun built up a slow, steady rhythm, nudging past the barrier of Theo's throat with a bitten-back curse, gripping his hair just tight enough on the right side of painful.

Theo had never experienced anything so perfect with anyone else. It was as if Jun had walked right out of his filthiest dreams.

By the awestruck look on Jun's face, it was even remotely possible Theo had walked right out of his too.

Another strangled curse, and then Jun's voice rumbled through Theo in time with his thrusts. "Touch yourself."

Theo had never been happier to obey. His hand flew over his throbbing cock, his pleasure amplified by the thick slide of Jun down his throat, the tight clench of fingers in his hair.

Jun choked back a low moan as he watched Theo, squeezing with his knees to cradle Theo's shoulders while his boots slid out to nudge against his folded legs.

The ridged soles pressed into the soft flesh of Theo's thighs, just above the bend of his knees, forcing his legs to spread wider and wider until they burned with the stretch.

Jun left his boots there, not exerting pressure, but resting firmly against Theo's thighs. It was the strangest sort of caress, hard and rough, yet still more personal and meaningful than the dozen carelessly gentle hands that had touched Theo there before.

Jun watched him with something deeper than lust lighting his eyes as his hips quickened their rhythm. "Good."

Theo keened high in the back of his throat as he spilled on the floor between them, shaking around Jun's cock.

No one had ever called Theo "good," simply because he wasn't. He was the bad twin, reckless and impulsive and irritating. Men had called him a "good time," but that wasn't what Jun had meant.

That wasn't what the light in his eyes had meant.

Jun's hips lost their rhythm, pushing harder and harder down Theo's throat until he came with a growled sound that might have been shattered fragments of Theo's name.

Theo swallowed every drop and chased him with his tongue as Jun pulled out with a satisfied groan.

To Theo's dismay, he took his boots away too. He then pushed to stand and stepped away as he tucked himself back into his trousers.

The chill of the room hit Theo with a slap, goose bumps erupting over his exposed skin as he wiped the back of a shaking hand across his mouth.

Jun picked up his coat, and Theo turned away, staring at the rumpled dent on the bed as he waited to hear the sound of the door.

He squeaked in surprise as the heavy warmth of black leather fell across his shoulders in a cloud of Jun's scent. Strong hands lifted him up onto the bed, and Jun tucked him into the folds of his coat.

Dark eyes studied him closely as Jun pushed Theo's hair off his face, broad thumbs brushed against his cheeks.

Without a word, Jun turned and went through the open doorway into the small attached washroom. He returned with a damp cloth and wiped Theo's mouth like he was cleaning a porcelain vase, his face set with concentration.

He cleaned the rest of him with the same focus, then swiped Theo's mess from the floor and tossed the cloth back into the washroom.

Theo melted against him as he sat beside him on the bed, posture as rigid as ever but breath still ragged in his chest. After a moment, the weight of his mouth pressed to the top of Theo's head. Theo lifted his face for a kiss, only for Jun to turn away, fisting his hands on his knees while he faced the wall.

"No kissing. Not on the mouth."

The odd request was one more jarring piece to this puzzle of a man, sending Theo careening into uncertainty. He sat up, holding the coat tight around his shoulders. "Whyever not? That's a fairly ridiculous place to draw the line, considering what else you would allow our mouths to do."

Jun's gaze flitted to Theo's swollen mouth with a flare of heat. He shook his head and looked away. "If we do this—"

At Theo's inelegant snort, Jun's mouth snapped shut into a frown. "Oh, I would say 'if' has quite flown past the view screen, wouldn't you? We are well past 'if' at this point, Captain. If anything, we are plotting a course for 'when.' Perhaps toying with a detour through 'are.'"

Jun continued with a brief sigh, his voice as stiff as his backbone. "If. We do this. We need to keep it casual. Impersonal. This can't interfere with my work. With our work."

Theo thought the bitter taste of Jun's semen lingering in the back of his throat was rather personal but refrained from commenting on such. Because he was a gentleman.

He focused on the slight movement of Jun's hands, the tattooed fingers trembling ever so slightly against his thighs. "I'm afraid I don't understand."

Staring at the wall as if waiting for it to move, June rubbed his Valor hand across his Honor knuckles. "I lost sight of it once. Never again."

Theo leaned close, running his hand down Jun's arm to cup his knuckles where he seemed to be trying to rub away the ink. "Lost sight of what?"

Breathing in deeply, Jun pulled his hand away and got up from the bed to step toward the door. He paused there, arms crossed tightly over his chest.

"Of what's important." He said it in such a way that Theo was acutely aware the term was not meant to apply to him.

Jun kept his gaze averted. The pattern of triangles shaved into the right side of his scalp shone pale and alien in the artificial light of the bunk. "Stay here. I'll bring your work to you."

Theo stood on shaky legs. He dropped the heavy coat from his shoulders and threw it at Jun, hitting the back of his knee with a satisfying slap. He didn't bother trying to cover himself, stood naked and brazen, glaring at Jun's broad back. "Is that a suggestion or a command, Captain? Am I allowed to move freely about the ship, or am I your prisoner here?"

Jun reached down slowly, picked up the coat, and held it over his shoulder. He hit the door panel, his voice as hard and impersonal as the polished steel walls of the ship.

"Stay."

Chapter Ten

The description had been accurate: pale, thin, male, green eyes, red hair. And yet Jun felt misled.

There had been nothing in the initial description of his search to prepare him for the reality of Dr. Theophrastus Campbell.

Nowhere had it mentioned that he was achingly young, and brimming with boundless babbling energy, and devastatingly beautiful.

Jun had been struck down by the reality of him, completely unprepared. That was the only explanation for his behavior.

Explanation. There was no excuse.

Theo had looked up at him with those big green eyes and long red hair; hair that was just begging for a firm hand to wrap around it and *pull*, and Jun was...

Jun was done. With that part of his life. He had to be. He didn't have time to take a beautiful brat like Theo in hand.

Theo was sweet, but he wasn't meek. It was the sharp edges that pulled Jun in like a loading beam. Made him itch to see Theo on his knees.

Holy shit, but he'd been gorgeous on his knees.

Sonnets could be written about the way Theo looked on his knees. Jun wouldn't read them, but he knew poetic beauty when he saw it.

Despite rumors circulating in certain pockets of the dark, Captain Park was only human. He sometimes found it necessary to make an occasional stop, drop by a bar and find a warm body for the night. But this? This was something entirely different. He couldn't do this.

He couldn't lose focus.

Theo was the definition of a distraction. Shining with temptation, drawing Jun's attention like a magnet.

Ripe and sweet, needy for direction and guidance and love.

Jun just couldn't be the man to give it to him. The thought that this meant there would be another man coming around to give Theo those things made Jun want to punch a hole in the wall.

Maybe if they had met a few years ago, but that was impossible. Theo had been deep in the Core attending university while Jun had been bashing heads with his old Crew. Piling on the mistakes until he had built a razor-wire cage of his own making. Cutting his own path up from hired muscle all the way to captain of his own ship.

Now, it was worse than impossible. Jun was running out of time, and wasting any fraction of it chasing after Dr. Campbell's adorable tail was unconscionable.

Jun pulled up the translation database on his pad and laid out the single precious hardcopy of his parents' notes alongside.

This was what Jun should be focused on. He owed that to the memory of the greatest minds he had ever known. A pair of Core scientists who had fled to the Restricted Sector with a terrible burden of knowledge. And one inadequate son.

He might have been a bitter disappointment for most of his life, but he was seeing things more clearly now. The path before him was set, and no amount of distraction, however lovely, could divert him off course.

The stakes were too high for that.

He chewed his lip as he flipped through his findings.

Twenty languages, and Jun was only three-quarters of the way through, every passage a new revelation and every revelation tightening the noose.

There was no denying the timeline. Two months and three days.

Seven hours, twenty-six minutes, and twelve seconds.

Five passages left, and within them, the fate of tens of thousands.

After opening a new document, Jun copied over the remaining passages, making sure nothing else carried over. The information was too precious to risk a leak.

As innocent and harmless as Theophrastus Campbell appeared on the surface, Jun had been burned too many times to lay his trust at the feet of a man he had known for less than three days.

Intimately, for less than two.

Shutting that chain of thought down and throwing it in a padlocked box in the basement of his mind, Jun transferred the document onto a carefully disabled pad. He had painstakingly disconnected it and rendered all but basic word processing impossible as a precautionary measure.

Sometimes it felt like every move Jun made was a precautionary measure.

Except the way he had moved on Theo, shoving him up against the wall like an animal, every gasp and slide of soft, pale flesh a lightning strike bringing Jun back to life after years out here in the dark.

Focus.

Padlocked box. Basement.

Two months, three days, seven hours, and twenty-five minutes now.

The galaxy didn't need him to get distracted by a pair of intelligent eyes in a pretty face.

The galaxy needed a hero.

Unfortunately for the rusted galaxy, all they had was Park Jun-Seo, prodigal son and reformed thug.

Mostly reformed.

He was working on it.

It would be easier if everything weren't so aggravating all of the time. His rage waited so close to the surface, only requiring a tiny scratch to burst through.

Mindfulness, Dr. Park Min-Seo would have reminded him in that light, disheartened tone he reserved for his only son.

Discipline.

Focus.

Jun closed and locked all traces of the notes and tucked the hard copy away in the small uncrackable vault he had sourced from a first sector bank. Sourced, selected, extracted, and rehomed aboard his ship.

"Stolen" was such an ugly word.

As riddled with regret as his misspent youth may have left him, there were some skills he couldn't have learned any other way, and for that he was grateful.

He'd still shoot his ex-captain in the heart if they ever came face-to-face again, but he was grateful for the lessons. Captain Barnes had been keen on instilling harsh lessons in his Crew. Prided himself on his callous, bloody mentorship of wayward youths like Jun had once been.

Kill or be killed. Trust no one.

How to take a hit without slowing down. Larceny and smuggling and the delicate art of infiltrating the data stream without detection.

Betrayal.

All important lessons, leaving him with as much self-loathing as self-reliance.

It was a fair trade.

Jun absently traced over the disconnected circuits on his neck, pressing against the phantom itch of data he was no longer plugged into, the remembered pain of disconnection keeping his touch wary.

He'd have had the empty circuits stripped from beneath his skin, but the process was as expensive as it was time-consuming, and time was the one commodity he was desperately low on.

Money was a close second.

He turned his head at a knock on the door of the command center, tucking the disabled pad away, down a hidden pocket of his pants.

"What," he barked, hoping an aggressive greeting would be enough to forestall whatever bullshit awaited on the other side of the door.

The door slid open, the heavy clomp of tiny feet in giant boots telling him he was out of luck before he even got a look at Boom's ticked-off face. "So we're trading Dolls now, Captain? I thought you left your old Crew because you couldn't stomach the business."

Jun turned away, pulled up a surveillance data stream of the surrounding area, and pretended to study it, still clinging to the hope that she might go away. "Not trading. And he's not a Doll."

Boom sauntered over with her distinctive aggressive sway and hitched her hip up onto the console next to him.

She stared him down. "Hmm, looks like a Doll, talks like a Doll, kept by some asshole against his will like a Doll, must be a fucking duck, then."

Jun groaned. Giving up on the pretense of working surveillance, he met her sharp gaze. "It's temporary. I need him to interpret the last of my notes. So we can finally move forward. Then I'll set him free."

Boom shot him a scathing look as she flicked her fingers to load a charge of her wrist blasters, the augments glowing ominously brighter. "Yeah. I'm sure lots of houses tell the Dolls it's temporary. Because temporary enslavement is just fine, right? You're a regular hero, Park."

Jun set his jaw and turned back determinedly to his screen, each of her words salt in the wound of his guilt. "It's none of your business. Keep your mind on security, and you'll get your cut."

Boom sneered as she leaned into Jun's space, her augments whining with the building charge. Half his size and not an ounce of fear. Although that was probably because Boom was, arguably, his best friend.

If Jun had the time for friends.

Or the disposition.

"Me and Marco don't want a cut if it comes out of Doll trading. Either you set him free, or you admit that you've started a collection here on our ship so I can go ahead and slit your lying throat."

Closing out of the surveillance projections to give his hands something to slap away, Jun snarled, "My ship. And you're dismissed, Valdez."

Boom hopped down from the console, nose to sternum with Jun and eyes ready to set him on fire. She held a hand to his throat, weaponized fingers resting against his windpipe. "Get stuffed, Park."

Boom glanced pointedly down at the knuckles of Jun's Honor hand while he silently counted to ten and then twenty and then gave up and growled, earning only an unamused glare in response. "Not terribly honorable, is it? Taking advantage of a scared little Doll under your authority? I'm disappointed in you, Captain."

She removed her hand with a low drone of it charging down, and Jun turned to walk over to the navigations console. He pulled up their trajectory in an attempt to make it look less like the retreat that it was. "I'm devastated."

Boom's silence was worse than her angry tirade, weighing down the center of Jun's chest while he waited for the hammer to drop.

"I saw his face," she said finally.

Jun didn't have to look up to know her expression had hardened, to see her mouth set with fury.

"What happened? Did he try to resist? Disobey orders? Too much backtalk for big, bad Captain Park? He can't weigh half what you do, you prick."

Jun snapped his head to the side, matching her furious tone with a hard stare. "I didn't hurt him."

Jun would have loved to have been able to say he hadn't touched him at all, but—

That ship had sailed, at fucking hyperspeed.

Because Theo was a beautiful, brilliant brat. And Jun was an asshole with, apparently, no self-control despite years dedicated to building it up.

All of that hard work, and his control melted like candy in the rain under Theo's slightest advance. Jun had never met anyone who could have such a profound effect on him.

It was terrifying.

Boom lifted her chin, her heart-shaped face sharp with challenge. "That bruise says you're a liar."

With a breath of frustration, Jun turned to give Boom raised eyebrows. "That bruise says his seat on the dinghy collapsed into spare parts."

Fury melted away into consideration on her face, the steel loosening from her spine, vertebrae by vertebrae. "Oh. Yeah, Marco mentioned you brought it back in pieces."

Jun's expression said "no shit," but he kept his words civil. "Barely made it back across."

Boom stared at him with that weighted, expectant silence, and Jun leaned back against the console with a sigh.

"You know I don't run Crew with a raised fist, Boom."

She nodded and slid a small blade from her thigh holster. Picking at her fingernails with it, she made a perfect picture of threatening nonchalance. It made Jun grin like an idiot, his lips curling up at the corners before he could tame them down again.

"Yeah, but I also know you used to run with the big boys. You learned your leadership skills at the knee of a fucking sadist. I've seen you take down a man for looking at you wrong. Why would you be different with some Doll?"

Jun dropped his poker face, overcome by a rare wave of vulnerable honesty. "I'm different with you. And Marco. And even Axel, which is a daily struggle."

Boom shrugged, slipping her blade back into place. "Well, yeah, but we're—" She closed her mouth around words that might have started to veer too close to sentimentality for comfort, both of them relieved by the restraint.

An unholy light started to gleam in her eye; her full lips stretched into an evil smile. "Oh, I see. He's not just some Doll, is he?"

Jun tried to cut that line of thought off as quickly as possible, standing up straighter in alarm. "I told you; he's here to work."

Boom examined him up and down as if she might find clues written out across his body. Jun resisted the sudden urge to check his fly, arranging his face back to antagonistic blankness.

"Not just that," she continued, not giving him a chance to continue. "You've picked up another stray for your little ragtag band of misfits. Our ugly little family. You like him, don't you? You like-like him. Look at your face. That's adorable, Park. Really cute."

Jun pushed away from the console, opting for a strategic retreat. "Fuck off."

As he passed, Boom patted his cheek with a throaty laugh. "Adorable!"

Jun refused to respond as he made his way down the hall to the makeshift brig.

The fact that it was really just the first mate's cabin with three extra layers of security helped to alleviate the guilt of putting Theo under lock and key when he had done nothing wrong.

Among the endless line of dead philosophers Jun had been made to study, there was an ancient scholar who'd said something about ends justifying means.

Jun's end was so important it could justify far more than locking an innocent professor away for a few weeks.

According to Jun's moral compass anyway. Which he'd been assured was in very poor condition, but fuck it.

When he weighed destruction and death for countless, faceless innocents against unwarranted upheaval in the life of one man, he chose the lesser of two evils. No matter how appealing the man had turned out to be.

Seven hours, four minutes.

Jun had never gotten ocular or cerebral augments, but it felt like he had a digital timer in the top left corner of his brain, flashing numbers as the time scrolled by. Every morning, he opened his eyes to the new set of numbers, dreading the chunk of time carved away by the necessity of sleep.

He entered the code that activated the bio-locks and opened the chamber door without knocking.

It was *his* ship, damn it. The captain shouldn't have to knock. Boom could shove her personal privacy bullshit down the garbage chute.

Jun wasn't lurking. Boom always claimed he was, while throwing objects at his head when he entered a room without announcement.

He was the captain, and this was his ship. Simple as that.

Theo lay on his stomach on the bed, nude from the waist up, bare feet crossed at the ankle and swaying in the air above his pert little bottom as he lazily paged through a book.

He glanced up at Jun's entrance, tossing his silky hair over his shoulder, beautiful face a picture of unconcerned inquiry.

Jun's heart made an excellent impression of a battering ram at the cut of light across the delicate shadows of his collarbones.

Maybe he should have knocked.

Theo looked back down at his book, and Jun's skin grew tight with displeasure. He wanted Theo's attention as much as he wanted to put him right back where he had found him, and the conflict between the two made Jun irritable.

He stalked over to the bed, snatched the book, and held it up over his head. "Where did you get this?"

Theo sat up on his knees, feet tucked elegantly beneath him as he felt along the sheets for his discarded shirt. He held it up against his chest in a show of modesty that was far too little, far too late.

Jun had once been able to go about his days, blissfully unaware of the exact delicious shade of strawberry-pink of Theo's nipples.

He could kiss that goodbye, now. There wasn't a padlocked box big enough to contain all the images of Theo's perfect body seared into Jun's brain.

He was going to see creamy, freckled skin and bright, silky hair in his stars-cursed sleep.

Theo blinked wide, innocent eyes up at Jun as though he hadn't been deep-throating his cock like a rusted professional not an hour before. "Axel gave it to me. He didn't wish for me to die of boredom while you decided how long I was going to be locked away. He's quite a jocular fellow; I can see why you would want him on your crew."

Irrational jealousy threatened to rise in a surge of undeserved possessiveness. Axel was a good guy, if a little heavy-handed with his humor. He was personable in a way that Jun never was and never could be.

Despite knowing full well Theo was in no way Axel's usual type, Jun had to suppress the urge to stake a claim.

Theo was his. Jun had him first.

A guy like Axel wouldn't know what to do with him, wouldn't be able to give him what he needed. Wouldn't be able to make him shiver and cry out and roll those beautiful, intelligent eyes back in bliss.

No. Focus. No time for that.

Padlocked box, locked in the basement, flooded with ice water.

Jun dropped the book on the bed, pulled out the pad, and placed it alongside.

Theo let his shirt fall to his knees as he picked up the pad, his face an open question.

"There are five passages on that pad. Translate them. Tell no one what you find. Keep all notes on that pad only. I am the only one you can discuss this with. Is that clear?" Jun needed to keep this short, eager to leave before he did something he would regret. Again.

Theo fired up the pad, nibbling on his lip in a way that made Jun tighten his thighs against the urge to pounce and nibble it for him. "Nothing about this is clear, I'm afraid. You are something of an enigma, Captain Park."

Jun had heard that before, from men he had picked up for the night. Waxing poetic over how mysterious he was. People never seemed to realize that sometimes a person didn't talk about themselves because there was nothing good to say. "Get it done. I'll be back in the morning."

Theo sputtered out a protest that Jun allowed to bounce off of his back as he strode out the door. He locked it and sagged back against it in the empty hallway.

Six hours. Thirty-seven minutes and ten seconds.

Nine seconds.

Eight.

Theo's eyes were so green. Jun hadn't known eyes could be that vibrant without augmentation. He hadn't known eyes could reach inside you like that, shining a light on all of the places Jun worked so hard to hide about himself. Soft, vulnerable places he tried to cover up with plates of armor and hard expressions.

Places that didn't deserve to be seen, that he had hollowed out himself with a rusty spoon like a prisoner attempting escape.

Theo had cracked him open without even trying, and Jun was—

Six.

Five.

Four.

He was so. Fucked.

Chapter Eleven

"I thought you said you'd be back in the morning."

Theo congratulated himself on his nonchalant tone, keeping the tremor from his voice by sheer will alone.

If there was one thing at which Theo did not excel, it was being quiet. If there were two things, they were sitting still and being quiet. If there were three things, they were sitting still, being quiet, and being left alone.

There were actually many things at which Theo did not excel.

But those were the top three, easily.

The hours had seemed endless as he stared at the four walls of the empty room, too shaken to focus properly on his translations.

"Eat," Jun said, dropping a laden tray onto the small desk in the corner of the bunk where Theo sat.

Theo examined it, pleased to find better fare than the protein bar he had choked down that morning.

There was even some kind of fresh fruit, round and shiny green with thick, pitted skin. Citrus, perhaps, though nothing he had ever seen back home.

Theo looked up at Jun, who appeared to be settling in to watch him eat as he leaned back against the wall with his arms crossed.

His holster was still loaded. Theo's heart sank at the sight, his continued status as a captive unignorable.

He shoved the tray away, the metal clanking hard against the wall. "What, no knives, Captain? Don't you trust me? Precisely how far do you think I could get on your ship when all of you are armed to the teeth? It's not as though I would even be able to make my way back home, even if I managed to escape."

"Wouldn't want you to hurt yourself." Jun watched him with faint traces of humor lining his eyes and coloring his tone.

The easy humor sent something tumbling in Theo's chest, something with the sharp edges of rage banging against his ribs. He glared at Jun, straightening his posture in his chair. "No, that's your job, isn't it?"

Jun's whole body jolted. He pushed up from the wall with a wave of concern crashing over his face. "Did I hurt you? When I—" He stared down at the floor for a full three seconds, then looked back up at Theo and walked over with sure, decisive steps.

He curled his hand softly around Theo's throat, but it didn't feel like a threat.

It felt like the opposite of a threat.

Like a comfort.

Theo's pulse leapt beneath the warmth of his palm; his eyes fell shut as though a switch had been flipped, all of the rage draining away.

Jun's hand slid up Theo's throat to cup his jaw, and his thumb brushed across his lips.

"Did I hurt you?" Jun's voice was soft and deep, and Theo felt himself falling into it like a warm bath. "Answer me."

Something beyond the phantom warmth of Jun's hand blocked Theo's throat, and he had to let out a breathy sound before he could speak. "No, you didn't. Not in the way you mean."

Jun pulled his hand away, but Theo bobbed closer as he tried to chase the contact. Jun crossed his arms tightly, the hand that had been touching Theo now balled into a fist.

Jun's face was solemn, mouth set in a determined line. "You know you don't have to do those things with me. I only want you of your own free will. I will never ask for more than that."

Theo sighed and picked up the fruit. He tried to remove the peel but failed to lift any of the edges from the stem, the peel waxy and slippery in his grasp. "I know. Difficult as it may be to believe, I can assure you I have a knack for only doing things I want to do. I'm rather notorious for it back at home."

Jun took the fruit from him and deftly dug his thumbnail in beside the stem to lift up a thick strip of peel. "Tell me if you don't like something"—he addressed his words to his hands, keeping his face hidden—"if I push too hard or... Or anything. I'll always stop when you ask me to."

He continued to remove the peel until the pale-green fruit segments were revealed, coated in white, pithy threads. He pulled some of them away, broke off a cleaned section, and held it out to Theo.

Theo leaned forward and bit into the fruit, spilling tart juice down Jun's hand. Jun's eyes widened, his lips parting on a sharp exhale as Theo's teeth scraped against his thumb.

Theo watched him while he chewed, a drop of juice falling from Jun's frozen hand onto the floor with a quiet plop. "You hurt me when you left me here alone. I don't like to be alone; I'm not any good at it. I don't want to do that anymore. I can't stare at these walls a moment longer."

Jun stared down at the spot of juice. He held out another segment and met Theo's eyes. "I can't stay in here with you. I have a ship to run, and I need those translations as soon as possible."

Theo nodded, plucking the morsel from Jun's hand with nimble fingers, secretly thrilled at the flash of disappointment in his eyes when he didn't use his mouth. "I will help you. I've given my word on that, Jun. I will work on these passages until they are translated to the best of my ability. But I want something in exchange for my expertise and effort."

"What?" Jun asked in a flat, sharp tone. More juice spilled from between his fingers as his hand convulsed around the fruit.

"I want my freedom."

Jun started to speak, brow furrowing, but Theo pressed sticky fingers to his lips before he could make a sound.

"Not like that. I'll stay here until the work is done, just as I've told you I would. I want the freedom to move about the ship, to be out among you and your crew. I don't want to stay in here all alone anymore. Please don't leave me here alone, Jun."

He almost made it through his entire plea without his voice breaking, right up until the end.

Jun's eyes softened even as his lips firmed against the pads of Theo's fingers, and shadows of longing rippled beneath the surface of his face.

Theo moved his hand to Jun's shoulder, trailed down his arm, and wrapped it around his wrist. He brought

Jun's empty hand to rest against his throat, and then Theo lifted his chin.

Jun didn't move, eyes wide and hand perfectly still where Theo had placed it. Theo swallowed just to feel the slight pressure against his Adam's apple, something warm settling in his stomach like a cat curling up to sleep. "We can continue doing this too. If you want. As long as I'm free."

Jun ripped his hand away, took a step backward. "You don't need to barter your body for your freedom. I would never ask that of you."

Not to be dissuaded, Theo stood and followed Jun as he retreated another step. He reached out and took the rest of the peeled fruit from his hand, pulled a segment away as he continued with a shrug. "I'm not. I'm only saying that nothing has to change except I won't be locked in this room any longer. I'll still work on your translations, and we can continue to explore this thing between us. I'll simply have other people to talk to, as well. Really, you'd be doing yourself a favor by widening my audience."

Jun crumpled the bits of peel and pith in his fist, dark eyes hard on Theo's face as he chewed the fruit in a show of nonchalance he didn't feel.

"If I let you go around the Crew, I need your silence. On the translations and also on—" He glanced at Theo's throat and then back up to his eyes. "They can't know. That we do this, sometimes."

Theo tilted his head, swallowing down a mouthful of fruit before he had quite finished chewing. "Why not? I was given to understand that Outliers were less socially restrictive. While this kind of thing enjoyed between men is accepted back home, it is still frowned upon in certain extremely boring circles. I always thought it might be better out here. Shame to find out I was wrong."

Jun shook his head, then walked over to hit a panel beside the desk, opening a refuse hatch and dropping the peels inside.

"It's not that."

Theo watched him close the hatch, memorizing its location and waiting for Jun to look back at him. "Then why must we keep our relationship a secret?"

Scowl firmly in place, Jun wiped his hands down the side of his trousers. "First, this—" He gestured between them with a flat, sharp hand. "—is not a relationship. Second, I don't want my crew to know I do this with you. My business is my own."

Theo nodded absently, "with you" echoing inside his head on an endless loop and the tangy fruit turning to ashes in his throat.

It wasn't that he was especially new to being someone's dirty little secret; he could trace that pattern all the way back to his secondary school dorm-mate, with a few scenic stops along the way for various married men and professors. It was just that he had thought this was different.

He had thought Jun was different.

Jun felt different.

But Theo was the same, and perhaps that was the problem.

He spoke more loudly, trying to drown out the sound of Jun's voice snarling "with you" in his head. "Do we have an agreement, then? I can have free run of the ship as long as I complete my translations and keep mum on everything to do with you?"

With you. It was as if the words had been branded in the back of his mind. Inescapable. His heart ached as though there was a thorn lodged inside.

Jun was looking at him oddly, eyes scrutinizing as though trying to puzzle out something wrong with Theo's face.

So Theo tacked a guileless grin on for good measure.

Jun nodded once, slowly, chin tilting and lifting even as his gaze remained fixed on Theo's face. "If you step out of line, I'm hauling you back in here and welding the door shut."

Theo suppressed a shiver at the mental image of Jun hauling him down the hallways of the ship, over his shoulder perhaps, like in those illicit novels his aunt had liked to read. He and Ari used to steal them to giggle over together in their bedroom.

"With you" finally began to fade away, only the ache left behind.

He smiled up at Jun, enjoying the way the expression on his face seemed to stop Jun in his tracks. "Excellent. We have a deal, Captain. I shall do my best to make sure that won't be necessary."

Jun headed toward the door, stepped out, and hesitated, leaving it open behind him. He gave Theo one final glance over his shoulder.

"We'll see."

Chapter Twelve

The ship was huge.

At least, it was far larger than Theo had ever traveled in before. His family had always kept small personal craft intended for jaunts across the Core.

Jun's ship was something else entirely.

Multiple decks equipped with winding corridors and mysterious doors, rust-streaked tunnels with rickety rungs leading between the decks at seemingly random intervals.

It was dim and eerily quiet. Theo's steps echoed off the dark metallic walls as the ceiling panels either failed to light above him or flickered to life with a petulant whine of electricity. It should have been intimidating, and perhaps it was, but Theo couldn't be bothered to worry about ambience when he was finally free to move about.

It was an absolute delight to explore after hours and hours of staring at the same four bare walls.

The three unlocked doors Theo had come across this far had all contained stacks of storage crates, all of them sealed except for one empty one. It was equal parts disappointing and intriguing.

He assumed some of the other doors lead to other bunks. He wondered how many people were required to man a ship this size. Surely a dozen at least.

He'd only met three of the crew besides Jun, and that was when they had first arrived.

Theo had been exploring the ship all morning and had yet to encounter another living soul besides Jun.

Jun, who had personally delivered another tray for breakfast—a second green fruit along with a bowl of dehydrated grain.

The fruit had been peeled.

Theo had thoroughly enjoyed their breakfast conversation, even if Jun's contributions had largely consisted of monosyllabic grunts before he disappeared with a stern admonishment for Theo to finish his work.

It had taken Theo less than an hour of focused translation to abandon it for the option of exploration.

He could turn the translations over in his head as he wandered anyway.

He did his best work when he wasn't concentrating too hard on it, to a lifetime of tutors' and professors' consternation.

Around the bend of the next corridor there was a lift, sparse and bare the way maintenance lifts often were. The doors appeared to have lost several battles with something the size of a rhinoceros, judging by the layered dents and scratches.

Theo trailed his fingers over the rough surface of the metal as he stepped inside, grateful when the lights blinked on without complaint, along with a control screen.

Three levels were indicated on the screen, showing that Theo was currently on the second level.

He put less than a second of thought into it before slapping the panel blindly, pleasantly surprised to discover he was to go down to the third level.

As soon as the doors of the lift opened, Theo was accosted by a wave of mechanical noise, accented by a repetitive metallic banging pounding away down the corridor.

Never one to leave a mysterious noise uninvestigated, Theo headed toward the source of the sounds.

The pounding was coming from what Theo now recognized as the engine room. Hulking pieces of machinery chugged away all around him in a calamitous din of clanking, banging chaos.

Marco was crouched over some kind of pipe, bringing a hammer down on it with considerable force.

Theo did not mind taking an extra moment to admire the way his arms bulged with the effort.

Marco's curls were shaved close around the sides in what Theo was beginning to recognize as something of a trend in Outlier fashion, or at least among Jun and his crew.

He shifted on his feet, clanging noisily into another loose pipe. Marco's head snapped up at that, and he nearly dropped his hammer as he startled at the sight of Theo.

Theo held up his hands, smile still in place. "Hello, I didn't mean to alarm you. I was just exploring and found myself down here; thought I ought to make myself known."

Marco pushed to stand, the enormous hammer dangling from his hand as he stared at Theo's face. His brow furrowed as Theo spoke more and more rapidly from nerves.

It occurred to Theo rather suddenly that he was in a remote, enclosed space with a strange, large man holding a strange, large hammer.

"Although perhaps you would prefer that I didn't," Theo continued. "I can see that I'm disturbing you, so I'll just make my way back. Wander out the way I came in. So sorry. Please, continue with whatever it is you are doing down here in such a manly fashion. Terribly sorry to have bothered you!"

Theo turned before Marco could speak a word or swing a hammer, and fled back the way he had come, bolting into the lift and only feeling silly about it once the doors began to close and he could glimpse Marco's puzzled face through the small smudged window of the lift.

He hit the panel again. Heat rushed to his face as he considered his own awkwardness. Not the impression he had hoped to make upon the crew and his only possible allies out here in the dark.

The doors opened onto a well-lit corridor, with wall panels clean and maintained in a way he had yet to see elsewhere on the ship.

The lift screen indicated he was on the top deck. He stepped out into the immaculate corridor, and the doors closed behind him with a dull thud.

Laughter drifted down the hall, coming from a central room with double doors half-open to the corridor.

Theo made his way inside, then paused to watch Axel throw something into the air before catching it in his mouth, laughing once again at something on one of the seven vid-screens he had open in front of him.

He was sprawled across his chair, chrome-accented boots crossed on top of the dash of one of several control stations in what Theo was beginning to realize must be the bridge of the ship.

"Captain let you out for walkies?"

Theo jumped guiltily at Axel's voice, then stepped farther into the room. Axel kept his eyes trained on his screens, several of which seemed to contain navigational data and numerical calculations while others showed entertainment vids, one of which was undeniably pornographic in nature. Theo wrinkled his nose at the sight of bouncing breasts.

Axel turned his head with a grin, and with a lazy swipe of his bionic arm, closed the entertainment vids, leaving four navigational screens open.

He popped another morsel into his mouth, managing to chew with a smirk as he looked Theo up and down, pale eyes glowing with mischief. "Didn't expect to see you in here all alone, dollface. I kind of expected the captain to put a tracking band on you at the very least. But here you are, clogging up my cockpit with sunshine. You really are a looker, huh?"

Theo straightened his shoulders, tossing his hair out of his face as he stepped closer to Axel's station. "I have free rein of the ship, just like you."

Axel's eyes fell to Theo's lips knowingly, leaving Theo fighting a blush and the urge to wipe his mouth on the back of his hand. "How long did you spend on your knees to earn that? You should ask Park to invest in some quality kneepads. These floors can be hell on the joints."

Theo bristled at the implication, never mind that in this instance it was indeed based on fact. He had spent the entirety of his academic career combating dismissive and patronizing responses to his work based on his age and appearance and, occasionally, his sexuality.

One crass green-haired pilot wasn't going to shrink him down with a smirk.

"My name is Dr. Theo Campbell"—Theo put a biting edge to his voice, sharpening his accent until it was crisp and bright—"and I am working for Captain Park as a consultant in my field of expertise." His rounded, plummy vowels emphasized his intellect. "I wouldn't expect someone like you to understand the value of my academic contributions, but I will demand the respect due to me as a fellow member of your Crew."

Axel's face went blank, then broke out into a slow grin, mouth softer and eyes sharper on Theo's face. He held out a handful of puffed grain pellets, fragrant with cheese powder. "Fair enough, Doc. Want some cheesy puffs?"

Theo stepped closer with a shake of his head, looking over the dash of Axel's control station with interest. "No, thank you. I find they don't agree with me. What does that button do?"

Axel glanced at the dash, crowded with buttons of varying size and color, then back up at Theo and said with a wry tone, "Which button?"

Theo stepped close enough to touch the dash, his fingers hovering over a row of candy-colored buttons glowing faintly against the chrome. "All of them."

Axel's answering smile was as swift as it was bright, lighting up his face until he glowed like the dash. He dropped his boots to the floor and scooted closer to the buttons, eyes twinkling up at Theo. "You ever flown a class nine freighter before, Doc? Don't tell the captain, but it's easier than it looks. C'mere, I'll show you a few things to get you started."

He wiped his cheese powder–coated fingers on his tight-fitted gray trousers. Leading Theo's fingers to a pale-blue button, he started a lesson on basic navigation and instrument flight that Theo found as intriguing as any lecture he had ever attended.

Axel, it would seem, was a born instructor. Theo had a feeling the pilot would not take that as the compliment he'd intend it to be, so he kept the thought to himself.

After a quarter hour of engaging lessons and intermittent supervised button pressing, Theo built up the confidence to start asking questions. "How many of you are there?"

Axel winked up at him as he guided Theo's fingers through a complicated code sequence. "Can't you tell? I'm a singular sensation, baby. One in a million. Often imitated but never repeated. The real deal."

Theo bit his lip through a burst of laughter. Axel's confidence was so overblown it went right past irritating into endearing. He could relate to that. "I meant to inquire about the crew. How many people are on Captain Park's Crew? I've been exploring all morning and hardly come across a single soul. Though there is every possibility they may be avoiding me. It has been known to happen. Why, when I joined the faculty, professors practically made a sport out of ducking down hallways to get away from me."

Axel shrugged, leaning back in his seat as he watched Theo slowly repeat the sequence with only one correction necessary, all the while switching idly through three different attachments at the end of his arm with a muted click and whirr. "Just the four of us—five now that he's brought you on board. You already met everyone down in the loading bay. Don't tell me you forgot Boom because I wouldn't believe you." His face assumed a dramatic far-off look. "She's the terror in the night that haunts the dreams of wicked men, the scrape of metal down an abandoned hallway, that creeping sensation on the back of your neck when you hear footsteps in the dark."

His eyes flitted up to Theo, gleaming with amusement at his shocked expression. "But seriously, she can be scary as shit, so let the captain deal with her if you get on her bad side. Also, don't get on her bad side. Like, ever."

He shuddered for effect.

Distracted from the buttons, Theo considered the small crew. He thought of all the closed doors down the winding corridors. "So few of you for such a large ship."

Axel scoffed, fingers flying across projections over his screen. "She's a big girl, but nothing I can't handle. Never met a girl who didn't fall for my irresistible charm immediately, and this ship is no different. Besides, what more do we need but an incredibly talented and handsome pilot, a terrifying security chief, a dedicated engineer, and, of course, our fearless leader?"

After closing out the screen he'd been working on, Axel turned to Theo. "Oh, and you. I guess we needed a pretty face on the team. I'm more dashing than pretty, myself."

Theo tossed his hair back from his face at the compliment. He knew he had a pleasing countenance, but it was always nice to hear.

A quick snap of his fingers and Axel pointed at Theo. "Oh shit, no, you're the brains, aren't you? Well, we definitely needed more brains on the crew. We've been pretty heavy on the brawn. Captain Park is, like, 70 percent brawn, 30 percent scowl, 0 percent fun."

The assessment earned a grin from Theo as he deemed it accurate, if incomplete. One must take into account Captain Park's other qualities. Such as his steadfast dedication to his mission, or his strong, capable hands. Or his thick, beautiful— The point was, Jun was much more than brawn with a scowl.

Theo observed over Axel's shoulder as the pilot squinted at a scrolling stream of data on one of the remaining screens. "Boom and Marco, they're siblings, are they not?"

Axel nodded distractedly, fingers nimbly working across the screen. Theo watched in fascination as he flipped his arm to a stylus attachment and sketched out a diagram next to some calculations.

"Isn't it lovely that they get to work so closely together? I have a twin brother, back home. We do everything together. Sometimes I wonder if we delved so far into academia just to be able to stay close, why we keep working in the same place even though our areas of interest differ so greatly. I miss him terribly, actually. His absence is like a stone in the bottom of my shoe, painful and constant and difficult to ignore. Are Marco and Boom anything like us, do you suppose?"

Axel gestured absently, frowning at his data as the numbers changed more and more rapidly. "Something like that. Captain couldn't have hired one without the other; they're a package deal. Paranoid, you know? Neither one will let the other out of their sight, too afraid to be separated again. Probably because they used to be Disconnects, grew up on one of those nature communes. You know the type. All farmland and sing-alongs. Basket weaving and hand-holding type shit."

Theo had no idea what that meant, but it sounded lovely. Idyllic, in a pastoral sense. He cast a skeptical eye around their decidedly non-pastoral surroundings. "However did they go from a life like that to this?"

Axel's face closed off, his gaze shifting as if he only just realized he may have said too much. "They hit a rough patch. Hey, you know what? I think you're ready to graduate from buttons to switches; let's try some of these."

Theo allowed himself to be distracted by flicking switches for a few minutes. He waited until Axel started to relax before speaking again.

"I had the occasion to meet Marco earlier. Well, I say 'met.' Rather, I accidentally ran into him and tried to start a conversation, but the engine room was so loud I doubt he could hear me."

Axel's mouth softened with fond amusement. "Yeah, He's not much for talking anyway. Can't relate, personally. He may not have much to say, but he can take an engine apart and put it back together blindfolded, and it would run better than it did before. Plus, he's stupid-fast on repairs. Park couldn't get a better engineer if he wanted to."

"And I don't want to."

They both jumped at the deep rumble of Jun's voice.

"A better pilot, however"—Jun slowly walked closer—"I could definitely use one of those." He glared at Axel. "What are you doing?" The expression on Jun's face sent Axel straight to his feet, chair spinning slowly behind him.

Theo leaned against the dash with a smile. "Axel's teaching me to fly the ship!"

Axel sputtered, putting distance between Theo and himself with a studied casualness that was anything but. "Not really, Captain. Just keeping him busy, you know, out of trouble and—"

"Look! I'm allowed to press all of these buttons!" Theo crowed with glee, demonstrating the code sequence Axel had taught him.

Jun looked at Axel the way a bored lion might look at a mouse. Not like he was hungry enough to eat it, but like he planned to kill it anyway.

Axel's arm whirred and clicked through a few attachments, lightning fast. "Would you look at the time? I need to go do a thing real quick. On the other side of the ship, probably. You guys just chill here; I'll be right back. In the morning. Maybe."

Jun's glare followed him until the door hissed shut and left them alone on the bridge.

Theo waited impatiently for Jun's attention to return to him before toggling one of the switches Axel had assured him was harmless. "See? Another few days under Axel's tutelage and I'll be flying the ship!"

Jun stalked over and closed his hand around Theo's wrist as he reached for another button. "You're not going to be under Axel's anything."

Theo deftly turned his wrist to catch Jun's hand, lacing their fingers together, and Jun puzzled down at their joined hands like he hadn't been aware they could do that. "Oh? Is there another position open, then, Captain?"

Narrowing his eyes, Jun yanked his hand away and crossed his arms tightly. "I know what you're doing."

Theo stepped closer, allowing a single finger to trace the lines of Jun's muscular arms with a grin. "Do you? Oh no. I thought I was being so subtle."

After a glance up at the roving eye of a camera in the corner of the room, Jun stared back at Theo meaningfully. "Keep it off the bridge. No public areas. Understood?"

If anything, Theo only grinned harder, dutifully removing his finger from Jun's forearm. "You would prefer for me to focus on your private areas, Captain. I understand perfectly."

Despite Jun's eyeroll paired with a groan, the corners of his mouth lifted just enough for Theo to suspect him of a smile. A smile was definitely implied. "Where are my translations?"

Theo hummed noncommittally, studying the wall of instruments to the rear of the command center. "I am still in the first phase of my work process."

The wall was about as hard and unforgiving as Jun's face. "Procrastination?"

Some of the screens had been left open. Theo couldn't help reaching out for one, only to have Jun nudge him aside and close it with a harsh swipe. Theo shrugged at the loss and turned to perch on the edge of Axel's station. "Less procrastination and more intentional distraction to allow my mind time to process without undue stress."

Jun's face remained within the realm of a scowl, but he managed to make the scowl appear skeptical. "Distraction is part of your process?"

Jun's dry tone was unwarranted, in Theo's estimation, given that he knew nothing about Theo's work beyond a single barely published academic paper. "Oh yes, always has been. You are certainly not the first to doubt my process. You should see the behavior notes from all of my professors over the years, absolutely abysmal, every one. It was always 'Theo is a chatterbox, Theo won't stop daydreaming, Theo is incapable of maintaining his focus, Theo is easily distracted' and never anything in the least complimentary; whereas, my brother always received a glowing report."

For which Theo was not in the least resentful, or envious, or anything of the sort. Would it have been nice to have, just once, been the twin most deserving of praise? Of course, but it really wasn't Ari's fault he was such a quiet little delight of a mouse. Not any more than it was Theo's fault he was a chaotic disaster.

Theo in no way resented the fact that Aristotle was a perfect student, and son, and colleague, while Theo had been more often described as "something of a nightmare." He simply accepted what was, and stomped firmly down on any nagging, negative emotions associated with the comparison.

Theo picked up the tangled bit of wire cast aside on the dash and pulled at it carefully to wind into a coil around his finger, twisting the ends into little loops and lines. He held it up triumphantly after a few moments of concentration. "Ha. Look, Jun, I made a star in miniature!"

Jun's face twitched into something very strange that was neither irritation nor amusement yet managed to convey a little of both. He plucked the star from Theo's hands but didn't crush it, the delicate figure held carefully in his palm.

"Get back to work. Now." Jun's voice held a familiar note of exasperation underscored by something warm. Theo hesitated to label it as fondness, painfully aware of the seductive powers of wishful thinking.

Theo thought back longingly about the still unpressed buttons as he trudged toward his room.

No one ever understood his process.

Chapter Thirteen

The bridge was fully manned by the time Theo returned the next day, pad in hand and new translations on the tip of his tongue.

Jun stood at the central console, upright and alert, bringing to mind the oft-revisited image of Professor Gladwell at his lectern.

Although, Theo's memory of Professor Gladwell paled in comparison to the sight of Jun commanding his ship.

It was not unlike comparing a poodle to a wolf, actually. One, all elegant lines and placid restraint, and the other, bristling with barely contained raw power. Axel sat in the same place Theo had first discovered him, only five screens open and none of them noticeably pornographic. Theo was sure that had something to do with Jun's stance at the console directly behind Axel's station.

Boom leaned over another console off to the side, surrounded by dozens of tiny screens streaming images from all over the ship, both interior and exterior. Theo could see Marco working with some wiring on the engine room screen.

Boom's head swiveled in Theo's direction as he walked in, eyes raking him over, and then she turned back to her screens in clear dismissal.

Once he had scanned the room, Theo decided on the console across the wall from Boom. He tried to walk over quietly and settle in the chair with minimum disruption, but in the time-honored tradition of Theo's efforts to keep quiet, he failed in spectacular fashion. He carefully, slowly placed his pad directly on top of something that set off flashing blue lights and a wailing siren throughout the ship.

Axel cursed loudly in Patch, slamming his hand over one of his ears as Jun turned with full-bodied disapproval in Theo's direction.

After stalking over to yank Theo's pad away, Boom pulled up a projection screen and entered in a series of complex codes. The lights and siren cut off abruptly, Axel's continued shouting amplified in the sudden absence of sound.

Boom reached behind the console and retrieved a thick plexiboard. She slammed it down across the panel and locked it in place with efficient movements.

It was a scramble for Theo to catch his pad as she tossed it over her shoulder and stomped back to her console with a long-suffering sigh.

The heat of a deep blush crept along the roots of his hair and ran beneath his open collar. He had decided, given the casual apparel of his crew mates, to forgo his waistcoat and cravat. There was something deliciously thrilling in going about his day half-dressed. Now, however, he felt a trifle too exposed under their universally disapproving glares.

Plastering on a winning smile, he waved his pad cheerily as he swiveled his chair side to side. "I suppose that is one way to wake everyone up, isn't it? While I have your attention, allow me to wish a splendid morning to you all! Isn't it a perfectly lovely day? I was just thinking how delightful it was to begin the day with fresh fruit. Exceedingly rare to enjoy such a luxury on interplanetary journeys."

Axel turned his glare on Jun, who twisted his face in a slight wince, avoiding Axel's eyes. "Wait. I thought you said we were out of fruit? Why does he get fruit, Captain?"

Jun ignored Axel entirely and focused on Theo. He rolled his shoulders beneath his holster and clasped his hands behind his back, standing straight and tall and about ten times more still than Theo had ever managed in his life. "What are you doing here?"

It was difficult for Theo to maintain his smile under the blunt force of Jun's scowl. "I thought it might be nice to continue my work up here with all of you. I am not much of a solitary creature, I'm afraid. I do my best work in the company of others. Silence and solitude are never my companions of choice."

Scrutinizing Theo from his fidgeting spats to his finger-combed hair, Jun gave a sharp nod and turned back to his console.

Axel watched Jun's every motion with a slowly spreading grin. His eyes twinkled at Theo as Jun turned away. "Whatcha working on, dollface?"

Jun stiffened at the nickname and turned the heat of his frown on Axel. Axel appeared completely immune as he unconcernedly picked his teeth with a narrow, sharp attachment on his arm.

Attention on his pad, Theo remained determined to keep his word. "I'm afraid I'm not at liberty to say."

Axel whistled obnoxiously, boots thunking as he propped them on the dash. "Top secret, is it? Bet the captain's got you keeping all kinds of secrets, huh, Doll?"

"He's not a Doll," Jun snapped. "And boots on the floor, pilot, or I'll take every scuff and scratch on that console out of your pay."

Axel dropped his boots, muttering petulantly in Patch.

Ignoring him, Jun turned his head fractionally in Theo's direction. "Dr. Campbell."

Theo frowned, confused by his formal address. He waved a hand magnanimously. "Oh, do call me Theo, please. Dr. Campbell has always suited my father and brother far better than it ever suited me. I'm not one to stand upon ceremony. There's something about the air of authority the title lends that has never seemed to agree with me. Perhaps because I never seem to agree with authority either."

Jun's expression glazed over as Theo rambled, then sharpened when he paused for breath. "Theo. Have you made progress?"

Everyone on the bridge seemed focused on their conversation. Theo arched an inquisitive brow at Jun. "Am I permitted to discuss the particulars, Captain?"

Jun's face hardened. Theo had not realized how relaxed the captain had been until suddenly he wasn't anymore. His whole body shifted into something bigger and meaner, and oh, stars, Theo really ought to be concerned with his own lack of self-preservation instincts. Because a bigger and meaner Jun looked absolutely scrumptious to him.

"No details. Just tell me how much is left."

Theo concealed his shiver at the rolling depth of Jun's voice by fidgeting with his pad. He shifted to cross his legs in his chair. "It isn't an entirely linear process, you understand. Sometimes, I can translate bits and pieces that lead me on a meandering path to entire phrases, but the initial translations tend to be quite scattered."

"Percentage," Jun barked, sending Theo jolting in his seat and scrabbling to catch his pad.

"Oh, well, maths are hardly my area of expertise, but I would say perhaps 20 percent of the passage has been translated. Given considerable room for error in my statistics."

Jun continued to stare him down, face hard and shoulders square. Theo did his utmost to avoid either melting into the floor or climbing those shoulders. He had the distinct impression that neither response would be appreciated.

"Acceptable."

The release of pressure when Jun cut his eyes away left Theo inhaling shakily as he squirmed in his seat.

His mind drifted through poetic raptures over the captain's spectacular rear view when he turned to bark at Boom in Patch, sending her swiping through vid feeds of the ship exterior with a frown.

Theo explored new ways to sit in his chair after he refocused on the passage, curling one knee underneath himself as he lay on his side, head propped against the armrest.

The rest of the crew settled into acting as if he wasn't there. Axel provided running commentary on everything from funny animal vids to exotic cuisine while Jun and Boom answered with monosyllabic grunts and the occasional mild threat.

Theo rather enjoyed the novelty of being the quiet one in the room. It had never happened to him before.

Possibly due in part to the constant presence of his painfully shy twin.

There was a sharp twinge in his chest at the thought of Ari, back home and alone. By now, he must have spoken with everyone who Theo usually interacted with so Ari didn't have to. Even their gregarious postman, whose insistence on small talk practically gave Ari hives. Poor darling.

Theo hoped Ari was not holed up in his laboratory, gazing lovingly at his rocks while he wasted away from malnourishment. Never mind the fact that it was typically Ari who had to remind Theo to eat. Without Theo bustling around, would Ari ever consider leaving his beloved laboratory at all?

He had always preferred rocks to people. "Minerals," he would have corrected Theo scathingly. Honestly, one would think he had never—

Theo straightened in his seat, fingers flying across his pad as words slotted neatly into place within his mind, each one building upon the next as they sharpened and honed down into coherency. The familiar thrill of discovery coursed through his veins, sending him to his feet as he finished decoding a new chunk of text. "Jun?"

Jun's shoulders tightened as he glanced over his shoulder with eyebrows so daunting Theo might have thought twice about approaching. Had he been the type to think twice about anything. "Pardon me, *Captain*." He corrected himself with a roll of his eyes, ignoring Axel's snort of amusement. "Would it please you to know the translation of the first significant portion of this passage? I can always return later if this is an inopportune time. You do seem to be terribly busy with distributing your unpleasant disposition evenly amongst your crew."

Boom's snort outshone Axel's in both volume and duration.

Jun didn't spare her an ounce of his attention. Instead, he made a sharp gesture with his chin toward the door, then stalked through with the clear expectation Theo was to follow.

Scrambling after him, Theo knocked his elbow into a switch that thankfully did not seem to trigger any lights or sirens. He flipped it back to the original position as discreetly as possible, just in case.

Jun waited for him in the corridor, arms crossed and brows lowered.

Theo held up his pad as he approached. "If you would care to look here, I can explain the—"

Without a word, Jun snatched the pad and turned away. He stepped into the battered lift and slapped the control panel. Theo barely made it inside before the door banged shut behind him. Had he been wearing his jacket, his tails might have been caught. The near miss spiked his heart rate as he stumbled into the lift.

When the door opened onto the second level, Jun tucked the pad under his arm and slid his hand loosely around Theo's wrist. The line where Theo's shirt cuff ended and their skin pressed together buzzed with awareness. He found himself staring down at Jun's rough hand around the fine bones of his wrist.

Theo barely noticed where they were headed until another door shut behind him, this time with a generous inch to spare. Jun released his wrist, and Theo shook his head to get it out of the clouds.

Jun took a step into his bedchamber, tucking his Honor hand into a fist as he held up the pad with the other. "Show me."

Suppressing a shiver at the memory of those words in this room, Theo rolled his lips in his teeth against a smile. He must not have been entirely successful, judging by the flash of heat in Jun's face. Jun shut it down with visible effort, and his expression went hard and cold once again.

"Sometime today, Doctor."

It wasn't an endearment, not really. More a statement of fact, the use of Theo's academic title. But that didn't stop his heart from doing a happy little skip as he took the pad and pulled up his translations. "I've been working on this passage, and it seems to be part of the notes for some kind of schematic—for an extremely large barrier field. Impossibly large. The notes express concern over catastrophic failure."

Jun nodded as though this was no surprise, every line of his body tight with impatience as Theo continued.

"The real giddypony of it is that even once I have translated a passage, it still appears to be in some sort of code."

Jun's forehead scrunched as he mouthed *giddypony*, then waved his hand for Theo to go on—something that had so rarely happened to him that he did a little wriggle of excitement.

"Yes, so, as I said, there's a secondary code. But luckily, it was the work of a few hours for me to open it up and begin to parse my way through—"

He made an indignant sound as Jun seized the pad and proceeded to scroll furiously. He then stopped and frowned at Theo menacingly.

Which, really, ought not to have the tightening effect upon his trousers that it did, but, alas.

"You cracked the code?"

Theo fell back a step as Jun advanced, wielding the pad like a weapon. "Well, yes. It was quite a twister, but I muddled my way through, which, you'll be pleased to know, should help me accelerate the rest of the translation."

Jun did not appear particularly pleased to know that. He appeared irate. Volatile. Dangerous. "There is no way you cracked this code in a few hours."

Despite the flat, even delivery, Theo still heard a familiar and unwelcome emphasis on the word "you." He drew himself up to the same posture he used when confronted with skeptics in his field. "There is one particular manner in which I cracked this code, and it was the method that I used. You're welcome, by the way."

The expression on Jun's face was not particularly thankful as he tucked the pad in his pocket and stepped toe-to-toe with Theo, using his extra inches of height to his advantage. "Who are you?"

Offering a smile didn't seem to have any effect on Jun's intimidating stance, but Theo gave his best effort anyway. "I believe we have already been introduced, Captain Park. And made each other's acquaintance. Quite well, as a matter of fact."

The breath shot from his lungs as Jun grabbed the front of his shirt and lifted him up on his toes with a snarl. "Who do you work for?"

Slowly, carefully, Theo wrapped his hands around Jun's fist, lightly tracing the spill of ink across his knuckles as he blinked up into his face. "Technically, I'm still employed by the Department of Linguistics, but in actuality, I appear to be working for you."

He gasped, tilting his head with the motion as Jun shot one hand out to lightly circle his throat, two fingers pressed to his pulse.

This close, Theo could see that his irises weren't black, not really. They were closer to the swirling dark of space, lit by the burning wreckage of stars all around them. Not flat black at all, but limitless. Drawing Theo irresistibly in as Jun growled low in his chest, "Are you lying?"

Theo swallowed against the hand over his throat, rubbed his thumb softly across the knob of bone at Jun's thick wrist. There was no pressure on his air supply, but his voice rasped nonetheless. "I speak only the truth, Captain."

Jun's face struggled through anger and confusion before finally settling upon astonishment.

He lowered Theo's heels to the floor. Flattening his grip on his shirtfront, he slid a palm across his chest and cupped his shoulder. "You're not lying."

Theo would have shaken his head were it not still held in place by the gentle grasp of Jun's rough, warm hand gliding up his jaw to frame his face. "No. I'm not."

Jun's lips parted as if to speak, but nothing came. His gaze fell to Theo's lips instead, his nostrils flaring as his brows drew together. "You cracked the code I've been working on for two years." His growl had fallen away, leaving his voice soft and low. "By yourself. In a day."

Theo squirmed a bit under his scrutiny, accustomed to the irritation of his peers when he sailed ahead on some project they seemed to struggle with. "Yes. It would appear so. I'm terribly sorry if—"

Shaking his head slowly, Jun grazed the broad pad of his thumb just below Theo's bottom lip and whispered softly, "You're astonishing."

Oh.

That.

Well.

Something rattled loose in Theo's chest beneath Jun's honest regard, thumping madly against his ribs, bounding free and unfettered for the first time.

His skin burned with the force of his blush, sneaking down his hairline all the way to his chest, surely radiating heat beneath Jun's hand. "Oh, no. I simply worked out the pattern through cross-analyzing the languages chosen, and—"

Jun cupped the back of Theo's head, fingers gentle in his hair, and angled his face up to meet dark, thoughtful eyes. "Theo. Stop."

With a click of his teeth, Theo shut his mouth, his skin still burning as his hands fluttered in the scant space between their bodies.

Gently massaging Theo's scalp, Jun pressed their foreheads together for a brief, endless moment. His warm breath battered Theo's parted lips with a heavy sigh, and then he released him and stepped back. "You're amazing. Thank you."

If Theo's chin had lifted, just a little, they could have kissed. Easy, simple.

Impossible.

He burned with the absence of it. The heavy weight of longing held him captive in Jun's arms.

Without Jun to hold him up, Theo slumped back against the wall. "It was nothing, really. I—"

Some of the growl came back into June voice as he stared him down, stars still burning in his deep-space eyes. "No. It was not nothing."

He pulled the pad out of his pocket and tapped on the deactivated screen insistently, his face as youthful and open as Theo had ever seen it. "Theo, this could—you could be saving countless lives with this. You have no idea."

Theo brushed the tips of his fingers over Jun's tight knuckles as he gestured at the pad. "Then, tell me, Jun. I could have plenty of ideas if you would just let me help."

Jun gave the pad back to Theo but kept hold of it when Theo tried to tug it free. He wrapped his fingers over Theo's on the pad, his touch light and warm and reaching all the way down into the center of Theo's loneliness. "I know you could. I'm beginning to suspect there may be nothing you can't do. But this isn't something you want to be involved in; trust me."

Theo hooked Jun's pinky with his own and held tight when Jun started to retreat, capturing his gaze with a rare serious expression.

"I think you should let me decide that for myself, Captain."

Chapter Fourteen

Jun was ready to pace out of his skin.

Three days and no further progress. The first day had been spent in the rare effervescence of building hope, the second in slowly dawning frustration, and the third in a state of impotent rage that left his section of the ship largely unoccupied.

Except for Theo.

Undeterred by Jun's black mood, Theo simply continued to wander in and out of Jun's personal space, either maintaining a meandering monologue or studying his translations quietly while every inch of his body jostled with excess energy.

Until very recently, Jun had been unaware that it was even possible for a person to fidget with their elbows.

There did not seem to be a single part of his body that Theo was unable to fidget.

It did not help with Jun's efforts to pretend he didn't notice the way Theo had commandeered Jun's bed and lay sprawled across it like an offering.

Which was, truly, an enormous effort on Jun's part.

Theo yanked his head up from where he had been staring down at his pad and spat out the lock of hair he'd been noisily sucking. He scrambled onto his knees.

His shirt was rumpled, from where he'd been spread out on his belly across the mattress, and askew, revealing the pale blade of a hip bone jutting up over his trousers.

Jun found it difficult to look away from the scant three inches of unknowingly bared skin.

Which was ridiculous.

He could go to any station and find acres of flesh on display if he wanted, day or night. Could pull up a vid on the stream of anyone willing to do practically anything in the nude. It was easily, readily accessible, at all times. Jun had never bothered with or been particularly interested in any of that. It was cheap and easy and so omnipresent that he'd grown desensitized to it.

There was just something about the combination of Theo's modest manner of dress and his cavalier attitude toward his own nudity that struck Jun as highly erotic.

Inconveniently so.

Theo's shirt was buttoned up to the base of his throat. As he tugged at the hem, the top button let loose quietly and unceremoniously, and the placket fell aside, revealing a hint of delicate collarbone.

Jun wanted to press his teeth just there. He wanted to hold Theo down and lick every beautiful inch of skin beneath that prim clothing. He wanted to fuck him deep and slow for hours until he broke down and cried. He just. Wanted.

Hellaciously inconvenient.

Jun didn't want things. It was always a bad idea, and he knew better than that, now. Wanting led to craving led to needing, and Jun didn't have time for any of those in his life.

A man on borrowed time didn't fall in love. That would be incredibly stupid, and incredibly selfish. Jun just needed to try harder to ignore the distant roar of feelings coming for him from the depths of his heart.

Theo's lips were slick from his distressing habit of chewing on his hair. Jun couldn't help but compare them to the way they had looked after swallowing him down as though Theo was made for it.

Delicious. They looked delicious.

Kissable.

The most annoying thing was, Jun had never particularly enjoyed kissing.

It was always a means to an end. It could be pleasant enough, with the right partner, but it just hadn't appealed to him as an act in and of itself.

Until Theo.

Until now.

Now, it was never far from his mind.

Just kissing.

It had been an impulse, to forbid it as a ground rule. A last-ditch effort to protect the heart Theo wore on his delicately embroidered sleeve. A mark of delineation between the trappings of an actual relationship and...this.

Whatever mess this was between them.

The magnetism Jun could not deny, his dragging heels leaving scuffmarks on the floor as he was pulled closer and closer.

There could be no deeper emotions involved, no attachment formed. Jun knew where that ended—with a load of heartbreak for sweet Theo and another gallon of guilt for his own ever-deepening well.

He was doing the right thing, keeping his distance.

Maintaining the walls he'd built around his heart, brick by careful, painful brick.

Walls that shook beneath the impact of every sunny smile and coquettish glance through golden lashes.

Walls that seemed significantly less solid now than they had a week ago.

It was time to fortify them again, reinforce them with stern words and harsh expressions, until Theo stopped trying to chip his way inside.

It was the right thing to do.

So why did Jun want nothing more than to pull the last clinging strands of hair away from those rose-petal lips and kiss Theo until he swooned?

To knock him backward on the bed until he blinked up at him with wide, startled eyes and reached up for him with elegant hands?

Why did Jun want to kiss those pale, unblemished hands like some mythical knight? Shower him with flowers like the Core-based tales of courtly love his mother had told him as a child?

Because Jun was an idiot, apparently.

A fully rusted idiot.

Those rose-petal lips twisted into a frown as Theo planted one hand on his hip, gesturing with the pad.

"—aptain. Jun! It's all very well to demand results when you have no intention of actually listening to them!"

Jun guiltily released the little wire star he kept in his pocket to roll between his fingers while he was lost in thought.

He hadn't kept it for sentimental reasons.

There was no sentiment to be had.

It just happened to be the right size and shape. That was all.

He would probably toss it in the incinerator tomorrow.

Along with the embroidered handkerchief he'd carefully washed and tucked away. The initials were starting to come loose, anyway, from Jun rubbing his thumb over them.

Giving Theo his full attention, Jun cleared his throat, crossed his arms, and leaned back in his chair, knees splayed. "Proceed."

Jun would have to ignore the way Theo mimicked his deeper voice with a little sneer of his rosebud lips, murmuring the word back to himself before continuing.

He would have to ignore the way it made his body buzz and hands ache, wanting to reach out and grab Theo by those skinny arms. To throw him on the bed and show him the meaning of the word "proceed."

To have Theo gasping and begging beneath him, stripped down to his most essential self. As brilliant and beautiful as any star.

Jun's fingers dug trenches into his triceps as he restrained himself, listening intently to the lilting tenor of Theo's voice as he chattered a mile a minute.

"As I was saying, this word occurs multiple times throughout this passage, and I couldn't quite make it out. I was thinking that it couldn't be 'rock,' yet that was what it said, and that doesn't make any sense at all, does it? Not in the context of the phrase. But—"

He broke off to tap furiously on the pad, brow scrunched low as his loosely buttoned shirt started to slip unnoticed down the crest of his shoulder. Jun swallowed against a suddenly dry throat at the sight. He could envision him in candlelight, wearing nothing but that shirt, shoulder decorated with marks in the shape of Jun's mouth.

He nearly fell out of his chair when Theo exploded into motion, limbs flailing in every direction as he scrambled off the bed and trampled over Jun to get to the door. "Mineral! Of course it means mineral! I need to access my notes on the bridge."

He cast an irritated glance behind him as he paused in the open doorway, hair sticking up on one side and shirt still twisted around his waist. He looked edible. He looked like something that was going to eat Jun alive from the inside out. "Please get a wiggle on, Jun; we have work to do!"

Jun followed him to the hallway and watched as Theo trotted to the lift, still tapping at his pad and muttering to himself and generally being a beautiful, oblivious, brilliant menace. And Jun...just.

Wanted.

Craved.

Needed.

Lethally inconvenient.

Chapter Fifteen

Theo shuffled through his notes, ignoring the papers that flew and fluttered to the floor of the bridge until he found what he was searching for. "It appears to be some sort of recipe. Only, instead of dry goods, it calls for powdered minerals. Oh, on second consideration, it isn't a recipe at all. It's a chemical formula. Unfortunately, quite outside the realm of my expertise."

Jun took the pad from under Theo's arm and quickly scanned the translated Standard.

Peering over his shoulder, Theo had to rise up onto his toes in order to see the screen. He pointed at a sentence that had given him particular trouble, riddled with modern language difficult to translate from ancient text. "See, here it says something about an excessive amount of tantalum. I'm not sure if you're aware, but that's a mineral that's been banned in the Core."

Jun, still focused on the translation, made a short, stilted bob of his head that might have been intended as a nod. "Yes, I know what it is. Keep talking."

It took concerted effort not to wriggle with joy over hearing those words in Jun's voice. "Well, isn't it lovely to hear that for once rather than the reverse? Alright, then, there's this word, which I am unfamiliar with, but I could surmise from the context to be another type of mineral. I'm sure Ari could tell me everything about the blasted rock from its weight to its favorite way to take tea, but I'm at a bit of a loss. We could search for it on your stream to find out more about it."

Theo's heart stopped in his chest, then picked up double time when Jun reached for his hand. Holding Theo's hand in his, he jabbed Theo's finger at the pad.

"Point it out to me."

After underscoring the word in question, Theo then turned his hand to circle Jun's wrist lightly, just to hold him for a moment while he was too distracted to notice the presumption.

Jun cursed softly in Patch, knuckles whitening as his grip tightened on the pad to the point that Theo began to worry for the quartz screen.

Jun held it back out to Theo, breaking Theo's hold on his wrist. He wiped a hand down his face with a long, shaky inhale, and then returned to his station and flicked on the coms. "Crew to the bridge. Now."

Theo followed just behind his heels, bursting with curiosity. "It means something significant to you, doesn't it? I've made a bit of a breakthrough in whatever you are planning. I knew I would prove a valuable member of your endeavors. If you would share more about it with me, I could be an even greater benefit."

Jun's hand landed softly on the center of Theo's chest, large and warm and just edging beneath the (whoops) open edges of his shirt. Ari would have been scandalized to see Theo in such a state of disarray. Jun glided his hand over to Theo's shoulder, then let go with a quick squeeze that sent an echoing squeeze through his chest. "Quiet, please, Theo. Just for a minute."

It was the use of his name, as much as the pleading, that gave Theo pause. The raw, weary note in Jun's voice that scraped down his spine like a rusty knife. He never wanted to hear that defeated tone creep into Jun's usually strong voice ever again.

Perhaps he had made a breakthrough, but whatever Theo had uncovered did not appear to be good news.

He dared a hand on Jun's arm with a squeeze of his own. "Alright, Captain. I'll be at my station if you need me."

Theo's station had been what Boom liked to call "idiot-proofed," all panels shut, and access to buttons limited. Apparently, it was an unused communications station, which, really, was quite within Theo's wheelhouse.

He had once been told he could have a full conversation with a brick wall.

It hadn't been intended as a compliment, but Theo liked to look on the bright side of things and decided to take it as a recommendation of his communication skills.

The crew started trickling onto the bridge, first Boom with her determined stride, then Marco, fiddling with something Theo couldn't identify comprised of parts which he also couldn't identify.

Marco offered a small smile at Theo's cheery wave, waving back with his mechanical thing, and then cursing loudly when he dropped it, narrowly missing the tip of Boom's boot.

It was something of a surprise to see Boom stoop to pick it up without complaint and hold it out to Marco with a gentle, amused expression on her face.

Theo wouldn't have called it a soft look on anyone else, but coming from Boom, it was practically a pile of meringue served upon a feather pillow.

It made Theo ache for his brother, for the even softer look on Ari's face when Theo made a mess of things, and he'd swoop in to help clean up. He hoped Ari wasn't too terribly sad over his disappearance. If Theo had known it would go on this long, he would have made more of an effort to reassure Ari of his wellbeing.

Ari tended to fuss when Theo got a cold. He feared his reaction to this situation might be a trifle more overblown. But at least he knew Ari was safe at home, working in his laboratory even as he worried for Theo.

It would be such fun to regale Ari with stories of his adventures when he got back home. Tucked up, side by side on that awful brocade couch Ari had insisted upon purchasing, cuddled beneath the lopsided throw Theo had crocheted during one of his fits of obsessing over a hobby for a week before dropping it flat.

He thought Ari still used the misshapen mug he'd made out of clay, as well. Ari was and had always been Theo's greatest supporter. Missing him was like a scoop had been taken out from between Theo's ribs, leaving nothing but a hollow ache behind.

Watching Boom and Marco, he thought he saw a glimmer of much the same in their own sibling relationship.

"What the hell? I was taking a well-deserved nap, Captain!"

The way Jun's face scrunched up with irritation at the sound of Axel's voice reminded Theo of Ari as well.

Jun turned to stand at parade rest, surveying his crew with a lift of his firm jaw, and suddenly there was nothing resembling Theo's brother about him. "Alright, listen up. Dr. Campbell has discovered something that will alter our course."

Axel snorted, leaning back in his chair as he pulled up two vid screens and started watching cats trying to jump onto things and failing. "What, did he run out of—tea?"

Marco slammed his contraption down on Boom's station and ignored her hiss of disapproval. "Be nice, Ax."

The lazy smile Axel aimed Theo's way showed too many teeth to be entirely friendly. "What? That's what they like down in the Core, right, doctor? Tea and repression?"

It wasn't as if he was wrong, is the thing. Those were certainly Theo's parents' main interests. Theo just lifted one hand to wave it back and forth in a "more or less" gesture.

Jun ignored the exchange; instead, he snapped out with command, "Dr. Campbell has made a discovery. We need to acquire holozite. In significant quantities. Quantities Axel might categorize as something like an 'assload.'"

Boom's rounded jaw actually dropped in surprise, Marco echoing her expression about a foot above her head. She was finally able to gather herself to speak. "Where are we going to find something like that, Park? They don't exactly sell that shit at the multimart. It has a tendency to, you know, explode and destroy everything it touches?"

Shoulders slumping, Jun let out a sigh, then leaned back against his console as though he'd been deflated. "Do you want the good news or the bad news?"

"Good news!" Theo chimed just as Boom said "Bad news," followed with a quelling glare at Theo.

Jun addressed his answer to the ceiling, scowling up at it like he'd found a leak and expected it to come down on all of their heads any minute. "I know where to find it."

No one said anything for long enough that the words burst out of Theo like a highly pressurized cannon. "Wait, is that the good news or the bad news?"

Jun grimaced, finally looking back at his crew and locking on Boom's severe face.

"It's both."

Chapter Sixteen

"No, Park. You can't go back."

Theo sat up straight in his seat at the thin thread of fear in Boom's voice.

Jun had turned to his console to pull up a map, expanding it out to cover the main screen. The sparse, scattered planets of the outer zones of the Restricted Sector dotted the chart, interspersed with clustered stations and asteroid belts. It was so different from the tightly packed Core maps Theo was used to that he was momentarily distracted by it.

"I don't have a choice," Jun said. "He holds the main cache—of everything. Hoards it all in his rusted Dome compound. You know there isn't a better way."

Boom kicked her console, heavy boot giving a dull *clang* against the metal. "I know there isn't a better way for you to get yourself killed."

Neither she nor Jun reacted to the light sound of Axel's laughter, their faces remaining dour when he said, "Sure, there is. I can think of, like, four, off the top of my head."

"You don't understand, Axel." Boom didn't look away from Jun even as she answered Axel, staring him down while Jun pulled up schematics alongside the map, his lips a tight, hard line. The schematics expanded to display the largest space station Theo had ever seen, topped with a massive dome. All around it, smaller stations were clustered in a wavering band.

"This isn't a joke," Boom continued. "He's talking about walking back into the blood-soaked cesspit he clawed his way out of five years ago when he stopped running Crew with Barnes."

The absence of Axel's laughter was far louder than his voice. "Oh, shit."

A chill crept onto the bridge, settling cold in Theo's bones as he searched their stark expressions. Marco looked as if he might be sick, face pale and huge hands clutching the console behind him like he needed it to hold him up. A sense of foreboding shivered down Theo's spine.

"Is there, perhaps, an alternative to said blood-soaked cesspit? I'll admit it doesn't sound particularly appealing. It might be prudent to consider your options before settling upon certain doom."

Jun didn't move apart from flinging one of the schematics off his screen with a sharp flick of his wrist. "No."

With a gentle hand on his bulging bicep, Boom guided a stricken-looking Marco down into her chair and ran her glowing fingers through his curls. She then approached Jun's console to examine the map with him and focused it on the largest section with a slide of her hand. "Alright, well, if you're going to be a suicidal dingus, you're going to be a suicidal dingus with a plan."

It was somewhat shocking to witness Jun's companionable nudge of Boom's shoulder with his own, hints of a grateful smile on his face. "Thanks, Boom. This is going to be a hell of an undertaking."

Boom reached across Jun to open up a new screen, tapping on it until hundreds of flashing red dots appeared across the station on display. "If any asshole can do it, it would be you, Park. You're just filled to the bottled-up brim with—what's that you've got written on lefty, there? Fearless stupidity?"

The flat lack of amusement on Jun's face was practically a beacon aimed in Boom's direction as he lifted his left hand and displayed one tattooed finger in particular. "You know what it says, Boom."

Boom wobbled her head from side to side as though that were debatable and continued tapping the screen, turning half of the red dots yellow. "It's all pretty much the same to me. Valor, bravery, stupidity. That's you to an emotionally constipated *T*, Park."

Jun shoved her aside with his shoulder. He bent over his console, typing furiously and muttering low. "You weren't complaining when I blasted you out of that rust-bitten holding cell in Zingaria."

Boom shoved him back with her hip. (Theo noted he didn't budge.) "I'll admit that occasionally your ridiculous heroic nonsense can be beneficial. But only occasionally. Usually, it's annoying and dangerous."

Sensing an opportunity to jump into the conversation, Theo leapt with both proverbial feet. "Oh, I have plenty of experience with both of those. Possibly more the former and less the latter, but, nevertheless. Ignoring danger and providing annoyance are both well within my skill set."

The glint of appreciative humor in Jun's eyes lightened his dour expression sufficiently that Theo was willing to make an utter fool of himself if it helped to keep that light going. "Yes. I've noticed."

Boom looked between the two of them, brows climbing as Jun hastily looked back at his projections. "Seriously, Park? You're gonna involve him in this?"

The lack of immediate denial from Jun was promising. Excitement bloomed through Theo like a morning glory beneath the rising sun. "I would like to be as involved as the captain will allow me."

Axel talked around some kind of neon-colored gummy snacks he had retrieved from his station. "I think we can all see the two of you are plenty involved already."

"Get my ship ready to navigate the crowds around the Dome, and keep your sticky mouth shut," Jun barked as he closed out two schematics and opened a third.

His clipped tone didn't seem to deter Axel at all. The pilot just tilted his chair back with an ominous metallic creak and chewed louder. "Sure thing, Captain. We got nothing to worry about on my end. Sylvia's a good girl; she'll cooperate if I ask her nicely."

Marco made a sound of disgust off to the side but remained focused on his odd contraption.

It was baffling. Theo would have noticed another crew member. He needed clarification. "I'm sorry. May I inquire, who is Sylvia?"

Marco didn't glance up from his work, but he answered nonetheless while everyone else ignored Theo's question. "She's the ship."

Oh. How exceedingly odd. Back home everyone referred to ships by their make and model. "I see. The ship is a girl?"

A metallic creak, and Axel's chair was upright again while he goggled at Theo, aghast. "Of course she's a girl.

All ships are girls. Well, I should say, she *was* a girl. Until I made her a woman."

Axel finished with an unholy grin and a waggle of his bright green eyebrows.

Marco and Boom gagged in theatrical stereo, Marco still pretending to retch as Boom gave her scathing remarks. "Wow, there's so much to unpack there that I'm just gonna leave it in the box. Please never say anything like that ever again."

Jun expanded a section of the map filled with red dots. "Seconded."

Arm flipping to a pointer attachment, Axel aimed it at Boom accusingly. "Oh, come on! I've seen the way you practically lick your knives clean. You have no room for judgement. If anything, I'm the only one on this ship with a healthy investment in my job! You're obsessed with destroying things, Marco's obsessed with fixing things, and the captain is obsessed with kidnapping brainy little Doll-faced professors, apparently."

The balled-up piece of paper Jun threw his way bounced off Axel's face right between the eyes. He scrunched up his freckled nose as Jun aimed a severe finger at him. "No more creepy talk about my ship, Axel. I will fine you for every cringe."

"Not fair, Captain!" Axel tilted his head back at Marco and Boom with an exaggerated pout. "Daddy's playing favorites again."

"That's your first fine," Jun snapped over Axel's flailing protests.

"That wasn't even about the ship!"

Jun made a short, sharp gesture at the entire bridge, expression flat. "Who cringed?"

Everyone but Theo raised their hand. Jun counted them out while staring Axel down. "That's 300 chips so far. Care to keep going?"

It seemed like the right time to interject, so Theo did. "Well, I, for one, didn't mind the Daddy bit. And you can't fine me because you don't pay me."

The groan Boom gave sounded as though it had originated in the depths of space before exiting her mouth at full volume. "This is all frankly traumatizing to hear, so could we just move on, or should I start stabbing things? Starting with my own ears?"

Marco elbowed her lightly, his soft voice barely carrying across the bridge. "You can do my ears too. I'd thank you for it."

The posture Jun assumed—finger and thumb pinching the bridge of his nose while he scrunched his eyes closed and tightened his mouth—was so reminiscent of Theo's brother that it sent a pang through his chest.

"If we're going to crash Barnes's Dome"—Jun's voice rang out across the bridge—"we need funds. Chips to flash around and drop into all the right pockets. The floor is open for your terrible ideas."

He turned to Boom, who didn't even pause in scanning her security feed, answering with a sardonic tone. "I don't know; we could pick up a hit on somebody?"

Something in Jun's sigh indicated this was not the first time he had refuted this suggestion. "No, terrible. Next?"

To say Marco spoke up would be to say he spoke at a normal, conversational volume rather than his usual quiet tone. "Petty theft? Strip some abandoned fleet for parts and sell them off to junk raiders?"

Jun gave that one some thought, furrowing his brow, then tilting his head in Marco's direction. "Better. Takes too much time. Next?"

"Sell your fucking Doll and make a stack of chips right off."

Theo sat up straight at the unexpectedly sharp snap of Axel's voice.

Only Axel and Theo jumped when Jun swooped down to cage the pilot in, with his hands gripping both armrests of Axel's chair. His expression brooked no argument as he stared Axel down. "We don't joke about the Doll trade on this ship. You will speak to your fellow crewmates with respect. Apologize."

Leaning back as far as his chair would allow, Axel turned his face to side, words tumbling over his shoulder. "Shit. Sorry, dollface—" He winced as Jun flicked him once, hard, directly over his larynx. "Ouch, fuck! Okay, okay. I'm sorry, Dr. Campbell. Won't happen again."

Jun waited until Axel reluctantly met his eyes and then growled, gripping the armrests. "No. It won't."

To Theo's complete surprise and secret delight, Jun turned to him next, lifting expectant eyebrows like he had not just intimidated his pilot into submission. "What would you suggest, Dr. Campbell?"

Finances were not exactly Theo's expertise. No one had ever asked him for his input on something like that. He gave it careful consideration before asking, "Well, what do you usually do for money?"

It was astounding, the way every member of the crew abruptly found something very important to focus on at each of their consoles. Marco even poked at a blank panel as if it was a screen.

Axel finally answered after a few beats of silence. "Didn't the captain tell you? We're in the delivery business."

Was it the kind of profession Theo had imagined it might be? No. But he was intrigued nonetheless. "Oh, well. Could you make a delivery?"

It wasn't the kind of question Theo had anticipated might provoke laughter, but Axel seemed to find it hysterical. "I don't know, Captain, could we?"

Jun stood facing the schematics with a thoughtful expression, the fingers of one hand tapping restlessly against his thigh. It was the closest Theo had ever seen him come to fidgeting. "He's right. We need to make the next drop ahead of schedule."

Theo bounced over to Jun's console to stand alongside the captain and Boom. "What are you dropping?"

Boom turned to Jun rather than acknowledging Theo. Jun pretended he didn't notice her scrutiny as she said, "Seriously, why is he here, again?"

The obnoxious crack of Axel's knuckles resounded in the room. He had rolled them into a fist to press against a flat attachment on his other arm. "Let me put it to you this way, Doc. It's best in this business if you don't ask too many questions."

Hopping up onto the small stretch of empty space at the end of Jun's console, Theo gave a delighted gasp. He dismissed Boom's warning snarl with a wave of his hand. "My word! You're criminals!"

Boom scoffed while she closed out her screen and pulled up something that appeared to be an encoded inventory list. "There's no crime when there are no laws. You're not in the Core anymore; this is the deep dark."

Theo clapped and pointed at Jun, who continued to pretend like he was all alone on the bridge, poring over the list. "Brigands, then! Scoundrels. Rapscallions."

Even Axel seemed to be working now, furiously typing something out on his console, strings of numbers flying across his screen. "Yeah, no, we're definitely not whatever that last one was. That sounds like the opposite of awesome."

"I'd kind of like to be a rapscallion, actually." The soft sound of Marco's voice made Theo smile as he gestured to Theo with his contraption, which appeared to have nearly doubled in size with clear tubes now protruding in all directions.

For once, Boom's disgusted sigh was tinged with warmth as she slanted a glance at her brother. "You would. Probably because it sounds like some kind of food."

Theo swung his legs, drumming his heels against the metal panels of Jun's console and beaming at the crew. "I've fallen in with a band of ne'er-do-wells. How utterly thrilling! I demand that you teach me your scofflaw ways."

The balled-up bit of candy wrapper that Axel threw at him got stuck in his hair, leaving Theo to tease it out. Axel laughed at that, while Jun's jaw just continued to tighten. "Sure thing, Doc. First lesson—stop talking like you know someone who owns a rusted castle."

Theo winced guiltily.

Axel's eyes widened. "No shit? You really do know someone with a castle, don't you?"

Twisting the candy wrapper between his fingers, Theo gave a halfhearted shrug. "It's more of a palace, actually. The battlements are hardly fortified, and I doubt the portcullis is even functional. My aunt married up, you could say. It's not as though I've spent more than a few nights there; I haven't even visited since I was fifteen. There may have been an incident involving an overpriced yet terrifically ugly vase and a third story window; although rumors of my involvement remain unsubstantiated."

The entire bridge crew grimaced at the volume of Axel's appreciative whistle. Theo just relished the novelty of being the least irritating person in a room.

"Damn," Axel said. "A palace. Imagine that. Hey, they gotta have, like, loose valuables in a place like that, right? What was it you were saying about it wasn't fortified?"

"Shut up, Axel."

As Jun stared them both down, Axel leaned back in his chair, arms raised in surrender, and Theo sat up straight, hands folded on his lap, blinking back innocently.

Jun rubbed his temples with a low sound that made Theo want to bat his hands away and offer to rub there himself. And maybe other places. Just as a bonus kindness. Theo was nothing if not giving of himself.

"The drop. Axel. What's our ETA?"

The numbers paused on Axel's screen for just a moment. He screwed up his face in concentration. "Looks like it's gonna take another cycle and a half, give or take a few hours."

Chin dipping once, succinctly, Jun moved on. "Good. Boom?"

Solid heels were already clunking away from the console and out into the corridor as Boom tossed her answer over her shoulder. "On it."

"I'm still only about three-quarters of the way through repairs to the combustion chamber," Marco offered with an apologetic frown. "It doesn't want to cooperate." He held out his odd tube-riddled contraption as if it was proof of such.

Jun sucked his teeth, habitual scowl sliding back into place. "Damn. Do what you can to optimize fuel consumption in the meantime."

Marco gathered his tools and left with a jaunty salute at Jun's rigid back.

"Well, isn't this cozy?" Axel's attention bounced back and forth between Theo and Jun as if watching a tennis match, his mouth still chewing something. "Tell me, Dr. Campbell, do you have to manually remove the stick from the captain's ass or does he prefer to leave it in?"

He flinched so hard that he fell out of his chair when Jun feinted toward him with a snarl. "Okay! Okay, I'll leave you to it. It's not like I work here or anything."

One of his brightly colored snack packages fell from the pile in his arms when he stomped away, muttering in Patch.

Theo stooped to pick it up, puzzling over the sickly yellow font declaring them to be Power Blasted Fruit Nuggets.

When he turned to Jun to ask about them, he caught Jun's gaze jerking away from his posterior in a move Theo had gotten most adept at picking up from a certain type of gentleman.

The type of gentleman who was interested in Theo.

Snack forgotten, Theo stepped closer, grinning when Jun backed up a step and crashed into the console behind him with a metallic ringing sound. Theo pitched his voice into a soothing purr, offering a sympathetic pout. "Don't worry; I'm not going to climb all over you, Captain."

Jun's shoulders dropped incrementally, the harsh lines around his mouth softening a little. Theo leaned in closer to watch the lines deepen again, his own gaze falling to Jun's supple lips. "Unless, of course, you asked me nicely."

Never in Theo's life had he witnessed someone appear so furious over their own arousal. Jun's face

contorted into a sneer even as his pupils dilated, and his attention slid down to Theo's mouth, watching him lick his lips with a low growl. Theo found the reaction rather...
Motivating.

Chapter Seventeen

Unfortunately for Theo's raging libido, Jun remained focused on his plans for the rest of the day. He barely gave Theo a second glance despite his near-constant chatter.

Theo had resigned himself to resolving the issue through his own handiwork as he retired back to his bunk for the evening.

A tiny gasp escaped him when the door slid open to reveal the strong back of his captain, standing perfectly still in the middle of the modest chamber with his hands clenched behind his back.

He had stripped out of his long-sleeved knit shirt and stood now in just a fitted gray sleeveless undershirt, along with his tight black trousers and shoulder holster.

There was nothing overtly reassuring about his appearance, but Theo found it oddly comforting to observe Jun so exposed.

Even more ink climbed up his wrists all the way to his shoulders, disappearing beneath the edges of his top. Mostly black lines with tiny pops of color, Theo wanted to trace them with his tongue in a lazy, meandering path until Jun pulled him up by his hair and told him to stop.

Well.

There went any hope of concealing Theo's desire. His fitted velvet trousers were not particularly suited for camouflaging his rising interest.

Jun spun in place to face him, fists going down to his sides as he regarded Theo for a long, silent moment, waiting for the door to slide shut behind him.

Theo opened his mouth to inquire about the nature of his visit when Jun rushed to speak first.

"This is me. Asking nicely."

Asking?

Oh.

If Theo had possessed the power to dissolve his own clothing away with a single blink, this was the moment he would have done so.

Instead, he crossed his arms over his narrow chest and leaned back against the wall, allowing his gaze to sweep slowly over Jun from head to toe.

The fact that his feet were bare sent Theo's heart into overdrive, for some odd reason. It was only the tiniest hint of vulnerability, but it was—

Enough.

"Asking for what, Captain? Something quick and casual? Impersonal? Am I allowed to call you by your name or am I to address you only by title? I wouldn't want to act too familiar and cause offense."

The tiny thread of hurt that wove itself through Theo's voice surely gave him away despite his caustic words. He was usually better at hiding his hurt feelings in his affairs. Everything was just different, with Jun.

More.

Jun didn't answer as he stepped closer. Theo soon realized he had pinned himself to the wall through his own posturing. Jun didn't touch Theo so much as displace the air around him, a phantom pressure against his skin.

It made Theo tip his head back and drop his hands down to press against the wall behind him as Jun dipped to nuzzle into Theo's throat with a harsh exhale.

"Say my name." Jun brushed his lips against his skin. "Say anything you want. Just let me."

He didn't elaborate on exactly what Theo should let him do, but the particulars were immaterial anyway.

Because Theo would let Jun do anything he wanted to him. Including sweep him away across the galaxy after just a single glimpse of his heart-stopping face.

Theo had always been more prone to leaping than looking. He couldn't even find it within himself to regret it, not while he stood here in Jun's embrace.

Not while leather and ozone filled his lungs with each deep, greedy breath.

The humid heat of Jun's open mouth slid across his throat as he nudged his open shirt aside to get to his skin. He latched onto the crook of Theo's shoulder with blunt teeth and a muffled growl.

He pulled back when Theo made a soft, wounded sound. And Jun's shining lips tugged down in a frown as he lifted one hand to trace over the mark. "I'm not—I don't know how to be gentle. Not like you deserve."

Theo let his hands drift slowly up Jun's chest to rest over the thumping beat of his heart. "Yes, you do."

Jun shook his head, scowl slipping into place like a well-worn blanket, familiar and comfortable and covering all of his softest parts. "No, I don't. I never learned. I never had anything to be gentle for. Soft things don't last very long, where I come from. They never held any appeal for me, before."

The last was said sotto voce, as if Jun was speaking to himself, gaze drifting dreamily across Theo's face.

Theo arranged it into a teasing smirk as he grabbed one of Jun's wrists and led his hand down to Theo's tented trouser front. "One could hardly say I'm soft, Captain."

Jun gave him an obliging squeeze, just the right side of too tight, scowl fading from his face as Theo pressed up into his grip with a whine. Then he released him and lifted his hands to Theo's hair, tangling his fingers in the long silken strands. "Soft. Pretty." He tightened his grip abruptly to tug Theo's head back against the wall. "Sweet."

Theo shook his head, more to feel Jun tug harder against the motion than to express his opinion, the tiny pinpricks of pain shooting a thrill straight to his cock. "I'm really not. I'm a bit of a pill. Hard to swallow."

Jun's hand returned to Theo's trousers, yanked open the button placket with a flick of his wrist, then slid inside. His warm, rough palm was devastating against Theo's skin just as his warm, rough voice was devastating against his ear. "I think I'm up to the challenge."

And then Theo nearly swallowed his own tongue because Jun just...dropped.

To his knees.

It was beyond unexpected.

Theo could count on one hand the number of times a man had gone to his knees for him. That was usually Theo's role. Reciprocation had always been more of a hope than an expectation in his affairs. He yelped with surprise when Jun bypassed his cock entirely and instead, shoved Theo's shirt up and rubbed his face against the pale skin of his stomach. "Jun! What are you—?"

Jun's hands circled Theo's ankles and yanked them apart until he had to grab onto the expanse of Jun's shoulders for balance.

A shiver ran through Theo as Jun dipped a long, wet tongue into his navel, his sparse stubble scraping Theo's skin. He dug his fingers into Jun's shoulders as his head made an embarrassing hollow thunk against the metal bulkhead.

To his surprise and building distress, Jun stopped. He got to his feet and brought one hand around to rub at the back of Theo's head, his eyes dark on his face. "No."

Panic bloomed in Theo's chest like an insidious weed, shooting out in all directions as he sensed his time with Jun slipping from his grasp.

That was what he got for acting selfishly, for letting a man like Jun lower himself to Theo's level. "Oh, of course. Here, I'll just—" But when he attempted to get to his knees, Jun caught him beneath the arms, burning gaze unwavering from his face.

"No. Not like this. On the bed."

The "get" was implied, and Theo rushed to follow orders only to come up short, limbs flailing uselessly through the air and feet sliding across the floor when Jun didn't release his grip.

The noise Theo made when Jun lifted him from the ground should never have been granted a witness. Certainly not one who smirked at the sound, walking steadily across the room with his armful of blushing, rumpled disaster.

To his delight, Theo discovered that his legs did indeed wrap quite nicely around Jun's waist as he carried him to the bed.

A proven hypothesis at last.

Ari would have been so proud.

On second thought, Ari would have wanted to know absolutely nothing about this situation and would stubbornly plug his ears were Theo to attempt to tell him about it.

The thought made him giggle, giving Jun pause as he laid Theo flat on the narrow bed. A spear of anxiety shot through him at Jun's puzzled expression. Theo had been punished all his life for laughing at inappropriate times, and he didn't want to ruin this. "I was just—I didn't mean—there is nothing amusing about this situation. I wasn't laughing at you, and I beg your pardon."

If anything, Jun only appeared more puzzled. He tugged Theo's shirt off over his head, gaze hungry on his slender torso. "You have a nice laugh. I like it. Laugh all you want."

Oh.

Many words had been used to describe Theo's laughter.

Annoying. Incessant. Piercing.

But never, not once, nice.

The medical impossibility of Theo's heart melting into his spine did not deter him from experiencing the sensation of it.

Jun's face rubbing up his stomach and over his chest didn't exactly help either. Nor did the loose grasp of his hands around Theo's wrists.

Heart pounding against his ribs like it was demanding to be heard, Theo moved his arms slowly and deliberately up over his head, dragging Jun's grip along. Theo crossed his wrists on his pillow, monitoring Jun for his reaction.

Jun's breath whooshed out of him as if he had been gut-punched, unable to decide between focusing on his hold around Theo's wrists or into his anxious face.

Theo's confidence wavered as the silence stretched on, Jun frozen above him. He started to move his arms apart. "I suppose that isn't what you wanted after all. I apologize if—"

He squeaked as Jun's hands squeezed firmly around his wrists, pressing them into the pillow. His hard stare was all pupil, desire, and command reflected within.

And, something rather remarkable happened.

Every second of every day, Theo's mind was a hornet's nest, buzzing and stinging and throbbing with frantic activity. His gift and his curse, never quiet and never still. Always going full tilt, careening into ideas and notions and out again just as quickly, without a moment's rest.

But, like this.

Like this, pinned beneath the weight of Jun's regard, held solid under the steady pressure of his hands, Theo's mind went blessedly still.

Quiet.

It was transcendent.

Jun finally opened his mouth to speak. "Good. That's good." His voice was low and crumbling around the edges. "You're good, like this. Stay."

Theo shivered as Jun took his hands away, leaving it up to Theo to decide whether to comply. It was nice and quiet in his head, Jun encompassing every thought, looming so large that he pushed out all the buzzing nonsense until Theo couldn't hear it anymore. Until there was only the solid warmth of Jun's body, all slim curves and harsh angles pressed tightly to Theo. The deep, dark scent of him coating Theo's tongue when he swiped a taste of Jun's throat, finally chasing one of those dark lines of ink up to his jaw. The harsh exhale against Theo's cheek as Theo went limp beneath him.

The thrill of it sent bolts of lightning streaking through his body, cock aching in his trousers as he whispered up at Jun. "I'll stay. As long as you want me to."

Something complicated flickered across Jun's face. Then he ducked his head and caught Theo's nipple in his teeth.

Theo arched into the sensation, choking on a moan shaped like Jun's name.

Jun sucked hard, only pulling off once Theo's nipple was red and sore, giving it a swift lick, then granting the same treatment to the other side.

Theo twisted and writhed beneath him, wrists anchored to the pillow as if by some invisible force, simply because Jun had asked it of him. There was nothing Theo had given more gladly in his life.

He was a squirming, gasping mess as Jun trailed his plush lips down the thin skin over his ribs in long, openmouthed kisses. Jun took it slow, stretching out the moments until Theo felt as though he were floating, tethered to the bed only by Jun's will for him to remain there.

It was enough.

Strong, ink-stained hands hooked into his waistband and tugged his trousers and small clothes off in one heavy yank that nearly dislodged Theo's wrists, to his dismay.

He checked that they remained in place, nearly missing the gobsmacked expression on Jun's face when Theo's stockings were revealed.

His velvet trousers hit the metal floor with a heavy slap as Jun dropped them to focus on Theo's garters. The fingers of his Valor hand traced over one of the red satin ribbons around his thighs. "Holy shit. What the fuck are these?"

Theo curled up into himself a little, bringing his knees up to press his stockinged legs together just in front of where Jun kneeled on the mattress. His wrists remained on the pillow. "They're nothing. Standard practice, back home. I'm beginning to realize that the Outlier mode of dress is quite different from my own. Disregard them, please."

Humiliation burned hot through him like a shot of liquor taken too quickly. Back on Britannia, everyone wore stockings as a matter of course. Some of Theo's previous lovers had even taken an interest in gifting him with embroidered stockings or elaborate garters specifically designed for the boudoir. He wasn't wearing any of those, of course. Just thin black cotton with his plain daily garters tied in a modest bow.

It was immediately clear by Jun's reaction that out here, beyond the Verge, even this much attention to undergarments was considered peculiar. He didn't say anything else, his attention never straying from Theo's legs.

The silence jerked Theo into action, and he began to lift his wrists to take the garters off, himself. "I'll just get rid of these, so we can—"

"No." Jun was above him in a flash, both of Theo's wrists in the grip of one hand, pressed back into place against the pillow. "Stay."

Theo wasn't sure he could have moved if he wanted to as Jun settled back on his knees.

And he really, really didn't want to.

Jun's hands slid up his legs from ankles to knees and further still, until he could hook his fingers behind both garters.

Theo gasped when Jun pulled his legs apart with a single, strong movement, the garters now digging into the soft flesh of his inner thighs. Jun released them only to untie each bow one at a time, slowly and carefully, until his palm was slashed in half by two red ribbons.

He turned his hand to consider them, the drape of red satin flowing seamlessly against the ink across his skin as if it were a part of it. Theo tried to stifle the fanciful notion of leaving his mark on Jun, of getting so far beneath his skin that Jun could never forget about him. Ridiculous, since Theo had once bumped into an ex-paramour whom he had entertained for some weeks, and the man had not so much as remembered Theo's name. Theo was apparently not the kind of lover one didn't forget.

A thick, dark fall of hair obscured Jun's face as he dangled the ribbons until they skimmed over Theo's spread thighs. He trailed them in a sweeping, curving line up Theo's body. Theo cried out when Jun brushed them across his swollen nipples, and Jun made a harsh, satisfied sound in his throat, grip tightening around the ribbons.

Theo tipped his head back as Jun laid them across his throat; one firm thumb lifted Theo's chin to get a better view.

"You're unbelievable." Jun's lips barely moved around the words.

It was difficult to choke out a false laugh when Theo had sunk so deeply into this strange, beautiful place Jun was leading him through, but he managed. "Yes, so you've said. You can hardly believe a person such as I could exist, with all my irritating oddities."

Jun traced the line of the ribbons as he shook his head, and he gathered them up in his fist once more to pull them away from Theo's throat, following their path with his glittering gaze. "No, I can't believe, just— The galaxy is so ugly, but here you are. So beautiful."

His touch skated up the inner curve of Theo's arm. "So soft."

Red satin ribbons encircled Theo's wrists. He focused on the bob of Jun's ink-stained throat as he tied them loosely, and on the muscles rolling beneath his shirt.

Jun completed his work and sat back on his heels between Theo's legs. His palm pressed flat and warm against Theo's cheek. Theo's breath hitched at the brush of Jun's thumb over his parted lips, the deep rumble of his voice. "So sweet."

Theo wanted to deny it, wanted to point out that he was anything but sweet, only—only it was so lovely to hear those words in Jun's voice. Paired with the expression on his gorgeous face, it nearly made Theo believe him.

Jun tapped the ribbons lightly tied around Theo's wrists, his face serious. "Do you want it like this? Tell me when I push too far."

Not if. When. As though Jun was used to pushing until he ran up against a barrier, time and time again. Theo spoke over thirty languages, yet he didn't have the words to tell Jun that he was liquid in his hands, that Jun could dive as deeply as he desired, and Theo would only flow around him, welcome him in.

So he used the words that melted off his tongue when he opened his mouth. "I want it like this. I want you like this, Jun. I'm under your command, Captain. Of my own free will."

The first time Theo had left planetside and ventured into the stars, he had been transfixed by the view. The hypnotic swirl of sparkling light throughout the endless dark. There was something of that same view in Jun's face just now.

The same beauty, only made sharper by the edge of danger within the depths. The same relentless, magnetic pull, like a hook behind Theo's heart. The same sure knowledge that he would never be as he was before.

Jun spread Theo's hair out over the pillow, then petted down to his throat and let his hand curl lightly around it. "Perfect."

There had to be a limit to the amount of bliss that could flow through Theo's veins at the sound of a single word. A body could only withstand so much.

Jun released Theo's throat and rolled his sore nipples between relentless fingers, his attention never leaving Theo's face as Theo whimpered and pushed into the too-sharp flare of pleasure. "Good."

He swooped down to use his tongue, alternating between soft, soothing licks and quick, harsh flicks until Theo was leaking against his stomach, breathing out tiny little moans on every breath.

Jun discovered the small puddle as he braced against Theo's heaving chest, holding him still beneath his attentions, and his wrist dipped into it. He lifted his shining wrist to his mouth, making sure Theo watched him as he licked it off with a satisfied hum. Then he swiped the rest up on his fingers and brought them up to trace Theo's lips. He slid two inside until Honor was pressed up against Theo's teeth.

Theo sucked them clean, trying not to think about how much he wished it was Jun's tongue that filled his mouth, his lips on Theo's lips. This would have to be enough. It was already so much.

Jun took his fingers away and shuffled back on the mattress. He began to remove Theo's twisted, sagging stockings, unmoored without their garters to hold them in place. Theo kicked his leg to help, then cried out with shocked arousal when Jun admonished him with a light slap on his thigh. "No. Let me."

Jun didn't miss the way Theo's cock jumped at the slap, and his teeth flashed in a rare, broad smile. He fell to his belly on the bed and threw Theo's legs over his shoulders.

"Oh, gracious! Jun, you really don't have to—"

Those flashing teeth sank into Theo's leg in a gentle bite, and Theo was a live wire in Jun's hands, twisting and moaning and begging for more. Jun soothed the bite with a broad swipe of his tongue, then turned his head to focus on Theo's cock.

To his dismay, Jun skirted around it, laving at his belly, tongue slipping beneath Theo's cock and barely skimming his shaft.

Theo tossed his head against the pillow, his wrists nearly slipping from their loose bindings. "Please, Jun! Don't tease me."

Jun gave a thoughtful hum as he sucked on Theo's balls, rolling them on his tongue while his thumb pressed hard on the stretch of skin behind them. Theo was suddenly reminded of how achingly empty he was, how desperate to be filled. "Fuck me. Please, fuck me. I'll be so good; I promise. I'll even do my best to keep my mouth shut, to be quiet, please!"

A promise he was already showing evidence of being unable to uphold. It had been the primary complaint of his previous lovers, and Theo was determined to correct it if that was what he needed to do to have Jun.

Jun surged up with a fierce snarl, hooked the tips of his fingers behind Theo's bottom teeth, and tugged his lower jaw down. "Keep your mouth open. I want to hear you."

The tip of Theo's tongue caught on those fingers as he answered quietly, muffled by Jun's firm hand, "Yes, Captain."

Chapter Eighteen

Theo had been expecting a small acknowledgement of his compliance. Perhaps a hint of a smile or a kind word.

He was not expecting Jun to immediately reward him by slipping his fingers free and sliding down to suck his cock.

Jun's strong hands held him by the hips as he bobbed his head, sucking so hard Theo could feel the pull in his toes.

"Oh stars! Jun. Captain. You really, truly ought to stop that if you wish this to last more than a moment."

Jun pulled off with a wet pop that made Theo's balls draw up tight. His voice was even lower than usual, as dark as deepest space. "Getting close?"

Theo nodded somewhat desperately, chewing on his lower lip and shifting fitfully on the bed.

Jun clamped one hand tightly around the base of his cock, letting the head rest against his lips as he spoke. "Don't come until I tell you."

He sucked Theo back down as if the matter was settled, as if Theo could simply stave off his own orgasm through sheer force of will.

Theo arched with a cry as he hit the back of Jun's throat, and Jun just swallowed around him. "I can't—I'm going to—"

Jun's head came up with a growl, bared teeth pressed against Theo's thigh, his fingers an iron ring around Theo's cock. "You can. Be good for me."

Maintaining focus had always been a problem for Theo. Yet somehow, like this, he could think of nothing else but Jun. His strong body and rough hands, the silken touch of his tongue, his deep, harsh sounds as he let Theo inside.

Be good, he had said, and Theo wanted to be that for him above all else. Only for Jun.

"Alright. Yes, I will. I'll do my best, but you feel so—ah!"

Jun swirled his tongue on that sensitive spot just below the flare of Theo's cockhead, and it was nearly all over. In an effort to get away, Theo twisted his hips, desperate not to disobey command. Jun chased him, holding his cock steady while he changed course. He flicked tiny little licks up and down Theo's shaft that hit him like a jolt of electricity. It made him shake and huff out sharp little sounds on every breath.

Dark eyes flashed up at him through thick black lashes, and Theo finally lost his very last shred of dignity. "Please. Please, Jun. Captain, please! I need you."

No response came beyond a slow, leisurely suck at the very tip, Jun's tongue working him like a kiss, dipping sweetly into the slit. Theo dug his heels into Jun's shoulders, speaking through gritted teeth. "Jun, I swear by your giant, ugly, rusted ship. If you do not get up here and take your clothes off, I will shoot down your throat in the next three seconds."

That got a reaction.

Possibly more of a reaction than Theo had bargained for.

His spit-slick cock slapped against his belly as Jun released him. Theo waited, legs tossed to either side while Jun prowled up his body on hands and knees, his clothes scraping against Theo's skin. Jun leaned down to take Theo's jaw in hand, eyes snapping. "I thought you said you were going to be good. What happened to that?"

Theo squirmed with a plaintive whine, grasping the ribbons tightly. "I'm sorry. You feel so incredible, and I'm not used to being on the receiving end of that particular act. I want to—I want to be good, but I'm not. I'm just not. No matter how I try. Please don't stop."

He shut his mouth against the building overflow of humiliating, pleading words that crowded his throat. Asking Jun to stay, to keep Theo close even though he wasn't any good. Promising to try harder, to do anything, to let Jun do anything he fancied, anything at all.

Jun seemed to hear him anyway, brow furrowing as he softened his grip on Theo's jaw. He stroked Theo's face lightly, tenderly, and Theo had to blink against a sudden mortifying threat of tears. He let out a strained bit of laughter, instead.

"I'm sure it's no surprise to you that I can't manage to control myself for more than a minute at a time. That I can't even pretend to be good for you."

Jun's forehead pressed so hard against the side of Theo's face that Theo could feel his lashes flutter, and then Jun was gone, moving away. Theo bit back a harsh cry of disappointment when Jun sat up and climbed off the bed entirely. He turned his face into his upper arm to hide as he began to work his hands free of their binds. It wouldn't take more than a moment's work to escape the loose ribbons.

"Stop."

Every molecule in Theo's body halted at the command, breath frozen in his lungs for half a second before he released it on a sigh and turned to face Jun.

Jun, who was—

Nude.

Entirely, gloriously nude.

The sound of air whistling back into Theo's lungs was nearly as humiliating as the way his cock blurted a drop of excitement into his stomach at the mere sight of Jun.

There was a lot of him to see.

Not overly large in build, but every inch of him carved from warm stone and decorated with dark ink. Ink covered his arms in dozens of intertwined images Theo would like to dedicate some months to studying in detail.

Black lines traced the contours of his abdomen, pausing to form geometric shapes along his ribs and then thinning into bare lines again through the dip of his Adonis belt and down his thighs. Dark hair obscured some of the imagery on his calves, but it only made Theo burn to take a closer look.

Jun came back to the bed and dropped a bottle of lubricant by Theo's hip. He made a space for himself between Theo's thighs. His cock jutted up dark and hard and insistent as he took a moment to trail his fingers over Theo's skin. At Theo's shiver of response, his face brightened, his smile small but sharp. "Good. You're doing so well, baby."

Baby. It hit like a fist to the diaphragm, stealing Theo's breath. He had been called all sorts of things in bed over the years. Darling, sweeting, tart. None of it had ever drilled straight through his sternum to lodge so firmly in his heart in quite this way. He feared now that if one were to examine that organ, one would find Jun's name scrawled across it in indelible ink. Alongside the word "baby."

Theo shook his head even as he lifted his hips in a nonverbal attempt to spur Jun forward with the proceedings. "What utter nonsense, Jun. I haven't been good at all."

Theo's breath hitched when Jun picked up the bottle and lifted his leg.

"Yes, you have." Jun's voice was so hushed Theo could barely hear it over the sound of his own heavy breathing. "Better than I deserve."

And then Jun's fingers pressed wet and thick against Theo's entrance, and Theo's thoughts scattered like leaves to the wind. Nothing left behind but heat and pressure. He yielded, taking in two of Jun's fingers to the hilt, gasping at the realization that those tattoos were now rubbing against his walls.

Jun came up and buried his face in Theo's neck as he started to move his hand, opening Theo up and brushing against that small spot that made him see stars.

Theo let loose a sound he didn't recognize, something new and raw and entirely too honest. Much to his dismay, his open throat could only speak the truth under Jun's soothing tongue. He tried to gather his scattered wits about him to save face. "You don't have to—you can just fuck me. I've never had so much attention paid to me in bed, and I'm afraid it will quite go to my head if you do not stop."

Jun sucked a patch of Theo's delicate skin between his teeth, letting his fingers curl just so inside him. Theo tensed and moaned and tried not to feel claimed by the possessive mark left behind even as Jun finally let go to mumble against his throat. "I'm not stopping until you beg me to."

Theo didn't say that he was afraid of becoming addicted to Jun's intensity and attention only to have it taken away again. He didn't say that he was afraid nothing could ever satisfy him again after this. He didn't say that he wanted to wake up to Jun's grumpy face and fall asleep curled in his capable arms.

Theo didn't say any of that; he just let the sounds that climbed up his throat spill over his trembling lips until Jun began to grunt and rut against the bed with every thrust of his fingers, his own voice gravel-rough.

"Fuck, you sound so good. That's it, make some noise for me."

He added more slick and a third finger, and Theo started thrusting up against his hand, feet planted on the bed and thighs shaking. And when Jun pressed him firmly back down to the mattress with his free hand, he cried out so sharply it rang against the metal walls.

Jun was a strong, reassuring weight holding Theo to the bed, and it was as if something clicked into place inside him, something he had been searching for his entire life.

Theo melted back into the bed, legs falling open and arms going limp against the pillow as he slurred out his words, lids falling half-shut. "Please, Jun."

The rising satisfaction on Jun's face warmed Theo from the inside out. Jun carefully removed his fingers and braced himself on his elbows to either side of Theo's head. He nosed at Theo's cheek, lips damp against his skin. "Ready for me, baby? Damn, you're so pretty when you beg."

Jun slowly let the warm, solid weight of his body press Theo into the mattress.

Theo had been writhing above the flames of his need for so long that Jun's body fell on him like cool water, quenching the ache in a cloud of steam, fogging up his mind with desire. "Please. Please, Captain."

When Jun sat back up, the longer strip of hair atop his head fell artfully across his face, sticking to the sheen of sweat and emphasizing the glint in his eyes and his swollen red lips. Theo had never seen a man more beautiful.

Jun picked up the bottle and hesitated, his serious gaze pinning Theo to the bed far more securely than the flimsy red ribbons. "I've had my jabs, but I could go get a—"

Theo wrapped his legs around Jun's hips to pull him closer with a gentle shake of his head. "No, that's alright. I've had mine too. I trust you, Jun."

Jun's eyes went a bit wide at that, and Theo giggled as he fumbled the bottle with a curse in Patch.

Theo repeated the curse, grinning roguishly when Jun gave him a sharp glance. "I've been paying attention. If you'd give me data access, I could learn Patch on my own time in a few days."

Jun groaned good-naturedly, popping open the bottle with one hand as he gripped his hard length with the other. "That's all I need, another language for you to talk my ears off with."

Theo attempted a shrug in his bindings, accomplishing little more than scooting his shoulders up the pillow. "Well, if you don't want me to talk, maybe you should give me something more interesting to do, Capt—ah!"

Jun nudged his slicked cock inside with one long, smooth, powerful thrust. Biting his lip, he dropped the bottle and hitched Theo's legs higher on his hips. He bottomed out with a grunt, teeth bared like an animal.

Theo went a little wild beneath him, bucking and thrashing against his bindings. "Fuck! Untie me; I've got to touch you."

Those bared teeth flashed white and sharp as Jun shook the hair out of his face and adjusted his knees on the bed for leverage. The muscles of his abdomen flexed, ink rolling over the skin in undulating waves. "Not yet. I want you to beg first."

Jun gave him one hard thrust, and then another, until he had built up a brutal rhythm that set Theo's teeth rattling and his heart racing. He started begging in every language he knew, which only seemed to encourage Jun to go faster and harder until the obscene slap of their flesh filled the room.

Theo frantically tugged against the ribbons, wincing as they started to cut into his wrists.

Slowing to a stop, Jun shushed him while he stroked his hands up Theo's arms. "Shit, you're gonna hurt yourself. Here, let me just—"

He untangled Theo's hands from the ribbons and brought his wrists down to rest on Theo's chest between them. Jun rubbed at his arms and kissed the pinkened skin of his wrists in silent apology, then murmured into the marks, "Sorry, baby. Should've let you go, but you looked so good. I'll do a better tie next time, so you won't hurt yourself."

Next time.

The words sparked a chain of small explosions in Theo's chest, culminating in a flash fire that spread all over his body until he was nothing but flames in Jun's embrace.

He fisted Jun's hair in one hand as he trailed his nails down his back with the other, scoring the lines of ink with his own signature. Jun hissed Theo's name and bucked his hips, eyes reflecting the fire inside of Theo even as his hands remained gentle and sweet along his ribs.

Theo urged Jun down onto his elbows, lifting his hips to rub his leaking cock against the straining muscle of Jun's stomach with every thrust. "Jun. you're so—I want—"

He shut his mouth against unwanted words, biting them back with clenched teeth. Heavy, painful words he knew he couldn't say. Words that would undoubtedly prove unwelcome, since Theo's love and affection, once earned, was unrelenting.

Stifling—as it had been described before. Things Jun did not want from a casual liaison such as this.

Better to keep it to himself.

Their lips brushed, softly, unconsciously. Less than a kiss but more than nothing.

It wasn't nothing.

Theo's breath caught in his throat, lips trembling as he tightened his neck muscles against the urge to reach up for more. He clenched his hands over Jun's shoulders, nails digging in.

Jun pushed in hard, frozen in place as he watched Theo with an expression so open it seemed like it hurt. He took one ragged breath, then pulled out to flip Theo over onto his stomach. Jun then worked his way back in with short, smooth thrusts, picking up the pace.

His lips brushed over the nape of Theo's neck, mouth open and panting with punched-out grunts and softer sounds, whispered low.

His hands glided down Theo's arms to circle his wrists and brought Theo's hands up onto the pillow beside his head. Jun dug his elbows into the mattress and laced their fingers together.

That wasn't nothing either.

Carefully, tremulously, Theo stroked his thumb across Jun's knuckles where they interlaced with his own, and Jun gasped, hips stuttering.

Then, just as slowly, just as carefully, Jun began to kiss Theo's neck. Blatantly, unmistakably kissing him until Theo's own lips ached with envy.

Jun unlaced their fingers on one hand and dropped his to stroke Theo's cock in time with his thrusts. He made a soft sound of surprise when Theo reached out to take his hand again, holding it tightly.

"No, I don't need it. I can finish like this; just keep going. I'd rather—" Theo laced their fingers back together and brought them up to press his lips to Jun's knuckles. "—rather do it like this."

This time, the sound Jun made was anything but soft. "Fuck, yes. Come on my cock. Show me."

A minute shift of his powerful thighs and suddenly he was thrusting harder and deeper, dragging the head of his cock relentlessly over Theo's sweet spot. Jun shoved Theo against the mattress with every push, rubbing his cock over the sheets in too-much, not-enough bursts of pleasure that built and built until Theo was shaking in his arms, clutching at his hands.

"Right there! Right there, don't stop. Please!"

Jun caught the sensitive curve of Theo's ear in his teeth with a growl, and Theo shouted as he spilled across the sheets, squeezing Jun's hands even as his body tightened around his cock. Jun released his ear with a harsh, stuttering breath, barely able to pant out his words. "Good. That's so good, baby. Holy shit."

Jun lost his rhythm, pushing in harder and faster as he whispered praise into Theo's hair until he finished with a rush of warmth inside of Theo, muscles locking in place with a grunt.

Theo braced for Jun to roll away, clean himself up, and leave without another word. In Theo's experience, such was customary of a casual lover who held no interest in forging a deeper connection.

That was his only excuse for the tight, relieved sound he made when Jun's weight collapsed on top of him, crushing him into the mattress with a sigh.

When Jun finally rolled to his back with a muttered apology, Theo simply followed him and propped his forearms on Jun's chest with a bright smile.

"See? I told you that you could be gentle."

The height to which Jun's eyebrows aspired was rather ambitious, in Theo's opinion. "You think that was gentle?"

He took Theo's wrists in his hands, prodded at the rapidly fading marks, and then he brought them to his lips to lay the softest of kisses across his skin. For some reason, those tiny kisses echoed through Theo like siren bells ringing. Jun cut dark, satisfied eyes up at him, and it was truly a wonder that Theo's heart didn't break a rib with the force of its pounding.

Jun didn't whisper, but his voice hovered below conversational tone. It was husky, and sweet, and all the more intimate for the curving dip in volume. "I should never have touched you. I told you, I can't be gentle. I break things."

The regret written in two tiny parallel lines between Jun's brows shot through Theo like twin arrows, stinging his eyes with the threat of ill-timed tears. He sniffed them away and donned a brisk, no-nonsense tone, tapping Jun smartly in the center of his chest. "Well, you can practice with me. I won't tell anyone. You can still be big and bad and scary, and nobody has to know that you're gentle with me sometimes. That you can be soft and sweet, too, when you want to be."

Jun pulled a face at that, full upper lip lifting in a sneer, but his hands closed over Theo's shoulder blades, petting soft and sweet and, yes, very gently down his back. He ran a careful hand down the pale expanse of Theo's spine, still speaking low as if he didn't want to be overheard. "All of this blank, virgin skin. It isn't safe."

Tucking his hand under his chin, Theo blew a lock of hair out of his eyes in a habit that Ari had assured him was terribly uncouth. "What makes you say that? Everyone looks this way back home. Regeneration fluid takes care of any scars, and we don't do all of this lovely decorative ink either. Which I'm beginning to see is a terrible failing for us."

He slanted a glance up through his lashes as he dipped his head to trace one of the dark lines over Jun's collarbone with his tongue. It was just as satisfying as he had imagined.

Jun hissed and shifted beneath him but did nothing to stop Theo's meandering tongue, letting his own hands caress Theo's back in little circles. "It makes you look expensive. Valuable in a way you don't want to be around here."

Theo pushed back up to study his face. Jun was chewing on his plush lower lip as he ran his hands over Theo's skin with a soft reverence emphasized by the scrape of callouses on his tattooed fingers. He seemed as fascinated by the contrast as Theo was himself. It gave Theo a surge of confidence. "You like it, though, don't you? That I look so different from you. Like a— What did they call me? Like a Doll."

Jun's hands fell away as if Theo had slapped them, eyes wide on Theo's face. "No. You're not a Doll. Never say that again."

The slight tremble in Jun's jaw drew Theo's attention. And the thread of fear in his words. "Why not? That's what your crew keeps saying."

Jun shook his head once, sharply, and tugged the twisted sheets up until they covered Theo's hips. "Bad things happen to Dolls, Theo. You're not a Doll."

Ari had once likened Theo to a shark, with the way he latched onto things in conversation and refused to let them go until they had been torn to shreds. "What's a Doll, then?"

Sorrow flickered across Jun's face, leaving trace elements of sadness behind in the crook of his mouth and the corner of his eye. He sighed so deeply Theo rose and fell with it as though he were riding the crest of a wave. "People. They're people in a shitty situation. Traded like collectibles between Crews. Like, fucking, objects."

It was a concept Theo had heard alluded to but never discussed in polite company. One of the horrors that lurked beyond the Verge. It made his skin crawl to ponder it. "But, that's awful."

Jun's hands tightened over Theo's back as his jaw firmed with resolve, accented by the parallel lines of ink. "Yes, it is. And I'm going to stop it."

As he made that proclamation, all Jun needed was a cliff face along the moors as he stood facing the wind with a hand to his heart and a dark cape billowing in the wind. Or, at least, Theo's vivid imagination insisted that he did.

Theo tried not to let his breathless reaction to that mental image color his voice when he whispered, "How?" but objectively failed at the task. He could practically hear Jun's walls going back up, heavy emotional doors slamming shut with a mental clang.

"You don't need to worry about that. I told you I'd keep you safe, and I always honor my word."

Theo played with the tattooed fingers of Jun's right hand, humming with understanding. "Yes, I've seen your dedication to honor. Honor and Valor. Why did you choose those words?"

Jun pulled his hand away and lifted his index finger, rubbed his thumb across the characters. "It's a reminder."

Theo waited for further explanation, but it seemed Jun was finished. Theo angled his head inquisitively but Jun avoided his eyes. "A reminder of what, precisely?"

Burying the tattoos under Theo's curtain of hair with a sigh, Jun continued reluctantly. "A reminder of something I once forgot, but never will again."

The sudden fierceness in Jun's voice brought Theo up with a jolt, cutting through the peaceful air incisively. Alarm trickled down his spine like a slow poison. "You forgot your honor? What—did you accidentally leave it under the table in a tavern one night?" Theo continued with a little smile, trying to lift the mood, "I left mine out behind the stables when I was seventeen, so I know the feeling."

Jun sat up and swung his legs over the side of the bed. He grabbed his trousers from the floor and jumped into them with both feet at once. Theo made a valiant effort not to fixate on the still-visible shadow of dark curls at the open front to the exclusion of all else.

Jun hesitated, then slowly, gently combed through Theo's mussed hair and rubbed a few strands between his fingers. His expression was anything but distant when he met Theo's eyes. "You should get some rest, Theo. Tonight, you were— That was—was really, um…"

He looked so lost, floundering beneath that tough, inked-up, muscled exterior, it made Theo's stomach flutter with simmering affection.

Taking mercy on his captain, Theo stroked a hand up the outside of his thigh with an understanding expression. "Good?"

Jun's relief at not having to articulate the thought himself was palpable and gave Theo the oddest urge to gather him into his arms. He gusted out a grateful sigh. "Yes. That. You were. You are."

Theo padded after him to the door, carelessly nude and love-rumpled. Jun stopped in his tracks to stare at him like a starving man before a feast when Theo dangled one crushed red satin ribbon in front of his face. "Dream of me, Captain."

Jun's nostrils flared as Theo tucked the ribbon into Jun's front pocket with a conspiratorial smirk and a little pat.

The door slid closed across Jun's stricken face, his Valor hand raised to cover his pocket as if it contained something precious.

Something he didn't want to lose.

Chapter Nineteen

Theo wore his cravat to the bridge in the morning, the thin layer of linen and lace covering up the enduring marks Jun had left in the shape of his mouth.

It was strangely akin to the imagined sensation of wearing a lover's locket tucked away beneath his clothes. Something beautiful and secret, a trifle risqué, that only Theo and Jun knew about.

The very thought of such a thing brought a spring to his step. The rest of the Crew did not share his jocular mood.

Marco rushed in and out of the bridge with various small metal parts for Jun's inspection, until one finally passed muster and he jetted off to his lair in the bowels of the ship, cursing in Patch.

Theo now had a decent (or, rather, indecent) vocabulary built up in the language.

He had yet to use it and was waiting for just the right opportunity to catch Jun unawares. To make him smile, perhaps.

Every one of Axel's screens held maps and figures that scrolled too rapidly for Theo to follow as the pilot worked at his station with unusual focus, not a snack in sight.

Boom and Jun stood grim-faced before their stations, shouting back and forth with tense, clipped voices. "Orders, Captain?" Boom asked.

So many screens hung open above Jun's console that the translucent rectangles overlapped one another. He moved one angrily aside with the cut of his hand. "Commence defensive preparations. Our contact will be waiting on Drei X in six hours."

Grimacing, Boom entered something into her console that caused one of the dozens of closed doors on her screen to slide open and reveal a stack of metal crates somewhere inside the ship. "Drei X? They really don't want to be seen in our company if they're dragging us all the way out to the Wastes."

Still focused on his screens, Axel gave a low, foreboding whistle. "You gotta admit, we don't exactly have a stellar reputation. Makes sense to lay low. Keep our grubby little noses out of big Crew business."

Jun swiped away three more screens with a growl. "Cowardice is never rewarded."

Cracking his neck, Axel leaned back in his seat with a disdainful snort. "Yeah, okay. Thank you for that dour bit of wisdom, Captain. Where are you gonna get that one tattooed? I think there's still some space left on your pinky."

Theo stood up from his seat in objection, pad clutched in hand. "Surely adding a second condemnation of cowardice to his knuckles would be the height of redundancy."

A small scoff from Boom drew Jun's scowl. But Theo's attention remained on Axel when he made a high-pitched sound of epiphany.

"Oh, I get it, now," Axel crowed. "You're both pretentious assholes. That's why you go so well together. You know, me and Marco"—he blithely ignored Marco's shout of protest over the open coms at being included in the conversation—"we've been trying to puzzle it out. Like, is it just chemistry? Opposites attract? Novelty? But, no. There's more to it than that. You're both huge fucking nerds. You deserve each other."

The storm clouds in Jun's face gathered and intensified in such a foreboding manner that Theo stepped in to divert the next lightning strike, offering himself up as a sacrificial lightning rod. "I believe I would like to see these Wastes. I'm coming with you when you drop."

"Make the drop!" Marco shouted over the coms, then cursed and hammered at something that echoed through the speakers.

Theo was forced to raise his voice to be heard over the clanging. "Yes, that. I'm coming with you to make the drop. It would be lovely to take a stroll planetside after being cooped up on the ship for so long."

He didn't need to wait for the lightning strike.

Jun's hand clamped down around his wrist. "You're staying aboard."

Theo pretended to give it some thought, lightly tapping his chin, and then reached out to boop the rounded end of Jun's nose. "No, I don't think so. I'm coming along."

A smooth, sharp snick of metal on metal drew their attention to the side, where Boom had drawn a pair of wicked-looking knives from her thigh holster. She balanced one on her fingertip with a wide, friendly smile.

Jun abruptly released Theo's wrist and pointed a finger in his face. "No. You're not."

It was a struggle not to become distracted by either the tantalizing stretch of Jun's neck as he stood at full height to loom over Theo, or the dangerous juggling act Boom was performing off to the side, a third knife having been added to the array.

Theo focused on Jun's dark, flashing eyes, lifting his brow imperiously. "How do you propose to stop me, Captain?"

He wasn't imagining the way Jun swayed into him, nearly curled around him as Theo leaned back against the console.

"I could tape you to the chair again," Jun growled.

Marco shouted "Gross!" through the coms at the same time that his sister made a tiny retching sound in the back of her throat. One of her knives fell to the floor with a *tink*. Axel just started crunching something that sounded as if it could not be any good for his teeth.

Raising to his full height as well, Theo jutted his chin defiantly. "I would simply gnaw through the tape and start pressing buttons on Axel's console just to prove a point."

Jun's growl dragged so low it hit Theo in the gut like a ball of fire, melting his insides until his blood burned. "I could tie you up and toss you into your bunk to wait for me."

"Guys! Turn off your coms, please!" Marco's plaintive wail of protest was underscored by Axel spitting out a mouthful of shells and leaning over his com to shout back: "If we suffer, then so do you, Valdez!"

The rest of the Crew might as well have not existed for all the attention Jun paid to their antics. He was focused entirely on Theo.

It was the stuff of dreams, really.

Some of the molten devastation Jun had wrought trickled into Theo's voice as he refused to look away from

Jun's glare. "Yes, I suppose you could, if you wanted to. I have a plethora of ideas regarding that scenario if you'd care to hear them. Hand me your pad, and I'll draw up some diagrams for you."

Theo batted his lashes fetchingly, endlessly amused when Jun actually blushed and glanced away.

Her knives secured in their holster once more, Boom groaned at Theo over Jun's shoulder. "This is all very disturbing and far more information about Park's private life than I, personally, ever wanted to know, so if you could just. Not. That would be great."

Axel had to pitch his voice higher to be heard over the sound of his rapid typing and continued snacking, "Oh, come on, Boom. We knew. That scowl? That entire wardrobe of black synth-leather? Not to mention his raging, throbbing enthusiasm for being in command at all times."

"Axel. Airlock," Jun barked out over the tail end of Axel's list, his shoulders tense and cheeks still flushed.

Axel raised one hand palm out while his attachment continued typing. "Sorry, sorry. It's just, you're not exactly subtle."

"As subtle as a hunk of iron," Marco muttered darkly, then dropped something that rolled away from the com with a slowly fading rattle.

Biting back a grin, Theo leaned his hip against Jun's console and butted shoulders with the mortified captain. Stars, but he was cute when he was flustered. "He has a point, Jun."

Jun grabbed onto his shirtfront with one tight fist, forcing a gasp from Theo as he brought him up onto his toes. Jun's eyes were dilated, his lips parted around heavy breaths. It was only by the greatest force of will that Theo didn't climb him like a particularly grouchy tree. "Theo, if you do not shut your mouth, I swear you will not leave your bunk again until this entire mess is finished."

Sighing dramatically, Axel typed one last thing with a flourish. "See? It's shit like that, Park. You're calling yourself out, here."

Theo wound his hands around Jun's straining wrist. He allowed his thumb to sweep a tiny circle over the trail of ink that curved across Jun's wrist bone, and Jun let go as suddenly as he had grabbed onto him.

"You're staying here, and that's final."

Boom appeared astounded at the giggle that escaped Theo at Jun's proclamation. She seemed to think he ought to be intimidated. More fool, her.

"Ooh, an ultimatum. I'm quaking in my spats, Captain." Theo smirked.

Jun took in Theo's aforementioned spats with a slowly dawning expression of triumph. "You can't go to the Wastes. Not dressed like that."

There had never been a time in Theo's life when he'd been particularly receptive to criticisms of his wardrobe. A lifetime of bickering with his twin drew his spine up straight in affront. "Whyever not? I'm properly attired. I'll have you know that my tailor is very well regarded in the most fashionable circles."

Axel broke in with a wave of his arm, attachment switched back to the pointer. "Well, first off, wearing that? Around here? You're practically a walking advertisement for a kidnapping."

Theo smoothed down his admittedly rumpled shirt in a moment of contemplation. "Yes, I do seem prone to those."

The pilot's chair squealed with rusty springs when Axel hopped to his feet. "Secondly, I've got something that would help you fit in much better."

Jun made a threatening noise in his throat as he whipped his head toward Axel, who blithely ignored him, too busy sizing up Theo.

He swept a disdainful look over Theo's outfit, which Theo personally considered to be unwarranted. His trousers were excellent quality velvet, and as Theo's tailor had been quite intimately acquainted with his proportions, they were perfectly fitted. Horacio had been great fun, if a little too gentle for Theo's tastes.

Tailors had very nimble fingers, after all.

Arms crossed tightly over his chest, putting both muscles and guns on display, Jun glared at Axel. "Don't even think about it. Dr. Campbell wouldn't be comfortable outside of his proper little Britannian clothing."

Theo would like to think that he tossed his hip out coquettishly, hair streaming over his shoulders in a waterfall of silk. The reality was probably closer to an awkwardly bent knee and an invisible yet tenacious strand of hair caught in the corner of his lips.

He spit it out as discreetly as possible. "Propriety has always been nothing more to me than a monstrously heavy set of shackles, which I am more than willing to cast aside. It isn't a particularly good fit for someone like me anyway. I would be glad to be free of it."

Boom latched onto that, pausing at whatever she was typing into Jun's console. "Someone like you?"

It was incredibly refreshing that she didn't immediately know what he meant. That the entire Crew seemed to be at a loss. Theo wasn't used to being considered proper in any way. Much to his surprise, he was kind of enjoying it. "Oh, I suppose you may not be aware, but back home, I am considered to be somewhat unconventional. Those concerned with propriety often find me off-putting."

Jun's feet shuffled enough that his leg pressed against Theo's, and rather than moving away again, he left it there. Just...touching. Such a small thing ought not to have any effect on Theo's composure, but he found himself stifling a gasp at the contact. At the implications of familiarity. Intimacy.

The light in Jun's gaze only emphasized those implications, affection tinting his voice. "Unconventional's one way to say it."

The prickling burn of a flush started in Theo's scalp and washed down over his face. He waved his arms to distract from his undoubtedly pink cheeks. "Odd. Annoying. Dramatic. Overwhelming. Vulgar. Take your pick; I've heard it all. People have never suffered from a lack of things to say about me."

There was a moment where Jun pressed more firmly against him as if in support, and then he withdrew entirely. Theo barely restrained himself from reaching out for him in his retreat.

To his shock and delight, Jun was the one who reached out, skimming his knuckles over Theo's chin before he teased away the last strands of hair that were still caught in his mouth. "One thing you are not, is underwhelming."

He turned away so quickly Theo very nearly missed the blush that burned his ears. Nearly.

Theo gave chase as Jun began to walk off of the bridge, dogging his heels. "Wait. Was that a compliment? Jun? Say it again."

Jun paused at the door to tap something into the panel. "No."

The combined forces of Jun's blush and the embarrassed tone to his voice made Theo want to float to the ceiling with glee. "No, that wasn't a compliment, or, no, you won't be repeating yourself?"

Jun didn't answer, focusing instead on Axel with a severe expression. "Set our course for Drei X, and leave Dr. Campbell alone. Boom, follow me."

Theo held in his laughter at Axel's silent mimicry of Jun's face until Jun and Boom had left the bridge, but it was a very near thing.

It wasn't that he didn't love Jun's face and the effortless way he exuded a dark cloud of masculine rage; it was more that—

Oh.

Oh, dear.

Theo loved Jun's face.

He loved—

"So, you and Captain Park, huh? I was kinda joking before. But I gotta say, he's not reacting as if it's a joke to him. Park can take a surprising amount of razzing, but when you hit too close to the bone, he'll bite your head off."

Theo avoided the question by locking up his pad with a noncommittal hum. Thankfully, Axel didn't notice the slight tremble in his hands.

Chapter Twenty

Axel sauntered out into the corridor, paused, and then stuck his head back around the doorway to the bridge to call out to Theo. "Come on, legs, I'll hook you up with the goods."

Reluctant to be left alone on the bridge with the multitudinous tempting buttons and his own dubious self-control, Theo followed after. "Do you know, I've dedicated my life to the study of language, and yet, when you speak, I am often cast to sea."

Axel leaned back against the interior of the lift, leaving plenty of room for Theo to join him. "I can't understand half the shit you say, man, but I gotta admit, you say it with style."

That sounded somewhat complimentary, so Theo decided to accept it as such. He had learned long ago to take praise wherever he could get it. They arrived on the second deck, and Axel took off in the opposite direction from Theo's bunk, winding around the dimly lit curving hallway until he came upon a haphazardly decorated door.

Printed images in various states of distress plastered the dented metal. Some were faded and scratched, while others appeared shiny and new. There was no rhyme or reason to the arrangement, just brightly colored images of everything from a scantily clad feminine torso to what appeared to be a ham sandwich overlapping one another from top to bottom.

Axel didn't comment on the decor as he opened the door to a room filled with much the same, with the addition of multicolored lights glowing along the edge of the ceiling.

He bent to dig through a mountain of discarded clothing, then emerged triumphant with a bit of black cloth clenched in his fist. "Here, try these on. They're too small for me, so they might fit your scrawny ass. They're even clean, so you're welcome."

He smacked Theo in the face with the cloth, which turned out to be a pair of exceptionally tiny black trousers. They were made of some kind of strange, stretchy material that had a metallic sheen to it.

Axel threw himself back on the bed, dug through the rumpled sheet to recover a pad, and then pulled up a vid of some thumping musical performance with brightly flashing dancers in accompaniment. He focused on the screen, not even glancing Theo's way. "Go on and get changed. I'm dying to see Park's face when you walk out in those. Promise I won't peek, Dr. Campbell. On my honor."

There was something there, in the way he dropped his voice to say that last bit, that made it clear he was poking fun at Jun. Theo couldn't find it within himself to laugh.

The door remained open, but Theo had gotten undressed in riskier situations, so he complied with a mental shrug.

His linen small clothes were unfortunately too voluminous to fit beneath the trousers, so they had to go.

He had also ceased wearing his stockings since he had gifted one of his garters to Jun.

Consequently, there was nothing between the tight fabric of the trousers and Theo in his entirety.

They fit more akin to stockings than proper trousers, faithfully hugging the lines of Theo's body from just below the crest of his hip all the way to his ankles. He had never possessed something so snugly tailored in his life. A small smile graced his face as he thought of Ari's no doubt scandalized reaction to such a garment.

Followed immediately by a pang in his chest. He was really beginning to miss his quiet, straightlaced twin. Being scandalous wasn't half as much fun without Ari around to scandalize.

Theo turned to examine his backside with a critical eye in the smudged mirror stuck to the wall. He had to bunch up his shirt over his navel to see properly. "These trousers certainly leave very little to the imagination."

Axel's pad landed on the bed with a thump, and he pushed to stand and study the fit, himself. "Yeah, I bought them a size too small, hoping to attract the ladies with the siren call of my bulge."

This was accompanied by a rather unfortunate gesture toward the front of his own closely fitted trousers.

Theo winced. "Oh?" He made an attempt to be supportive and nonjudgmental, aiming for a light and inquisitive tone rather than openly cringing. (Ari would likely have fainted on the spot from sheer disgust.) "Did that prove an effective courting strategy, for you?"

Axel made a face that wasn't particularly confidence-inspiring, and then turned to hunt through the pile. He found a dull-gray sweater, which he thrust out at Theo insistently. "I got myself shot with a stun ray, so, no. But

I did get the contacts for one super snarly dude first, so I thought they might work better for you. It's not my thing, but snarly dude seems to be your type. Take off that blouse and put this on instead."

Theo started to work free his cravat, only remembering the marks Jun had left on his neck when it was too late. Axel's bright-green brows shot up, but he thankfully refrained from making comment.

"I can't deny that there is something compelling about a man with a scowl on his face." Theo's shirt slightly muffled his words as he struggled to get it over his head without entangling his arms. "Makes me want to see what it takes to get him to smile." He popped the sweater on, relieved to find that it had no odor, despite his fears. "I must inform you, however, that there is nothing of significance between your captain and me."

"Significance" being the key word, there.

Nothing of any significance whatsoever. Just Theo's nonsensical heart falling deeply and irrevocably in love with a man who wanted nothing to do with him outside of the occasional tryst.

Par for the course with Theo, really.

And entirely insignificant.

The rude sound Axel made was anything but an agreement. "Are we still going with that? I don't get why he's hiding it; it's not as if any of us care who he's nailing to the wall in his free time."

Theo tugged at the collar of his new soft, slouchy top. He was suddenly a trifle warm at the unexpectedly welcome notion of Jun nailing him to the wall.

A thought that required further study.

Preferably while he was alone, in his bunk.

Theo frowned at his reflection and fussed with the hem of the sweater. The garment was too short. It barely flirted with the waistband of his trousers, flashing skin whenever he moved in any direction. "I think it's more that he doesn't want me to get inflated ideas of my own importance. Doesn't wish for me to labor under the misapprehension that I matter to him beyond my work."

He couldn't decide if it was encouraging or disheartening that Axel's face fell at that revelation. "Shit. That sucks, man."

Theo gave up on the hem of the sweater and, instead, pushed at the overlong sleeves that hung low over his knuckles. "It's quite alright. I know my place; he doesn't need to worry. I'm aware of the importance of my work here, as well as the unimportance of myself as a person."

If there was something Theo excelled at, besides languages and making an unholy mess every time he entered a kitchen, it was accepting his undesirability as a long-term romantic partner.

It was a proven, tested pattern, after all. Ari would applaud his use of the scientific method to reach that conclusion.

Actually, Ari would wrap Theo up in their softest blanket and acquire his favorite Turkish delight and sit with him while he cried. A steady, sympathetic presence Theo could depend on even at his worst.

Which was also a proven pattern.

Stars, he missed his twin.

Axel tossed a pair of clunky black boots at him, narrowly missing Theo's ankles. "Throw these on, and you're ready to walk the Wastes with the rest of the Crew, Doc."

Theo gathered them up, surprised to find that he and Axel were of a size. He offered a soft, sincere smile of thanks. "I think these will suit rather nicely. Thank you for your assistance; you've been ever so kind to me."

Axel clicked through the attachments on his arm with a furrowed brow, avoiding Theo's gaze. "That's me, kindness and light itself. I basically shit rainbows."

Which was an exceptionally colorful idiom Theo had never come across before. He mentally added it to his inventory, to be used whenever it would horrify Ari the most.

Axel seemed to be done with him now that he had garbed Theo in Outlier clothing; his body language screamed dismissal. Theo bundled up his things under his arm and stepped through the doorway.

Axel stopped him with a soft sound, faintly audible above the constant low grind of the engines around them. Theo turned back, but the pilot was still avoiding his eyes. His hand was clenched around the wrist of his attachment, knuckles bone-white. "Hey, listen. I know I joke around a lot, but this shit is serious. This mission Park is on, it's nothing to take lightly. People are gonna get hurt whichever way it goes. People already have. Just make sure you're not one of them."

Theo opened his mouth to respond, but Axel had already hit the panel to slide the door shut between them.

Thus, Theo found himself gaping at a cartoonish illustration of an ice cream cone with inexplicable cat ears.

*

By the time Theo made it back to the bridge, Jun was standing at his console, barking orders while multiple screens flashed information so quickly it made Theo dizzy just to watch.

"I want engines running at half power even after we dock. We're getting off this rock the second bay doors are shut behind us. And, Marco, I need you to— What are you wearing?"

Jun turned to face Theo and froze, brows thundering down ominously even as his mouth hung open with surprise.

Marco's voice rang out through the coms in the sudden quiet of the bridge. "I don't—like, shorts? And a shirt? Why, Captain?"

Rubbing a hand over his face, Jun erased his shocked expression and replied, "No, not you, Marco. Go check our fuel supply, and see if you need to make a crystal run while we're planetside." His eyes narrowed at Theo as he made a sharp gesture to his body. "You. What is that?"

Theo glanced down at his new Outlier apparel, and then struck a pose to best display the outlandishly close-fitted trousers. Jun's attention fell immediately to the exposed strip of skin just above the low-slung waistband. "I'm dressed to accompany you. Incognito. I appear just as any other Outlier, wouldn't you agree?"

Boom remained focused on snapping metal cuffs onto her forearms that connected to the metal lines embedded in her hands. The *click-buzz-click* of each connection was hypnotically rhythmic. "Yeah, maybe. Until the second you open your mouth and a bouquet of roses falls out."

It was impossible to tell if the statement had been meant as an insult or a compliment, so Theo chose to hear it as a compliment.

Life was better that way.

Jun continued to scowl in his direction, scanning over Theo's entire outfit but repeatedly returning to the exposed sliver of hip on display. "Where did you get all that?"

Axel's tapping at his console doubled in speed as he studied his screen as if his life depended on it. Jun's scowl proved ineffective when it was aimed his way, so Jun turned it back to Theo. Theo tried not to think about what Axel had said about his new trousers attracting snarly gentlemen.

"You're staying aboard," Jun ordered. "I can't have you walk around like that."

It had been fun, at first, to make Jun frown and grouch about his outfit, but now, Theo was done. He wanted to taste fresh, uncirculated air. He planted his hands on his hips, ignoring the way Jun sucked in air through his teeth as his sweater rode up. "Don't be ridiculous. Why not?"

Jun made a broad, sweeping gesture, indicating Theo from top to toe. He sounded a little strangled, voice strained. "You're too pretty."

"Aww, that's so sweet, Captain!" Marco piped up from the coms.

Axel snickered and Boom rolled her eyes in response, the pair of them continuing to work at rapid speed at their consoles. Boom's augmented fingers moved so quickly they blurred when Theo attempted to follow the motion.

Jun's ears turned scarlet, to Theo's delight, as he scrambled to save face in front of his sniggering crew, his tough facade crumbling away. "No, I mean. Yes, you are, but— It's not safe. You're not safe, like this. I need to focus on the job, and I can't be distracted watching you."

The new trousers made Theo hyperaware of the sway of his hips as he cocked them coquettishly and twirled a lock of hair around his finger. "You think I'm distracting, dressed like this, Jun? Apologies. Captain Park?"

Boom jostled Theo out of his pose as she squeezed between them to get to the other side of the console. She grumbled low, "I'll take your apologies for, once again, subjecting me to the painful experience of witnessing Park attempt to flirt. It's like watching him try to land a ship. Just pitiful and jarring."

Jun snatched one of the small metal devices she held out in her hand, ears still glowing. "I'm not— Shut up, Valdez. I can land a ship just fine."

Axel leaned heavily on a button that caused a harsh buzzing sound to fill the bridge for several seconds. "False."

Marco shouted over the coms, "Most of a ship, yeah," while something whirred in the background. "You leave the rest in pieces on the runway for me to pick up and tack back on later."

Theo watched as Jun unfolded the device and held it tight against his skull behind his ear until there was a muted click. Then he let go, but the device remained attached to his head, softly glowing around the edges. "All of you. Shut up. Focus on the drop. There's a reason they brought us out to the Wastes, and it wasn't to shake our hands and buy us a beer."

Grabbing his shoulder to turn him to the side, Theo peered up at the device behind his ear. "What's that? Can I have one? It would be exceptionally diverting to use Restricted tech, I should imagine."

Jun shrugged him off, but he leaned down to remove the device and hold it out on his palm. "Auto-coms. Keeps us connected to the ship, so we can, unfortunately, hear Axel while we're planetside."

Theo snatched it off his hand and held it behind his own ear, waiting for the click.

Nothing happened.

Jun took it back with surprising gentleness, running the back of his fingers down the curve of Theo's ear as he moved away. "You can't use them without a base. Ours are embedded behind the ears, see?"

He clicked it back in place and tilted his head for Theo to watch as he removed it again. Theo immediately shoved his fingers behind Jun's ears to feel for the base, but only encountered skin. Except, there. There was a small raised circle of some hard material just beneath the surface, bumped up against the cartilage.

"We've just received a message from our contact, Captain." Axel was all business as he cut in, harsh around the edges without his signature humor. "They're demanding that we go in dark. Disconnected. No live augments. No pads. And...there might be a problem with communication."

Jun went laser focused on his pilot, auto-com clenched in his fist while Boom gave a put-upon sigh at his side and started to remove her cuffs. The glow in her fingers faded once the cuffs had disconnected. "Explain," Jun demanded.

Ruffling his hair, his face screwed up with confusion, Axel sent the message to the main screen. "See, there? Halfway through, the message switches to something I can't read. It isn't Standard or Patch. It's not even Grunt. I'm a little rusty on that one, but I can usually make it out. I don't know what the hell this is supposed to be. Code, maybe?"

The assembled crew all read over the message in tense, ringing silence, finally broken when Jun muttered darkly in Patch.

Boom gestured angrily at the screen. "Seriously, what in the rusted stars is that? Did you run it through a translator?"

Theo had never witnessed a person angrily chew a stick of gummy candy, but Axel managed it.

"No, Boom," Axel drawled. "I just decided to show it to the captain without attempting to figure it out." He gave her an insulted glance. "I sent it through three translators. Nothing. That's why I'm thinking it's a code."

Theo read over the message thrice more just to be sure before he tossed his hat into the ring. "It is. Well, it is, and it isn't. It's a mix of six languages, five of which are no longer used in any capacity, including heirlooms. Most written records of them haven't been digitized. One must consult physical copies of samples in the literature simply to be aware of them."

The startled, assessing once-over Boom bestowed upon Theo after that revelation gave the impression she was completely rearranging her perception of him in real time. "You can read that shit, Dr. Campbell?"

Everyone at the bridge turned to Theo with varying degrees of surprise.

Jun appeared the least surprised. If anything, he seemed resolved. "Can you please translate for us?"

Theo suppressed a happy little wriggle at being deemed useful and continued in the professional, polished tone he usually reserved for lectures. "Certainly, Captain. The messenger seeks to convey that they will absolutely not be communicating in anything but these six languages for the remainder of your interactions and demand that you do the same. They believe that doing so will aid in keeping the exchange clandestine and undetected."

Theo jumped a little when Marco's voice sounded over the coms: "Sounds like they're trying to keep it undetected by us, as well. Pretty hard to negotiate when they refuse to speak to you. Also, Captain, turns out I am gonna need to replenish crystal stores while we're docked. I estimate about half an hour to get it done."

Jun leaned on the console, his head hanging low between his shoulders while he took a deep breath. "Thank you, Marco."

Boom reached over and grabbed the auto-com from Jun's hand, blithely ignoring his irritated grunt. "Dark and disconnected means you can't use your regular assortment of toys, Park. We're gonna have to get creative."

Jun flicked one of the metal lines embedded in her hands with a frown. "It also means you can't go with me. I'm the only one on the ship without live augments. Sounds like I'm going in alone and unarmed. Fantastic."

Theo grazed Jun's boot with his own to gain his attention, striking a confident pose. "Not alone, Captain. I possess no augments whatsoever, and I believe you are in desperate need of a translator."

Jun's bark of denial was overshadowed by Boom pulling out a six-inch blade from a hidden holster inside her top.

"How good are you with knives, Dr. Campbell?"

Chapter Twenty-One

It was universally agreed upon by the Crew, with the notable exception of Theo, himself, that Theo should not be given a knife.

He and Jun waited in the docking bay, surrounded on all sides by crates stacked higher than Theo's head, for Boom to return with alternative weaponry.

Theo snapped and unsnapped the dark hooded jacket Boom had bestowed upon him to cover up his hair. It was apparently crucial for them to avoid unwanted detection by passersby and surveillance equipment. He looked up to Jun, who stood close by.

Jun regarded him with a conflicted twist to his lips, and his voice dropped to a growl. "How? How are you the best thing that's ever happened to me?"

Theo had the singular experience of being both thrilled by the words and insulted by the tone.

He scoffed, pretending to brush imaginary dust from his trousers while he attempted to conceal his pleasure at the words. "I suppose you think you deserve better."

The bay was cold, but Jun radiated heat as he stepped closer. "You know nothing of what I deserve. Better is not the word."

Jun's hand wrapped around Theo's jaw, firmly but gently lifting his face to look into Jun's eyes.

They were naked and clear of the facade of irritability he had been wearing moments before. Jun leaned in close enough that Theo's ever-hopeful heart leapt at the possibility of a kiss.

But, of course, he stopped with a buffer of cold ship air still between them. "I meant it, Theo. You are."

Theo tried to twist away, disappointment bubbling in his stomach at the denial of a kiss. The wasted dream of Jun's lips upon his. "What am I, exactly?"

The only thing softer than Jun's steady gaze was the brush of his thumb down Theo's jaw. "The best thing."

Jun's attention fell to Theo's lips, the damp heat of his breath whispering across Theo's upturned face as he swayed even closer and closed his eyes in tremulous anticipation. Finally.

Finally.

Boom clattered into the room, and Jun wrenched his hand away with a long step back as she dropped an armful of weapons on the floor between them. Theo eyed the pile thoughtfully, trying to determine which he was going to use to kill her with for the interruption.

Jun refused to look at him and, instead, crouched over the pile. But it was clear he'd been affected, his back still heaving with uneven breath as a wash of color stole over his cheeks.

Theo would have found it endearing if he weren't so incredibly frustrated.

Boom squatted beside Jun, the cuff of her boots slouching low to reveal more than a hint of knife. "You're lucky we had this crate of outdated Verge tech. They'll use just about anything over there, and half of this shit doesn't even have the capacity to Connect."

With a sneer, Jun held up a battered, rusted ray gun pinched between his thumb and forefinger. "You really expect me to use this stuff, Boom? I might as well just hit them with a rock."

Theo picked up a rifle nearly as long as his arm, and yelped as Jun immediately yanked it out of his arms with an admonishing grunt.

"No. Absolutely not."

Boom handed Theo a palm-sized, square device with a single button covered by a plastic dome, currently latched shut. "Here. You get a single-use stun detonator. That should take out anyone within a twelve-foot radius. Just hit the button, drop it, and run. You've got about five seconds to get out of range."

It was blocky, and unattractive. Theo turned it over in his hands with a disappointed sigh. "It lacks a certain amount of flair, though, doesn't it? Couldn't I have something with just the tiniest bit more style?"

Jun decided upon an ancient-looking ray gun and a set of black iridescent metal blades. He tucked everything away so efficiently on his person that Theo would never have detected their presence if he had not personally witnessed the concealment.

Jun then turned his attention to Theo, tugging his jacket open. He shoved Theo's stun detonator into a hidden interior pocket of the jacket, tucked up under Theo's arm in a very discreet lump. "There. Do not use this except as a last resort. Basically, if I'm not dead, leave it alone."

Theo grasped his arm as he tried to pull it away, fingers tight with alarm. "Dead? Do you anticipate such an outcome as a likely possibility?"

Jun pried his grip away with careful fingers, allowing a fleeting squeeze, just once, around Theo's palm. "It's best to stay alert and prepared when making contact on these sorts of deals."

Theo observed as Boom examined and discarded several weapons, then decided on a discrete pistol that disappeared into her modest cleavage. "Why do you engage in such business ventures if they are so dangerous?" he asked her.

Boom shrugged as Axel joined them in the bay. She tossed another detonator at his head, laughing when he scrambled to catch it. "High risk, high payoff."

Axel clipped the detonator to his belt and made a rude gesture in her direction. She ignored it entirely, and Theo stepped back to get out of the line of the daggers Axel was glaring.

"I see," Theo said. "Nothing ventured, and all that. Still, couldn't you find employment less likely to result in catastrophe?"

Axel's anger turned to Theo with sharp, clipped words in a sarcastic tone. "Well, you know, dollface, turns out that galactic subterfuge requires funding and an absolutely massive set of balls. Right, Captain?"

"Shut up, Axel."

If Theo had thought Axel's tone was sharp, Jun's would have left the smaller man bleeding.

Axel made an exaggerated gesture with his organic arm, ending with a snap of realization. "No, yeah, I forgot. Your supersecret plan that only everyone on this ship already knows about, including your new boyfriend, judging by the work you've given him. Yeah, I'll be sure to keep mum on that, Park."

Jun took a heavy step toward Axel, who flinched away, face going blank and white as sim-parchment beneath his freckles. Jun took a slow, deliberate step back, hands held palm out at his waist. "I'm not going to hurt you, Ax. I don't run that kind of Crew."

Axel was still pale as he rubbed his hand behind his neck, but he faced Jun without fear. "Yeah, I know, Captain. Old habits die hard, I guess."

Jun's posture was rigid and his expression sincere as he spoke low and fervently. "I made you a promise, and I intend to keep it. You won't ever work for a rough Crew again, not while I'm around."

The bright, flickering lights of the cargo bay gave the illusion of tears in Axel's eyes, there and gone by the next flash of light. "Saving the galaxy one scrawny little shit at a time, right?"

With a surprising display of camaraderie, Jun clapped him once on the back. "If that's what it takes."

Marco scooted past them, his metal augment clanking more heavily against the flooring of the ship than his organic foot, despite wearing the same boots on each one. He opened the bay doors with a flourish and a broad, cheeky smile. "Stay safe, Captain. I'll go get Sylvia a bellyful of crystals and have her ready to go for you."

The unexpected sight of Axel and Boom descending down the ramp behind Theo sent him puzzling. "I was under the impression that the pair of you wouldn't accompany us."

Axel glanced up from where he was picking at his teeth with a narrow attachment. "Oh, we won't be going to the drop. I'm just running out to grab some nosh, and who knows what nefarious scheme Boom is up to?"

Shoulder checking him on her way past, Boom jogged down the ramp onto the scuffed metal flooring of the dock. "We're out of regen and bandages."

Theo grunted as Axel's elbow connected with his gut conspiratorially. "See? Med supplies. Nefarious." He pitched his voice to be heard by Jun and Boom up ahead. "For your victims, perhaps?"

Boom didn't check back over her shoulder, but there was no doubt to whom her response was addressed. "Keep talking and find out."

Axel stopped midway down the ramp, arms flung wide. "Did everyone just hear her threaten me?"

With hand outstretched, Jun waited at the bottom of the ramp (to Theo's delight and surprise) to assist Theo down onto the floor. "I dunno. That sounded more like a promise to me."

Axel clomped down the rest of the way, muttering under his breath, "Disgraceful, the way they treat me around here."

The group completely ignored him.

The dock was sparsely populated, with a few broken-down older ships being disassembled right next to newer freighters and speedships fueling up. There was a distinct lack of color, everything cast in shades of gray from the DreiXian's clothing to the ships. The only exception to the monochromatic theme was the occasional poison-bright flash of neon flickering beneath a layer of grime. It made Theo want to toss out a bucket of paint to brighten things up. Or an army of polishing cloths and some very strong cleaner. It was entirely possible that the buildings could be brightly colored beneath the muck.

He faltered as something soft dropped onto his head. "Here."

Theo batted at the material Jun had dumped atop him, struggling his way free of a thick, gray, circular scarf which bore a remarkable resemblance to the blanket on Jun's bed.

He clutched it against his chest, turning his face up to Jun, utterly charmed by the clumsy gesture. "You're lending me one of your scarves?"

Jun shrugged, eyes trained on the people bustling around them as they turned out of the docks onto a busy thoroughfare lit on all sides with dirty, glowing signage advertising myriad things. "It gets cold, sometimes."

Theo slung the scarf around his neck, rubbing the soft, thick yarn between his fingers. His shout of surprise was muffled by the material when Jun reached over and roughly pulled his hood up over his head. He then did the same with his own.

"Keep that on; don't let anyone get a good look at you."

Theo nodded, bumping shoulders with Jun as he held onto his new scarf. "Quite right. Wouldn't want them to discover how pretty I am, right, Jun?"

The fact that Jun actually stumbled over nothing at Theo's words lit a bank of warmth in his belly. It spread through Theo's limbs and brightened his smile as he laughed and laughed.

Axel spread his arms wide, casually stepping over a pile of refuse that oozed green slime across the grimy metal walkway. "Welcome to the Wastes. The crotch of the galaxy. Hot, damp, and reeking of piss. This is the spot where every rancid piece of flotsam this side of the Verge comes to do their dirty deeds. The land of shame and shadows, disaster and decay, regret and—"

Axel tripped on the foot Boom stuck out in front of him, but caught himself before falling face-first into a suspicious-smelling shimmering puddle while Jun and Boom cackled.

"We get it, Ax. It's gross. Not your favorite place." Boom sighed.

Slinging his mechanical arm over Theo's shoulder companionably, he gestured vaguely with the other. "Actually, my favorite grub stall is stashed in one of these shadowy corners. Best okonomiyaki in the galaxy, with a side of murder for hire if you're in the mood."

Jun turned a flat gaze on Axel, one eyebrow titling upwards lazily beneath the shadow of his hood. "You're definitely putting me in the mood, pilot."

Axel pulled Theo in close until they were walking cheek to cheek. He squished his freckled face into Theo's as he replied, "Aw, shucks, Captain. Not in front of the esteemed Dr. Campbell. You'll make me blush."

Boom gave a casual flick of her wrist to reveal a small blade that snapped to her metal-lined fingers. She flipped it in her hand, pulled out a tube of violet lipstick, and reapplied it using the knife's reflection. Pocketing both, she aimed a sharp smile in Axel's direction. "Besides, Park, why hire out when you can do it yourself?"

The rest of their walk was remarkably quiet.

It would have been tranquil, if not for the bustling city life all around them. Dark-faced buildings loomed tall enough to blot out the sky, and the sickly radiant light from omnipresent neon signage blurred together until Theo could barely make out the shape of the setting sun.

Where Theo was from, there were strictly adhered to clothing norms for men and women alike. There was nothing of the sort here.

Anyone and everyone wore trousers or skirts or very nearly nothing at all with a nonchalance Theo desperately wished to achieve.

It was exhilarating.

As drab as the garment colors may have been of those passing by, their hair, tattoos, augments, and cosmetics were another matter entirely, echoing the flashes of neon against the bleak metallic-black of their surroundings.

Axel's green hair blended in perfectly. Theo thought with vindictive glee about all of the times his own vibrant red hair had been deemed too bright and vulgar. He would be very nearly understated, here, especially with the absence of any augments. What an enthralling concept.

Several people had very similar tattoos to the lines and circles running down Jun's neck and torso that mimicked circuitry. Except, on the other people, the lines were glowing beneath their skin.

Theo pointed at a shirtless man so covered in glowing circuitry that he matched the flickering sign above him. "Why do their tattoos glow, but yours don't?"

Jun stiffened, and for a moment, Theo believed he wouldn't answer. But he held out his hand. The circuitry on his wrist terminated at the clusters of hexagonal shapes that spilled over the back. "They're still Connected to the Stream. I Disconnected when I left my first Crew."

Core-born though he might be, Theo could extrapolate that the Stream in the Restricted Sector must be similar to the data streams back home. However, those were only accessible through restricted-access nodes kept in university research buildings and Quorum centers. These tattoos appeared to allow anyone access. The shirtless man quaffing a carbonated beverage and belching loudly did not appear to be a member of the governing class.

Theo reached out to trace over the lines, half expecting them to feel raised, but there was only the warm, smooth texture of Jun's skin. "So, you don't have access anymore?"

Jun had slowed their walk to focus on Theo's fingers tracing over his tattoos, his expression wistful. "I can access with a pad or console; I just can't link in anymore. I had my circuits burnt out and my connections erased. It was necessary, to keep a low profile."

That sounded painful, especially the part about burning. Theo winced as he traced the lines up under Jun's sleeve, thinking about the way they covered him from neck to knees. "Didn't that hurt?"

Jun's voice dropped to a near whisper, wrist twitching beneath Theo's touch. "Most worthwhile things do."

Then, without another word, Jun grabbed Theo's hand and shoved it into the pocket of his coat, holding it in place as they walked.

Holding Theo's hand.

In public.

He couldn't suppress his gasp or the twitch of his fingers against Jun's.

Jun didn't respond beyond a single, slow caress of his thumb across Theo's palm, nothing in his rigid posture giving away the tender gesture.

There it was again, a touch. The slightest brush against his palm, soft and unsure. Such an odd, stilted expression of affection and support, and yet. Like all the other tiny, stifled gestures Jun made, it went directly to Theo's heart.

His heart was an idiot.

Axel stepped off into a shadowy alcove with a cheerful wave farewell. "Catch you later, lovebirds! Bring back some credits and try not to die. Or, if you do, send the credits first!"

Boom had already melted into the crowd, nowhere to be seen.

Jun didn't acknowledge his pilot at all, his hooded face trained forward as he strode purposefully through the crowd with Theo by his side.

Chapter Twenty-Two

They cut through a long, winding alley bereft of people, between towering soot-black metal buildings glowing green from the crowded signs overhead. Along the thoroughfare at the other end of the alley, strange chrome vehicles covered in acid-bright lights zipped past with a high, whining drone of sound. It echoed down toward them, hollowly meshed together with the raucous voices of passersby.

Long, wet streaks dripped sluggishly down the walls to either side as they entered the narrow space, and Theo found his normally inquisitive nature completely uninterested in determining the source of the dampness.

It seemed a mystery best left unsolved.

So, he turned his curiosity to Jun, who had slowed his walk, hand still loosely cupped around Theo's in his pocket. The casual gesture fanned the flames of something utterly inadvisable in Theo's chest. Something that would only end up burning him, in the end. It would be worth it, though, to have had this with Jun for even a moment.

Theo peered up at him, trying to make out his face around both of their hoods. "May I ask what we are dropping?"

"No."

"Very well, then. May I ask where we are going?"

"No."

"In that case, may I ask who we are meeting?"

Jun stopped in his tracks and turned just enough that the green glow lit his elegant profile. "Theo. I'm begging you to stop asking questions."

"No."

Jun turned the rest of the way, and Theo's arm followed with his hand still in Jun's pocket.

Theo scoffed at Jun's offended expression. "Oh, you don't like it when I give you curt, negative answers to your requests? How odd. You seem to think I should be overjoyed with the very same treatment."

It was endlessly entertaining to witness Jun relaxing his tough facade enough to roll his eyes petulantly. "Alright, alright. I get it. You can ask three questions, but they can't be about the drop." The tinge of affection in Jun's voice was more than enough to propel Theo forward with his inquiries.

Theo restrained his urge to jump for joy, clutching Jun's fingers instead. "The mind races with excitement. However shall I choose? Oh, I know! Pick a number between one and ten."

"Four."

"Where were you born?"

"Goryeo."

"What? But that's a Core planet! You were born in the Core?"

Jun's brow raised regally, the light and shadow of the alley blocking his face out in harsh angled shapes. "Is that your second question?"

Theo bent his knees with a groan, catching his hood as it threatened to slide off in his pique. "No. Damn it all,

Jun. You do make things difficult. Very well. If you were born into the Core, how did you end up out here, running dangerous missions such as this?"

For a long, silent moment, Theo thought he wasn't going to answer. The dim light reflecting off his irises made them appear deep pools of dark water into which Theo might very likely drown.

Then he blinked, and the illusion was gone.

"My parents were scientists. Brilliant, like you. They worked for the Quorum, but my mother discovered something. Something dangerous. We had to leave. I was six when we jumped the Verge. I grew up out here, an Outlier as much as any other, much to their bitter disappointment."

Parental disappointment, a subject Theo knew well. He could probably teach classes on it, instruct others on disappointing their parents. Make good use of his years of firsthand knowledge.

It was the first thing they had in common that Theo could not celebrate.

He stroked over Jun's hand in his pocket, softly and gently as he moved a little closer. "That must have been quite the discovery if it could cause a Quorum scientist to leave her prominent position for the dangers of the deep dark. I guess my final question would be—what was it?"

Jun scanned the empty alleyway in both directions, then tilted his head up to the rooftops, relaxing slightly at whatever he saw. Or didn't see. "I've spent the past three years trying to find out. My father left encoded journals. I barely managed to translate some of them, but it was enough to know there isn't much time left. There's a date buried in the numbers. Two months from now. He used every language he could find to make the code, and I worked on cracking it until I hit a wall. One language was so obscure I could find nothing on it. I put out watchers in every data system and nothing reported back until—"

Theo gasped with realization, yanking his hand out of Jun's pocket to poke him in the sternum with an excited finger. "Until my paper was published in the *Journal of Linguistica Obscura*."

Jun closed his hand around Theo's finger, squeezing lightly before he guided it away. "Yes, and you've made more progress in a week than I did in a year, Theo. You're just—you're amazing. I'm not like that. I didn't inherit my parents' intellect."

Another subject Theo was very familiar with— faltering self-esteem. He couldn't stand to see it in Jun. "Perhaps you didn't inherit their interest in academics, but you have shown your worth many times over. The notes had been so clearly organized that it was simple for me to apply my knowledge to them. You set that up for me, which was no small task."

Jun shook his head, mouth drawn in a tight line. "My parents were brilliant, brave, and honorable. We had nothing in common."

The noise Theo made with his lips would have gotten him thrown out of his mother's drawing room. "Poppycock. I'm sure you have much in common, such as stubbornness and a short fuse. A long second toe. And, as should be apparent to anyone who has spent any amount of time in your company, an abundance of bravery."

He reached out to take both of Jun's hands in his, rubbing over the knuckles with his thumbs. "It certainly took courage for them to do what they did, as much as it is taking for you to pursue their work now."

In their absence, he did not say. Jun had never mentioned, and Theo had never asked, but he got the distinct impression Jun's parents were no longer among the living. His heart ached for him.

Emotion crested in Jun's face as he leaned down to Theo, and it splashed over into his voice when he spoke quietly and fervently. "I must continue their work because I've seen what will happen if I don't."

Guilt, dread, and just the barest shimmer of hope were all plainly there for Theo to take in. He squeezed Jun's hands encouragingly. "What will happen?"

Jun's mouth twisted into a frown, unhappy creases appearing to either side. "Verge decay. Twenty years ago, the decomposition reached the point where integrity was compromised and there was a shift. The entire barrier contracted inwards, cutting off the three outermost Verge settlements and scorching away their water sources."

Theo gasped as a horrified shiver ran down his spine. "The Three Colonies disaster? I was just a child, but I remember the news flashes. So many Verge settlers died. It was terrible, but they fixed it—the programming error in the barrier that caused the disaster."

Jun nodded solemnly, his grasp tightening around Theo's hand just short of too much, and he spoke through gritted teeth, "The Quorum claims they fixed it, but it's a lie. If they delay long enough, then the Verge will contract, once again cutting off the outermost Verge settlements. Then it will stabilize for another twenty years and become someone else's problem. My parents objected and found their lives in danger."

It was chilling to even contemplate. Theo had never given much thought to the Quorum beyond vague annoyance at the restrictions the governing body placed on Core citizens. "Do you mean to tell me they plan to sacrifice innocent lives for their own convenience?"

Jun's face reflected Theo's horror, with a veneer of anger bubbling over the top like lava. "They deem it an acceptable loss in order to maintain the protection of the Verge for the Core planets."

If Ari were here, he would don his most disdainful face and drip ice in his words. All Theo could do was hiss with rage. "There is nothing about this that is acceptable."

Jun's rage mirrored Theo's, welling up in every line of his body, every twitch of his face, ticking like a time bomb in his clenched jaw. "No, there isn't, and I have no choice. I have to finish what they started. And I have—" He glanced away, and the sickly green glow overhead caught the sheen in his eyes. "—so much to make up for. Bravery doesn't enter into it."

Standing so close, Theo couldn't miss the bob of Jun's throat or the raw, wet sound of it as he swallowed against nothing. Jun pulled his hands out of Theo's grasp and stepped away, putting a good three feet between them.

Theo's hands were cold. He pressed them against his chest as Jun strode away down the alley.

"Come on," Jun said, casting his voice behind him. "We've wasted enough time."

Chapter Twenty-Three

Darkness had spread across the sky like a bruise by the time they exited the alley.

The glowing signage everywhere seemed brighter in contrast as the street was cut into pieces by bright light and deep shadow.

Peering into one of the shadowed sections, Theo recoiled and tugged on Jun's coat. "Jun, look. What in the stars are they doing?"

Theo gawked at a cluster of people of indeterminate age taking turns shocking themselves with a rusty phaser, screaming and laughing. Tears flowed freely in technicolor streams down their faces, bright makeup washed away in smearing streaks.

Jun tugged Theo's hood further up over his head, then crossed his arms over his chest with his right tucked in snug against his holster. "Just some stun-junkies and mist-mouths. Don't stare. Keep your head down; act natural. We don't want anyone to know you're from the Core."

Theo trudged along at his side, hands shoved in his pocket. He lent a mocking tone to his voice that usually got him pinched by his twin as he said, "Right, because then they might try to snatch me from under your nose, seeing as I am something of a hot commodity in the region. It would be terrible if someone were to try to kidnap me, Jun. Just awful. Could you imagine such a thing?"

Jun cut in over his sarcastic monologue with a short, quiet command. "Stop talking, eyes front. Let's go."

A lovely young lady smiled broadly at Theo from the other side of the walkway. Knotted lines of barbed-wire ink twisted down her neck, around her glowing circuitry tattoos. She licked metallic blue lips with a long tongue stained the same unnatural shade.

Theo lifted his hand in a respectful little wave, then yelped when Jun smacked it back down to his side with a particularly colorful curse.

"Don't engage. I don't want anyone to get the wrong idea."

It hadn't hurt even a little, but Theo still shook his hand out theatrically with a glare. "And what idea might that be?"

His theatrics had absolutely no effect on Jun, who simply continued to scowl at their surroundings. "That you're available."

Wasn't that an interesting thought?

A thought that required chasing all the way to the end. Theo bumped their shoulders as he hurried to keep up with Jun's long stride. "Oh? Are you saying I'm unavailable? That I've been taken off the market? Why would you say that, I wonder?"

It was as if he hadn't said anything. Jun didn't even twitch in his direction beyond a slight deepening of the line between his brows. He stopped in front of a building that held no distinction Theo could determine from the others to either side. "We're here. I need you to tell me everything they say to the best of your ability."

The weight of responsibility settled unevenly across Theo's shoulders, heavy and unfamiliar. He summoned up a nervous laugh as he contemplated the dark metal facade. "I'm amazed you would entrust me with something so crucial, having met me. Surely, you've realized by now what an unmitigated disaster I am."

It was disconcerting to suddenly have Jun's full attention when he had been chasing it fruitlessly for so long. Jun's coat flared dramatically as he turned to face Theo. He kept quiet but firm, leaving no room for argument. "I have never met anyone more capable. You're incredible, and I don't say that lightly."

A pleasant burst of warmth ran through Theo's veins at the simply stated praise, knocking his breath out in the soundless shape of Jun's name.

Jun watched his mouth for a moment before continuing, the beautiful lines of his face cast in stark relief by the shadow of his hood. "Stay close. If I have to pull out my weapon, you run. Understand?"

Adrenaline gathered in Theo's fingertips like rain dripping down until he was buzzing with it, shaky with nerves even as he lifted his chin against them. "Yes, Captain."

Rough, tattooed fingers grazed his cheek in the barest caress, and then they dropped away to disappear into the folds of Jun's coat. "Good."

It would have been remiss of Theo not to notice the bunch and strain of Jun's muscle as he hauled open the riveted steel door manually, then slid it halfway across the opening with a grunt.

Theo prided himself on his observational skills.

So, he definitely noticed.

The interior revealed some sort of warehouse, full of crates piled twice as high and in much worse shape than the ones crowding Jun's ship.

Nobody was inside, but a single, dim light switched on in the center of the space.

"Close the door."

Theo jumped at the sound of a soft feminine voice, his face scrunching as he realized she had spoken in a language he'd never heard beyond his own voice, reading aloud.

Damn, he had botched his pronunciation of some of the vowels.

Jun stepped in front of Theo, peering into the darkness with one hand inside his coat. "What did she say?"

Theo grabbed onto Jun's coat and pressed up close to translate quietly. "She asked us to close the door."

"That's enough Standard. You speak as I do, or not at all."

Scanning their abandoned surroundings critically, Jun edged a boot in front of Theo's. "Translate."

Theo released his coat to examine the space himself and discovered nothing to be seen. "She demands that we cease using Standard."

"No more."

Jun opened his mouth, and Theo rushed in to cut him off with Korean: *"Don't speak another word. Allow me to take over from here, please. You're going to have to trust me."*

"Cease now, or I leave."

Theo spun around to hold a placating hand out toward the empty space the voice had originated from.

"Apologies, friend. We have your package. You have credits for us?"

He winced at the awkward, rusty pronunciation and mixed-up articles. But for all that he was making a mess of it, there was a tiny thrill in practicing a language he had never used in conversation.

The contact stepped out of the shadows. A delicate filigree mask covered the top half of her face, leaving her unadorned mouth exposed. Her outfit left much of her body on display, bare skin peeking out between strips of black fabric.

It was disconcerting to realize that she was unmarked. No tattoos, no augments. Theo had grown so used to seeing Outliers with decorated skin that it was something of a shock to come across someone as plain as himself.

Theo took in the details of her appearance with avid curiosity, but she only had eyes for Jun. She never glanced away from him even as she addressed Theo.

"He doesn't remember me, but I remember him."

Twisting his head from one to the other, Theo could read no signs of recognition on Jun's stony face. *"You know each other?"*

She slowly lifted a hand in the air between them, as if to reach out, but held it back. *"Older now. Softer. Is that for you?"*

Theo shook his head in complete bafflement. *"I don't know what you mean."*

Her hand dropped to her side. Jun's hand hovered within inches of his hidden weapon as he remained vigilant and cold. She finally turned to Theo, her brown eyes wet behind her mask. *"He released me, along with many others. Nearly died for his efforts."*

Theo couldn't resist a tiny smile at that, pride blossoming. *"That does sound like him."*

She didn't smile back. Her lips were full but chapped, and she pointed at Jun with bitten nails. *"He has our support."*

Jun edged closer, examining her finger as though it might suddenly develop the capability to slice through Theo's chest. Theo rushed to move the conversation along.

"It's always nice to have friends, I suppose."

She wasn't large, but with a slight shift in posture, her petite frame hardened into something immovable. *"Not friends. Backup. Tell him I am ready to make the exchange."*

Theo translated, and Jun retrieved a small, cylindrical package from an inner pocket of his coat. Wrapped in plain brown paper and tied with a string, it was completely unimpressive and incongruent with their surroundings.

She held out her hand, cupping in it a simple black bag clinking with credits. The thick leather bracelet around her wrist shifted enough to reveal the raised edge of burned, curdled flesh, long since healed. The resulting scars had formed a pattern. The letter *B*.

A brand.

Theo opened his mouth to ask about it, but Jun's fingers dug into his arm as he gave a minute shake to his head. Theo flushed at the belated realization that it might be insensitive to inquire after a stranger's scars.

The lone light cut out just as Jun made the exchange, and then a bright, blinding spotlight switched on with the ominous, building buzz of a charger sounding off to the side.

With a curse, Jun shoved Theo between some nearby crates and hastily stuffed the packet in Theo's pocket. "Stay down!"

The stranger had fled, her frantic, slapping footsteps echoing off the maze of crates.

Jun withdrew his ancient phaser with one hand, and one of Boom's glinting, iridescent blades with the other.

Peering around the corner of a crate, Theo watched Jun drop low and roll out of the spotlight just as a beam scorched the concrete where he had stood.

Theo covered his mouth against a gasp, shrinking back at the sound of the door screeching open and boots hitting the ground without a care to stealth. Four men strode into the warehouse with phasers in hands, examining the area closely.

The tallest one sucked his teeth and barked out a command without pausing his perusal of the space Jun had rolled away from. "Park's in here somewhere. Scan for signatures and shoot anything that breathes. We're not taking any chances of going back to Barnes empty-handed."

Theo fumbled for his detonator, trying to remember Boom's instructions, just as the shortest of the group lifted his wrist to tap on the view screen embedded in his flesh. His circuitry tattoos flickered and glowed. He held the screen up as he turned in a circle, projecting the readings out in front of him in glitching red numbers.

Theo's heart stopped when he paused and scanned the crate in front of Theo again. "There. Picked up a signature. Definitely breathing."

The man with a shaved head chuckled softly as he took a step closer to Theo, phaser aimed just to the side of his chest. "For now."

Theo unlocked the detonator, thumb poised over the button as the man charged up his phaser. He started to press down, the plastic giving slightly before engaging, and—

Jun dropped down on top of the bald man, boots mashing his face into the ground. He kicked his phaser away, turned, and flicked his blade at the tallest man, embedding it in his wrist. The man shouted and dropped his weapon. Theo was so busy gaping at the running kick Jun aimed at the chest of the shortest man that he jumped in surprise when Jun slid over the crate, landed beside him, and snatched the detonator. "On the count of three, run for the door. Take this."

Jun shoved his charged phaser in Theo's hands and lifted him by the collar. "One—" He threw Theo over the crate in the direction of the door. "Two—" He let loose a hidden blade to pin the third man to a dilapidated crate by his loose jacket. "Three!"

Jun hit the button and dropped the detonator, swiftly gaining on Theo as they ran for the door. He hooked his arm around Theo's waist, turning them around the corner into the alley. Jun pressed Theo back against the cold metal wall of the building, damp seeping through his clothes as Jun covered his body, Theo's face tucked into his neck. The stun pulse gave a muted thud against the walls of the warehouse behind them.

Theo started to move, but Jun shushed him softly and took his phaser back with one finger held to Theo's lips.

Theo pressed a kiss against it, adrenaline coursing through him in hot, jittery waves. "Jun, who were they? What—"

Jun's quiet "hush" rustled the hairs on Theo's neck, and, oh stars, he was suddenly rock-hard in his trousers.

Achingly so.

He carefully, silently shuffled his legs until he straddled Jun's tense thigh, then let his hips slide, just once, against him.

Jun didn't make a sound, but his breath hitched, and his finger moved to trace over Theo's lower lip, then pressed just inside.

Theo swirled his tongue around the tip, and Jun pushed away from the wall and took Theo by the hand once more.

"They're down," Jun panted. "We've got to get out of here and off planet before they can trace us."

Theo gave a breathless agreement and stumbled after Jun as he set a punishing pace out of the alley.

They took a shorter, more circuitous route back to the ship, with Jun hissing at Axel over the coms to get everyone on board and prepare for launch.

Chapter Twenty-Four

Theo staggered to the side as Boom pushed past him, barreling onto the bridge with a snarl. "Security status report, Captain!"

Continuing to tap at the screens in her station, Jun stepped aside to make room as she seamlessly slid into place beside him and took up his work. "It's Barnes. The contact was one of his Dolls I set free after the firefight on Crovia Nine. He sent a team after me. Not Raiders, professional cutthroats. I took out four of them, but they'll be back."

Boom faltered, and then started tapping even faster, fingers moving more quickly than humanly possible with the help of her glowing augments. "Barnes. Shit."

Wiping sweat from his brow onto his shoulder while one hand and an attachment with ten additional fingers all tapped at his screens, Axel squawked from his station. "Shit is an understatement. There isn't a planet big enough to contain the pile of excrement you've landed us in, Captain. Congratulations, you've sealed our proverbial doom."

The ship lifted off the ground, and Jun careened into his console, then regained his footing quickly to pull up his own screens. "Anyone who wishes to leave my Crew can do so at any time without repercussions."

Axel blew a raspberry without taking his focus off his work. "Who said anything about leaving? Facing certain doom is like, an easy Tuesday for us here on Park's Crew, right, gang?"

A cheer came over the coms from Marco.

Theo strapped into his flight harness, struggling with the fastenings. "Quite right. It has been nothing but adventure and suspense from the moment we met. I've had a whale of a time, to be honest. Can't wait for more."

Axel sent him a fleeting grin and then turned back to curse at whatever was on his screen. "That's right, Doc. Life after abduction really suits you, I can tell. Plus, having your pretty face around makes the captain practically giddy."

The tips of Jun's ears flushed a slow, sure red that sent something joyful streaming through Theo like jets of bubbles.

"You mean he's usually even grumpier than this?" Some of the bubbles fizzled out in his voice, sending it floating up and away on a gust of levity.

The rest of the Crew's resounding agreement overwhelmed Jun's answering growl, interrupted only by Axel's sudden gasp.

"The station has a lock on us. I have to switch to manual to break it. Hold on to your butts, guys. This is gonna get a little bumpy."

Jun locked his feet into the metal braces beneath his console, holding on to the battered handholds at either side, as Boom rushed to strap in at her station. Jun swiveled to Theo, relief flitting across his expression when he saw his harness in place. "Marco, lock in and give us full thrusters on my mark."

Axel started to take slow, measured breaths, hands steady on his controls.

"One."

Boom cursed as her station lit up, fingers flying across her screens.

"Two."

Theo gripped the base of his chair, offering a small nod to Jun when he sent him one last glance.

"Three. Hit it!"

Nothing happened.

Theo released his held breath and was about to ask what was happening when the entire ship tilted onto its side. He ducked to avoid a flying cupful of Axel's snacks while Jun grunted and held on, muscles straining. Theo desperately wished he had taken a seat.

"Nothing to be alarmed by, folks. Just a little—" Axel hauled back and punched his attachment into a lever that had gotten stuck halfway. "—technical difficulty!"

Perhaps there was a solid foundation to Jun's method of percussive maintenance after all. Theo would have to apologize for his skepticism, assuming they survived this.

The ship righted itself with a jolt, shuddered, and then the buzz of maximum speed hit Theo's bones. It made his hair stand on end and his eyes water.

Jun checked on his Crew. "Everyone alright? Marco?"

Boom's rapid tapping paused for a fraction of a second when there was no answer, her gaze flickering to Jun and back.

Jun leaned over his station, his teeth bared. "Marco, report!"

"—ine, I'm fine! Just a bit—" He grunted as something crashed in the background with the telltale tinkle of broken glass. "—busy, Captain!"

The tense line of Jun's shoulders relaxed incrementally.

Boom let out a whoop that brought all their attention to her. "We're free! No readings indicate a lock or even a trace. We should be okay, for now."

Jun released his locked boots and went to her station. He gave her a curt nod. "Good. Axel, stand by for orders. Dr. Campbell, you're coming with me." He was across the bridge in a few strides to remove Theo's harness quickly and efficiently.

Theo's jaw dropped when Jun took his hand and led him out into the lift. "What's happening; where are we going?"

Though Jun's palms were sweaty, his grip was sure and strong. "You can't be here any longer. It's gotten too dangerous."

Theo decided to focus on one issue at a time. "Is this because of that man who doesn't like you? Barnes?"

Jun huffed out a humorless laugh and speared Theo with his gaze as the lift door opened. "Do you remember when I told you I had bad news?"

Theo usually tried to forget bad news, actually. It was Ari's job to remember that sort of thing. Life was much better that way. He trailed along behind Jun as he led them down the hallway. "Vaguely."

They came to a stop outside of the docking bay. Jun opened a wall panel and retrieved a small armory of defensive weapons, stashing them about his person as he spoke. "Well, it just got worse. Barnes's compound holds the main stockpile of holozite. The stockpile that we need, according to your translations."

Theo accepted a new detonator and tucked it into his empty pocket with a puzzled twist of his brow. "Okay, but— You haven't even gone after it yet. Why would he send men after you?"

Jun closed the panel and reached for Theo's hand. He faltered with surprise when Theo shrank back with a stubborn chin to await his answer. "He hates me. I used to work for him. Just a faceless grunt. Mindless muscle until he pulled me up to learn the business at his side. I was young and stupid and on the wrong path. And when I saw the error of my ways and finally left, I took some people with me. He didn't like that."

That didn't seem reasonable to Theo. "He lost a bunch of employees and holds it against you?"

The pain in Jun's expression squeezed Theo's heart like a fist. "No, Theo. Not employees. Dolls. He lost people he considered his property. He thinks I stole from him. I didn't. He was stealing from *them*. Stole their freedom. I merely restored to them that which was rightfully theirs."

It should have been obvious, from the occasional formality of Jun's speech patterns, that he had been Coreborn. Theo had been so dazzled by his stunning appearance and mysterious persona he hadn't read the signs. Too fascinated by and focused on their differences, he hadn't realized how much they had in common.

He beamed up at Jun with every ounce of the love that had been building inside of him for weeks now, finally letting it shine through. "You're a hero, Jun."

The pain on Jun's face darkened into something more akin to anger. "No, I'm not. I'm nothing like a hero, just an ex-grunt trying to set things straight in a tilted universe."

Theo inched closer and smoothed the scowl line between his brows away with his thumb. He cupped the side of Jun's face and let his voice drop low between them. "Don't you see? That is precisely what a hero would say."

Jun's lashes fluttered shut for a brief, sweet moment as he leaned into Theo's hand. And then he pulled away with a sharp inhale. "Come on. I'm getting you out of here."

Theo dug in his heels when Jun attempted to tug him by the hand. "What? Where am I going? Why?"

The force of Jun's sigh lifted his broad shoulders in a way that might have been distracting if Theo did not possess laser focus and an iron will.

Alright, so it was slightly distracting.

"As charming as your endless inquisitiveness usually is, I don't have time for it right now."

All traces of anger fled beneath the sheer driving force of his joy at the praise. Theo bounced on his toes and shoved his hair out of his face to better look up into Jun's. "You find me to be charming? Really? Tell me more."

The shadow of a smile passed over Jun's face before he reverted to his scowl. He slammed his hand on the door panel that opened into the docking bay. "Get in the dinghy. I'm sending Axel to take you home. I should never have brought you out here, into danger."

Theo peered in the doorway and then took a step back to lean against the bulkhead and cross his arms. "Hmm, no."

The sharp, precise way in which Jun turned to him sent a frisson of electricity up Theo's spine that he wanted to chase to the source. "What do you mean, no?"

Flicking an imaginary speck of dust from the wrist of his jacket, Theo affected a bored tone that had never failed to set his brother's teeth on edge. "Allow me to translate in plain Standard. No. I will not be going. I refuse."

Jun loomed over him, fists clenched, a muscle ticking in his jaw. It should not have been as alluring as it was. "I don't recall giving you a choice."

Theo scoffed as Jun wrapped a firm but careful hand around his arm and tugged him away from the wall. "Is this a reverse kidnapping? You're trying to send me back against my will? You are, truly, terrible at this, Jun. Just an abysmal abductionist. Don't get me wrong; I'm sure you have other talents I'm as yet unaware of. Baking, perhaps? Pianoforte? But, kidnapping? Not one of them. I would say you have ample room to improve in that arena."

Jun dragged him along a couple of steps, then halted with a low, frustrated growl. "Shut up and get in the dinghy."

Theo twisted and looped his arms around Jun's neck. He hooked one knee around Jun's thigh, tilted his head, and booped his nose against Jun's. "Make me."

It was as if a dam had broken. With a heavy grip beneath his thighs, Jun lifted Theo up and then slammed his back against the metal shell of the dinghy with just enough force to make his teeth rattle and his cock as hard as steel.

Jun swallowed his gasp with a heavy breath, hovering over Theo's lips, then dropped his face to Theo's throat. He sucked on a patch of skin, teeth skimming just right as Theo bucked his hips against his. Theo was so distracted he almost missed the words Jun started to growl against his neck. "Trying. I'm trying, but you—always—you—with your fucking mouth."

Theo dug his fingers into Jun's shoulders and arched back against the ship, already breathless with wanting. "You could always kiss me to shut me up."

The velvety fuzz of the shaved-close side of Jun's head tickled him under the chin. "That's not how I want to kiss you."

Theo let go of Jun's shoulders, grabbed the long fall of hair at the top of his head, and yanked him up to meet his shocked gaze. "I'm sorry. Did you just say that you want to kiss me?"

It was a good thing Theo had a tenacious grip with his thighs, because Jun might have dropped him otherwise. His mouth worked silently for a moment, and then he stammered out Theo's name, eyes as wide as Theo had ever seen them.

Theo wanted to scream. He wanted to jump for joy and also maybe bash Jun's head against the ship a little. "Jun. Are you serious? Because, I—"

The unwelcome buzz and whine of coms switching on overhead froze them both in place.

"Captain to the bridge! You'll want to see this. Bring Dr. Campbell."

Jun lowered him to the floor much less energetically than he had lifted him. He stepped away, clearing his throat as he tucked his mussed shirt into his trousers. At no point did he even attempt to meet Theo's piercing gaze.

Theo didn't bother to right himself beyond skimming a hand through his hair to shake it out. "Well, Captain, it appears your plan to be rid of me will have to wait. How tragically inconvenient for you."

Jun squared his shoulders to meet his glare head-on, hands held at his side as if they were preparing for a duel at twenty paces. "I'm trying to keep you safe. I don't want to be rid of you."

There was little Theo could do about the unruly celebration of those words clamoring around his head, sending a rush of relief through his chest, so he chose to ignore it. He put some bite in his words, teeth snapping.

"No? Then, tell me, what do you want with me, exactly? Because it seems you'd quite like to kiss me, despite your blasted rules. I'm beginning to suspect you have tender feelings for me beyond that of a convenient bedwarmer, and your continued silence on the matter does nothing to uphold your lofty ideals. Valor, indeed."

Not long ago, he had witnessed Jun face several armed men with less visible trepidation than he did this conversation.

"Theo—I—"

"Now, Captain!"

They both winced at Boom's distorted voice shouting overhead. The mechanical squeal of the coms shutting off went through Theo's head like a spike.

He gave Jun two more breaths to say something, and then he threw his arms up in exasperation. "Oh, sod this. I'm heading back. You can stay here and wade through your bottled-up emotions on your own, Captain Park."

Jun gave him several paces' distance before following after.

Chapter Twenty-Five

Boom fixed Theo with a long, hard stare when he entered the bridge, scanning him from top to toes, and then she gave a huff and went back to her screens.

Jun walked in with his shoulders back, not even glancing Theo's way as he went directly to Boom's console. "What is it? Security breach?"

She shook her head, dark curls bouncing as she tapped on one screen to make it larger and zoomed in on a low-quality vid feed. "Not exactly. Got a ping. Facial recognition code for Dr. Campbell. Something's screwy, but it's only off by a small margin. Take a look at this. It's a live feed."

Jun leaned over the feed, and then pivoted to give Theo the same scanning treatment. His face was guarded as it hadn't been since they'd left the dinghy to board his ship. "Explain this."

Theo was just as puzzled as everyone else. Why in the stars would a live vid feed send his code? Unless—

But that would be impossible, right?

"Out of the way, let me see." Theo squinted at the grainy feed, heart jumping into his throat with instant recognition. Drumming impatient fingers on Boom's arm, he hip checked Jun farther out of his field of view. "Can't you make it any larger? I need to know if it's— Oh stars! It is, it's him! But how?"

Boom worked steadily on the picture quality, the vid feed stretching and zooming in jerky increments until the figures moving across the screen became as clear as possible.

Undeniable.

Theo swatted Jun on the shoulder, ignoring the glare he received in response. "It's really Ari! Look, Jun, that's my twin brother! Where is this; can you find the origin? Why is he out here? This must be coming from beyond the Verge, correct? How could my sweet Ari possibly get all the way out to the Restricted Sector? He once had to take a breathing break because we needed to frequent a different post office than our usual."

He finally turned to Jun when he got no response, taken aback by Jun's slack-jawed, shocked expression. "You have a twin?"

They didn't have time for this. Ari was alone somewhere out in deep space, for some unfathomable reason. Ari was as gentle and timid as he was level-headed. He needed Theo to jump in and save him. This was the time for action.

He flapped his hand in Jun's face to convey the urgency of the situation, bones itching with the need to do something. "Yes, of course, which should be obvious by now from our very close resemblance, do keep up. I know I've mentioned Ari to you before, Jun."

A small line appeared down the center of Jun's forehead as he thought very deeply about something that, frankly, Theo did not have time for right now. "I thought— I thought Ari was your husband."

Boom recoiled from the console with a soft hiss. "Yikes."

Axel and Marco spoke over each other from the pilot's chair and over the static-bitten coms:

"Shit, Park."

"Oh, Captain. That's tragic."

A bubble of affront rose above the seething ocean of concern for his brother to pop in an explosion of words, index finger digging into Jun's solid chest. "I beg your pardon? You thought I was married? You genuinely thought I was a married man, who would comport myself in such a way with you? You insult me, Jun."

It wasn't the first time Theo had been assumed to be woven of loose moral fiber by one of his lovers, but it was the first time the assumption had hurt so badly. He felt a real connection with Jun, something deeper than physical attraction. He was even beginning to convince himself that his feelings might be returned.

Jun wrapped a careful hand around the finger drilling through his sternum, his face open and contrite. "Theo, I didn't—"

Yanking his hand out of Jun's grip, Theo spun back to the screen, teeth gritted. "No, I don't suppose that you did. I don't have time for this; can you find my brother, please? Quickly. He sets much stock in punctuality, and I would hate to be tardy for his rescue."

The light, jovial lilt to his words did little to disguise the way his voice shook, fear running ice-cold through his veins. He had never needed to fear for Ari before.

Ari was usually the brother one could depend upon to keep safe. To be sensible and solid and dependable. To stay put. Theo didn't care for the reversal of roles one iota.

He was going to have to murder Ari for putting him through this, once he was safe in Theo's arms.

Boom aimed a subtle, quick expression at Jun that did not bode well for Theo's nerves.

"What? Where is he? You've found it, haven't you? I can tell—" Theo tipped down closer to the screen with a gasp as Boom enhanced the image to show more detail. "Wait, that—that doesn't appear especially comfortable. Are those mag-cuffs? Is he being detained? Those don't seem to be Enforcers. Ari would never cross the law; he won't even jaywalk. What is going on, and who is *that*?"

He pointed at the large man being dragged along at Ari's side, his heavy boots scraping the floor. Ari walked close by with his head down, demure as ever. The occasional brushes of their limbs might have seemed accidental to anyone else, but Theo knew his brother. That was Ari seeking comfort. Or offering it.

Who was that man? Ari hardly touched anyone but Theo.

He had certainly never comforted anyone else.

Could it be? Had Ari finally fallen beneath the sway of Eros as he had bemoaned Theo doing time and again?

The man looked so rough, disheveled, and beaten bloody that Theo didn't know if he should hope for one way or the other.

Though he knew Ari favored men of a certain size, much as he tried to deny it—

Boom stepped back from the screen to consider Theo, one hand idly fiddling with a blade in her boot holster. "He's been picked up by Raiders. Him and his companion. You're sure you don't recognize him too? He's dressed like some Verge rat."

Theo hooked his fingers in Jun's belt to urge him closer, dread dropping through him like molten lead at Boom's tone. "No, I've never seen him before. That doesn't sound like particularly good news. Am I wrong in assuming one does not generally wish to be 'picked up by Raiders'?"

Jun's hand covered his on his belt, not to remove his grip but, rather, to cradle Theo's knuckles gently. "No. One—uh—you really don't."

It didn't take a doctorate in linguistics to understand the ominous undertone in Jun's few words. Theo straightened his shoulders with a deep, fortifying breath. "Well, then you know what we have to do, don't you? We must rescue him, with every element of haste. As soon as you can alter our heading."

Axel leaned back in his seat with a creak, hand hovering above his controls. "Orders, Captain?"

Jun didn't look away from the view screen in front of him, fingers on one hand tapping away unconcernedly as he slipped his other away from Theo's to pull up a swiftly scrolling stream of numbers that made Theo's eyes want to cross.

He twisted Jun's sleeve, an edge of desperation crawling over him as he watched the men on screen throw Ari into a dark room and shut the door. The despair on Ari's face as the door shut between him and his unconscious companion tore through Theo like claws through wet tissue, leaving him raw from the inside out.

"We have to save him, Jun! He has obviously gotten himself into a sticky situation. He never has had my flair for adventure, dear thing, I'm sure he's simply beside himself. I don't care what you say; I insist that we go there immediately and facilitate his heroic rescue." When Jun finally glanced at him with a slightly raised brow, Theo firmed his resolve. "No, no. I won't entertain any of your arguments to the contrary; we are going, and that is final!"

Jun shrugged the shoulder Theo was clinging to, then turned to him with an expression that reflected the sentiments of both of his knuckle tattoos. "Three hours. I altered our heading as soon as you recognized him."

It was a struggle for Theo not to drop to his knees and express his gratitude right there on the bridge.

Axel squawked, mouth dragging down in a petulant line around the string of candy dangling from it. "Captain, we've talked about this. Your override is for emergencies only. Just tell me to do it next time. Your flight codes are abysmal. I bet I can clean these up and get us there an hour sooner."

Two hours.

Just two hours, and Theo could see his brother again? He lost momentary control of his limbs in his excitement, wrapping them all around Jun like a clinging limpet.

It wasn't his imagination; Jun definitely wrapped both arms around Theo's back in turn, pressing warm and solid against him until tears sprang to Theo's eyes unbidden.

He dashed them away with a determined sniff as he pushed to stand on his own. He directed a winning smile in Boom's direction. "Now, I'll need to borrow a small arsenal to enact my rescue plan. Just a few of your detonators and a ray gun, for effect, if you please."

Jun scoffed behind him. "You have a plan?" he asked, using a tone that did nothing to indicate his support of Theo's mission.

Boom wasn't making any sort of move to provide Theo with the weapons he needed, so he decided to switch tactics.

He spun around to shine his smile on Jun, who froze beneath the manufactured brightness. "Of course, I have a plan! I'll simply arm myself, infiltrate the Raider ship, and retrieve my brother. And"—he squinted at the vid feed showing Ari's wounded companion being wrestled into too-small cuffs—"his paramour as well. It shouldn't be terribly complicated."

To his consternation, Jun started to laugh, and then he checked over Theo's shoulder, and Boom joined in with him, the pair of them practically rolling with laughter. Jun had to take three wheezing breaths before he could speak. "Oh, no, you're not setting foot on that ship."

Theo might have a preference for taking orders in the bedroom, but he refused to take such a senseless command at face value. "Yes, I am. If I don't board their ship, how am I going to rescue my brother and his friend?"

Jun didn't answer for a moment, busy switching out his ray gun for a newer model that Boom had stashed somewhere previously unseen. He looked up as he snapped his new weapon into place. "You're not going to rescue him. I am."

He accepted a detonator from Boom, leaving Theo to squint dubiously at her scant attire to determine where it had been kept. "And then, I'm sending you home."

Chapter Twenty-Six

He was building a wall out of hardened steel, ten sheets thick. Impenetrable by even the greenest, most intelligent eyes.

Jun would brick himself up into the wall until Theo had no choice but to go on his way and leave him behind.

So what if the wall made Jun feel like he was running out of air? Like he couldn't breathe at the prospect of losing Theo forever.

Forever probably wasn't going to be all that long for Jun anyway.

He could do this, bluster his way through a Crew of low-rate Raiders on the dregs of his old reputation, drop some credits he really couldn't afford, and bring back Theo's twin brother.

The only person Theo loved.

Jun could do that for him, and then he would let Theo go.

Because that was the right thing to do. The honorable thing.

He knew it was because it was the thing that hurt the most.

Pain was often a good indicator that his moral compass was pointed in the right direction, for once.

It wasn't difficult. The Raiders were a small Crew, not affiliated with anyone Jun needed to worry about. He would wager this had been their first successful Raid in a while. Striking low and easy, picking up a little Core scientist and his bumbling Verge boyfriend when their ship was out of order.

And, if he was a little rough in his dealings with them after seeing them lead a man who looked like Theo stumbling behind in mag-cuffs, well, that was his business.

Even having seen him on the vid feed, Theo's twin was a surprise.

Identical was an understatement.

Ari could have fooled anyone who hadn't looked into Theo's green eyes long enough to notice they were a slightly brighter shade, that his head was held at a jauntier angle, and his limbs were looser and more confident.

Then, of course, there was the hair. Where Theo's flowed wild and free, Ari's was cropped close to his head, disheveled by his misadventures but clearly meant to be neat and tidy.

Ari squinted dubiously at Jun with poorly disguised fear, the mouth Jun was so used to seeing wide open around a waterfall of words now pinched tight.

It was mindboggling to imagine the two contradictory brothers interacting. Jun couldn't wait to see it.

He kept up his full Captain Park act as he loaded them onto the dinghy and for the duration of the journey, savoring the anticipation of witnessing Theo's face light up when Jun delivered his twin safe and sound.

The bigger the buildup, the more spectacular the results, and if this was going to be the last time he saw

Theo's face, Jun was going to make sure it was spectacular.

The giant Verge rat had been a little harder to handle, for all that he staunchly remained at Ari's side. Jun would have been just as happy to leave him behind, if he could have borne the disappointment on Theo's face.

The man was clearly used to his size causing intimidation, but Jun knew that some of the most frightening people came in small packages. Barnes was short and stout, and Jun had never feared another man more.

When Jun docked the dinghy with Ari's shiny little ship in tow and opened the doors to Sylvia's cargo bay, the larger man busted out of his arm cuffs with unnecessary drama. He stepped in front of Ari and flourished the tiniest blade Jun had ever seen in his hamlike fist. Barely refraining from rolling his eyes at the man's posturing, Jun led them out into the cargo hold. He kept a careful eye on the Verge rat while he waited for Theo to arrive, an unfamiliar, bright emotion filling him at the expectation of Theo's joy.

He held his breath and kept his posture casual, trying not to reveal his building anticipation. If these were the last moments Jun would spend with Theo, at least he would get to see him rejoice at his brother's return. Jun could soak up the moment from afar, something he could hold on to in the dark, lonely days ahead.

It didn't take long before Theo careened into the bay, knocking over something that Jun could only hope was noncombustible.

For all their sakes.

Ari collapsed into Theo's arms, and Jun could sense the tension releasing from Theo's spine, the razor-sharp edge of anxiety he had kept carefully concealed all this time, melting away at a single touch.

It was as if, from the moment they saw each other, the twins fell back into roles so well-worn Jun could practically see the grooves.

He did his best to appear detached, steel wall holding steady, even as he took in Theo's explosive, contagious joy with greedy eyes and ears. Holding on tight to each moment with his stained hands.

The wall started to crumble when Theo turned his attention to Jun with full, fiery force, and Jun had to make his escape.

A tactical retreat, to regroup and rebuild those walls. He needed to tighten his resolve to send Theo away, to do the right thing. The painful, difficult thing. Jun walked away from the brothers' reunion to the rear of the dinghy, escaping unnoticed.

He cursed as he struggled with detaching the dinghy's hitch from Ari's ship. He needed to make sure it was ready for departure. If he was launching Theo into space, he was going to do it as safely as possible.

"Hey, watch it, now. You oughta treat a lady kindly if you're trying to get under her skirt like that."

Jun glared at the Verge rat—Ari had introduced him as Mr. Stone—who had followed him to the back of the dinghy. Stone was aptly named. He was already a stone in Jun's shoe, grinning at Theo's theatrics and dripping that syrupy Verge charm all over him. At least Jun wouldn't have to put up with him for long. Ari and his insufferable Mr. Stone would be gone as soon as Jun could shove them back on this little ship. Jun kicked the hitch open with the heel of his boot, ignoring a shout of protest.

Stone hurried over, clicking his tongue as though he were trying to soothe a child, and smoothed a loving hand over the small ship's hull. "Don't you worry, Delilah. I won't let the bad man hurt you again."

Jun got the feeling he was going to spend every brief moment in Stone's company attempting not to gag over that honey-mouthed Verge accent. He packed up the mag-hitch and shoved it back in the dinghy's hatch with a grunt while Stone cooed over the other ship. Jun slanted a skeptical glance at the man's bruised face. "You're a pilot?"

Stone cut off the simple little song he was singing to a hunk of metal and raked Jun over with a sharp gaze. "Sure am. Best on the Verge."

A dubious distinction, but it was better than sending Theo out on his own, just hoping he didn't press the wrong button and jettison himself. Jun kicked at the hatch until the lock clicked shut, ignoring Stone's sympathetic wincing. "You can make the jump back across?"

The Crew was going to kill him if Jun spent another hard-earned credit, but there was nothing he wouldn't pay to ensure Theo's safety. Verge pilots were notorious for overcharging, especially for their specialty services in crossing the Verge barrier without zapping their passengers into lumps of coal.

Jun would pay whatever Stone asked, and to make amends, Jun could let Boom use him for target practice at their next mandatory weapons training.

Axel would jump at the chance to hit Jun with a stun ray. Marco would miss on purpose. Boom would take him out at the knees.

It would be fine. Well worth it, to know Theo was safe.

Jun had known, as soon as he'd retrieved the twins' tiny ship, that his fate was sealed. Now, he could send Theo away on something more spaceworthy than the dinghy.

With a halfway decent pilot, even.

If he had been searching for an excuse to keep him here, Jun had run out of options.

Theo had translated enough of the code that Jun could probably work out the rest.

If he captured an entire linguistics department from another Core university.

He would have to worry about that later. For now, the priority was getting Theo off his ship and as far away from Jun as possible, before their affiliation became known.

Better to sever their growing attachment than to bring Theo down into the pit with him.

Because, once Barnes sniffed out a speck of weakness, he would strike.

And Theo was a glaring spotlight on everything soft that remained in Jun. Everything that he hadn't managed to burn away when he'd bitten down on a leather belt and screamed his way through Boom's hurried, unanesthetized disconnection of all his circuits. When he had detonated his former life and crawled his way free.

Jun had once thought there was nothing soft left among the pile of rubble inside of him, but Theo had pulled it out and dusted it off with a grin. Held it out with careful hands as if to say "See? You were only waiting for me, all along," with green eyes dancing. Just the thought of it sent a pang through Jun's chest.

And, as usual, Jun was left with no choice.

The only way to keep him safe was to make sure Barnes never caught sight of him, never marked Theo down as a weapon to be wielded with his trademark ruthless cruelty.

What was the saying? "If you love something, let it go"?

Jun had to let Theo go, because he—
There was a chance, that he—he might—
Love might be involved.

It was hard to see clearly under all the metaphorical dust flying off the surface of his heart as Theo cracked it open to crawl inside.

If this aching, yearning emotion that was eating Jun from the inside out was love, then he had never met a more destructive force or faced a more terrifying opponent.

And he had once battled a Raider in full mech with nothing but his bare hands and a broken chain for the amusement of his boss.

This feeling?

Much scarier.

Jun was about to demand Stone's price when the man spun on his heel and took off at Ari's sudden sharp cry. Jun followed after at Theo's answering shriek. The twins were right where they had left them, once in a loving embrace, now embroiled in a slapping, hair-pulling battle.

When Jun had imagined the twins' reunion, he had pictured something more tearful. Something less of a screeching brawl.

It was glorious.

During the dark, lonely weeks ahead, Jun was going to watch the vid feed of the fight over and over again, just to remember Theo at his wildest. At his best.

Theo was a blazing bundle of chaos, and Jun was going to miss him like sunlight on a deep-space mission.

Chapter Twenty-Seven

His scalp ached, his cheeks stung, and his left elbow twinged from landing on the metal floor. But the planet-sized hole in his chest had shrunk down to a manageable speck with Ari finally here by his side. Theo was so caught up in the joy of the moment, of discovering that he and his twin shared a love of adventure, and that Ari had finally found a man worth sacrificing a shred of his dignity for, that he forgot Jun's plan to send him away. Theo was too busy gleefully plotting his interruption of Ari's passionate interlude with his partner. He relished the reversal of roles after the countless times Ari had interrupted Theo with one of his paramours.

It was going to be splendid good fun, visiting upon Ari all of the torments he had put Theo through in his romantic endeavors. Theo couldn't wait to start.

Just as Orin Stone confessed his undying love for Theo's brother and announced that he wasn't going anywhere, Theo leaned in with a serious expression. He pitched his voice to break their concentration on each other.

"That's certainly good to hear, because we need your help."

The disappointed twist on Mr. Stone's rugged face made Theo giggle maniacally. His timing was impeccable, as ever.

Mr. Stone gave Theo a considering look as he tugged Ari close to his side. "What kind of help do y'all need?"

It was disconcerting to see Theo's prim and proper brother with this Verge tough. He almost couldn't fathom it, had always imagined Ari would end up with a quiet, boring academic by his side.

Something told Theo Mr. Stone was anything but boring.

Jun drew even with Theo, arms held in that loose cross he used when he wanted to display that he was armed, glaring at Mr. Stone. "I don't need your help—" He turned his glare to Theo. "—and there is no 'we.'"

Theo's blood was already up from fighting his twin. If Jun wanted to do this now, in front of Ari and his pilot and the watchful eyes of Boom's vid feed, then so be it. He stood toe-to-toe with Jun, lifting his chin with challenge and ignoring Ari's soft, worried gasp. "Yes, of course. Because you never need any help from anyone, right, Captain? Except, on occasion, when you are so desperate for help that you kidnap academics to assist you in your endeavors."

Jun scoffed, lips lifting in a sneer, but Theo continued before he could get a word in, pressing a firm hand to Jun's chest.

"And, as for the existence of a 'we.' It must have been my imagination a few hours ago when you had me up against that"—he pointed back at the dinghy—"hull, practically begging for me."

Jun loomed over Theo, wrapping a hand in his jacket.

Ari inhaled sharply at the move, and Theo vaguely registered his pilot reassuring him. He was too entranced by the flames dancing in Jun's eyes.

"If anyone was begging," Jun said, "it was you."

Theo batted his lashes, affecting a calculated pout that dropped Jun's gaze to his lips like clockwork. "Only because you like it so very much, Captain. I do try to cater to your unique preferences."

Releasing him with a snarl, Jun took a step back. He tossed up a rude gesture to the cameras, and Theo noticed for the first time that the coms were suspiciously silent. "Your brother's here. Your ship is here. You even have a pilot, if you can stomach that Verge smell."

The pilot in question growled, and Ari petted at his massive chest and cooed as though he were calming a horse. Theo would have found it amusing if he weren't steeped up to his eyebrows in righteous fury.

Theo pretended to check his nails, suppressing a smile at the way being ignored made Jun huff like a bull. "Did you have a point, or were you simply inspired to list my favorable circumstances?"

"You need to leave. Go back home to Britannia. Forget all of this." There was as much steel in Jun's voice as there was in the banged-up walls surrounding them.

The *forget me* wasn't spoken aloud, but it didn't have to be. It was clear enough.

All traces of amusement fled as Theo's heart dropped into his stomach with a dull thud. "I thought you needed my help. That only I could finish the translation. I thought you needed me."

I thought you wanted me. He didn't say it, but it was there in the tremble of his voice.

Jun's gaze darted over to their audience, then fixed on Theo. Jun curled over him in a semblance of intimacy as he lowered his volume. "Theo. You're incredible, and have already helped more than you can know—"

Theo grabbed onto Jun's hand, trying to pour every ounce of his sincerity in his face, to drown out the desperation he knew must be written there. "Then why would I leave? I know you must be tired of me, but I intend to see this through."

Slowly, sweetly, Jun's hand turned in his grip, lacing their fingers together. "I'm not tired of you. Not even close." He gazed down at Theo with stars in his eyes. "How could I tire of an ever-changing sky?"

Every word lifted Theo's heart back into place until he felt incandescent with strength and determination. "Well, then I have excellent news, Jun. I'm staying, and I'm going to help you see this through."

Jun blinked away the stars as he shook his head and released Theo's hand. "No. You have to leave; we're out of time."

Now that Theo knew for sure Jun had not tired of him, that his motivation stemmed from some as yet unrevealed self-sacrificing source, it was easy to resist. Effortless, really, to dig in roots and plant himself right where he wanted to be. Alongside Jun.

Theo focused narrowly on Jun's worried face, scanning the cracks in his stoic expression for points of access. "What about the holozite you intend to acquire? I suppose you have a laboratory on board to stabilize it?"

Jun turned his head away, mouth twisting unhappily at the corners under Theo's direct hit. "I'll cross that bridge when I come to it."

Nodding slowly, Theo pretended to contemplate that for a moment. He then held up his finger in a mock pose of discovery. "Or, you could simply ask one of the leading authorities on complex combustibles."

The lack of amusement Jun graced him with at that was nothing short of delightful, and Theo had to suppress a wriggle of glee at Jun's dry tone. "Great idea; I'll just go out and get one of those on my next run."

"Allow me to present to you—" Theo gestured to Ari, who startled as though he had forgotten he wasn't invisible. "—Dr. Aristotle Campbell, master geologist."

It was deeply satisfying to witness Jun's eyes widen with reluctant interest, snapping to take in Ari with renewed focus. "Geologist. But you'd need equipment to stabilize holozite. We don't have any."

Theo dug a jovial elbow into the solid muscle of Jun's stomach. "Did I fail to mention he has a fully equipped lab aboard our vessel?"

Really, Jun ought to have considered Theo with patent gratitude rather than teeth-grinding fury. "You didn't mention that."

Theo gave a loose-limbed shrug and took a few steps away as though preparing to board his ship after all. "Oh. Well, he does. But that wouldn't interest you, as you have no need of help, so I'll just tell him to pack it all up and head back to the Verge."

It was anything but a surprise to receive Jun's staying hand on his shoulder. "Alright. You win. He can help."

Theo accepted the hand as if they were dancing a waltz and turned into Jun's arms to pat him on the cheek. "How magnanimous of you. Truly, just astoundingly generous. However shall we thank you for your condescension to accept the assistance of two very well-regarded experts in their field?"

Ari made one of his small, squeaking Ari noises that meant he thought Theo was prevaricating but didn't want to call him out for it in public.

Theo sighed, dropping his hand with a reluctant gesture Ari's way. "Well, Ari is certainly well regarded. I'm generally well regarded until someone meets me in person. I tend to ruin whatever regard had been built up simply by virtue of my personality. Couldn't begin to tell you why."

Ari jumped in as loyally as ever. "Theo is renowned for his work in several prominent publications." He'd used the line to sell Theo to skeptical colleagues for years. It was as sweet as it was tiring to hear it, and know Ari considered that to be Theo's greatest, and only, accomplishment.

Theo muttered, "Yes, I do seem to come across much better on paper."

Caring, perceptive Ari sensed his deflation and offered a light touch to his elbow with a smile. "You're wonderful in person, as well, my dear. I shun the opinion of any who would disagree."

Theo caught his fingers with a swift squeeze, offering a smile of his own. "Thank you, darling. To be shunned by Dr. Aristotle Campbell is a dire fate indeed."

Mr. Stone leaned in, and Theo didn't miss the absent, familiar manner in which his hands fell to Ari's hips as his deep voice rumbled overhead. "I'd rather be bitten to death by warsnakes, myself."

Ari spun with a gasp to swat at Mr. Stone's chest indignantly. "Oh, don't say that, Orin!"

Theo had despaired of ever seeing his brother so happy; it lit a glow inside of him that tumbled out in laughter. "First names, Ari? My, my, it must be serious."

Ari aimed his stubborn chin Theo's way and the glow abated, subsumed by a rush of anger. "Don't think it escaped my notice that you have reached a similar level of familiarity with your Captain Park, Theo. We will be discussing that, I assure you."

He could feel Jun stiffening at his side, shifting with discomfort, and Theo rushed to prevent Ari from pushing too far. "There's nothing to discuss."

His brother rolled his eyes in a vulgar display of disbelief most uncharacteristic of his behavior in public. For the first time, Theo began to wonder whether this adventure had changed Ari in some permanent ways. The thought was nearly as intriguing as it was concerning. "Oh yes, there is," Ari responded. "For all I know, you have once again fallen beneath the sway of a dastardly fiend, and I shall not stand by in idleness while he takes deplorable advantage of your innocent and trusting nature!"

Jun made a choked sound at the word "innocent," but he was examining the ceiling when Theo turned a glare his way.

Ari continued in a soft, condescending tone so much like their mother that it set Theo's teeth on edge. "Theo, I mean no offense—"

"He only says that when he fully intends to offend me," Theo offered in an aside to Mr. Stone, who grinned in response as if their bickering was his favorite show.

Ari narrowed his eyes at Theo, hands planted firmly on his hips. "As I was saying"—his tone had lost a bit of its softness, hard edges pushing through—"I mean no offense, but you have not shown the best judgement in regards to your choices in romantic partners, historically."

Theo flung his hands out, smacking one into Jun's chest and eliciting a low grunt that was swiftly drowned out by Theo's raised volume. "One time! One time, I walked out with somebody who turned out to be a confidence man. We didn't need that month's allowance anyway, with my TA stipend. You must admit, Ari, that his mustache was very handsome. Had he been a foot taller and twice as wide, you would have given him a second glance and you know it."

Ari pinched the bridge of his nose, eyes falling shut while he counted to three under his breath. It was a funny little tic of Ari's that often cropped up when he was speaking to Theo. He finally dropped his hand with a sharp inhale, pinning Theo with his gaze. "I know no such thing. My point is that we can hardly trust you to be an excellent judge of character when it comes to love."

Jun's brows shot up as he glanced down at Theo and then quickly away as he directed his gaze back to the ceiling, a suspect wash of color tinting his high cheekbones.

Theo blew a lock of hair out of his face, his chest clenching at Jun's obvious discomfort.

Unrequited love was awful; Theo found little to recommend it.

"Oh fiddlesticks, Ari. Captain Park has, with the exception of his initial abduction, behaved most admirably."

He had nearly forgotten how amusing it was to watch Ari sputter with indignation.

"With the exception of— Theo, this man held you captive! He abducted an innocent person from their office, and—"

Theo cut in with a smirk, "Come, now. I would wager neither one of us has much claim to innocence any longer—" He tossed a wink to Mr. Stone, who, to his absolute delight, winked back at him. "—wouldn't you agree?"

Jun didn't seem to appreciate the exchange, his focus whipping to Mr. Stone with a chill Theo could sense over his shoulder.

It was just as amusing to watch Ari go bright red as it was humiliating when it happened to himself. His twin squawked with offended dignity and turned to Mr. Stone with wide, shocked eyes. "Why—I can't believe he would— The very nerve!"

Mr. Stone smoothed one big, rough hand gently over Ari's uncharacteristically mussed hair and settled it across the back of his neck with a squeeze, eyes sparkling. "He's got a point, baby. We've been pretty thorough."

"Orin!"

Theo had never known just how satisfying it would be to hear Ari screech someone else's name in outrage. He decided, right then and there, that he and Mr. Orin Stone were going to be great friends.

Chapter Twenty-Eight

"Are you going to introduce us to our new guests, or are we supposed to stay in the naughty corner until you let us out?"

Ari jolted and grabbed onto both Orin and Theo as Axel's voice buzzed overhead. The coms clicked off with a squeal, then clicked on again almost immediately after, Marco's mild voice wafting through. "I cringed at that, Captain. I vote for a fine."

Ari slowly started to relax, losing his vise grip, but Axel returned at twice Marco's volume.

"Treachery and lies, Captain! Marco just wants you to fine me because he's hoping the cringe bank will fund new parts."

Jun avoided Ari and Orin's curious gazes, glaring instead at the camera in the corner while Marco offered his response.

"Okay, yeah, but. I still cringed, and—"

"Enough! Everyone to the bridge, we're coming up." Jun growled at Axel's "oh, goody!" and stalked off in the direction of the door. He paused just before the bend in the crates, where he would disappear from sight, to find Theo over his shoulder. "Bring your friends."

He took off, leaving Theo behind to corral his brother and newfound friend through the ship.

Theo took Ari's hand in his, frowning at how cold it was. He chafed it gently between his palms as he led him after Jun. Mr. Stone followed so closely that Theo could feel his massive presence at his back, like a wall.

After a skeptical glance at the dented lift doors, Ari entered and held tightly to Theo as they rode up to the bridge. He whispered in his ear, "Do you trust these people?"

Theo gave his hand a squeeze and bumped their shoulders together, exactly the right height to line up perfectly. "Much to my astonishment, I absolutely do. They're loyal, hardworking, and they care about one another. I couldn't ask for more in a colleague or friend."

Ari's innate sweetness beamed through his small, sincere smile, and Theo absorbed it like a plant basking in the sun. "I'm delighted to hear that you've made good friends, Theo. You deserve it."

Mr. Stone wedged himself in front of them as the door slid open, feet braced against the floor as if he were expecting an attack.

Turning to them, Jun assessed his stance with a slowly raised brow, then jerked his head toward the bridge. "Come on; might as well get this over with. Apologies in advance—they're barely house-trained. Especially Axel."

The Crew stood in a jagged little line in front of Jun's console. Marco's calm face split the difference between Axel's open curiosity and Boom's suspicious stare.

Axel let out a long, low whistle, examining Ari as though he were some new variety of snack that might or might not be poisonous. "Whoa, that's creepy. You guys are, like, twin-twins. Super, crazy identical. Please don't murder us in our beds."

He flinched as both Jun and Mr. Stone took a menacing step toward him, both of them frowning to varying degrees. "Oh, shit! Now Park's pissed off in stereo." He swiftly aimed a wavering grin in the twins' direction. "Sorry, guys. You're totally not creepy."

Laughing at that, Theo noticed Ari's wounded expression and released his hand to hook their arms together. He couldn't stop touching his brother, just to feel that he was real, and solid, and there. "Don't mind him, Ari. Axel might be a fine pilot, but he has even less control over running his mouth than I do."

Ari's "That seems improbable" was overshadowed by Mr. Stone's sudden, keen interest in Axel.

"You're the pilot for this giant heap of metal?"

Marco dug an admonishing elbow into Axel's side as he burst into giggles.

"Sure as shootin', partner," he finally got out. "Boy, that Verge accent is strong, huh? Sounds like you've got a mouth full of gruel."

To Theo's astonishment, Ari let him go to surge forward. He stood between Axel and Mr. Stone with his hands on his hips. "Mr. Stone is as eloquent as any Outlier, and displays significantly better manners." His voice dripped icy hauteur in every word. "You will treat him with the respect he deserves."

Boom reached around Marco to flick Axel on the stomach with one of her metallic fingers. She relaxed her rigid stance and leaned back against the console. "He's feisty. I like him."

Rubbing his belly with an exaggerated pout, Axel turned to Jun. "You know, Captain, we can't help but notice an emerging trend. Every time you leave the ship on your own, you come back with a red-headed Doll. This one even brought along a giant cowboy accessory. We want to put it out there that you don't have to keep every one of them. Maybe we could implement some kind of a catch-and-release program."

"Shut up, Axel."

Theo raised his eyebrows at Jun as they spoke quickly and simultaneously.

Mr. Stone tugged Ari back against him with a gentle hand on his hip. The fact that Ari allowed such public physical familiarity was almost as mind-boggling as the naked adoration on Ari's face when Mr. Stone spoke. "Thanks, sugar. You're my knight in shining armor."

Lifting one of Mr. Stone's scarred hands to his lips, Ari gave him a gallant kiss. After a kiss of his own, Orin ambled over to Axel's console and sat in his chair with an ominous creaking of overtaxed metal. With a yelp, Axel hurried over to complain, which Mr. Stone proceeded to ignore, working the controls with a grin.

Ari focused his attention back on Theo. "You requested our help?"

Also turning from the bickering pilots, Jun chose to address Ari's inquiry. "What do you know about holozite?"

There was a subtle and distinct change in Ari's carriage when he spoke on his favorite topics, an authority that entered his voice and never failed to capture the attention of his audience. It was how he captivated entire lecture halls of students he would have stammered his way through a private conversation with. "It's as geochemically complex as it is scarce. And, much like tantalum, it's illegal to transport within the Core, due to its volatile technical capabilities. I've only had the opportunity to work with it in a heavily monitored university setting."

Ignoring the heat of Jun's frown, Marco leaned in to interrupt. "You're a materials scientist?"

Ari drew himself up to his full height with a tug of his waistcoat, fatigue melting away at the mere mention of rocks. Stars, but Theo loved his brother. "I'm primarily a geologist, with some experience in cosmochemistry."

Irritated with Ari's lack of confidence and perpetual modesty, Theo scoffed. His brother was a genius, and he should show it. "When he says 'some experience,' he means he has achieved multiple degrees in the subject and introduced groundbreaking research."

Marco looked a little starstruck, taking in Ari with newfound appreciation while Ari blustered and blushed.

"Well, yes," he said, "but I've only earned doctorates in geology."

"Two doctorates. He's brilliant," Theo cut in, chest puffed with pride while Ari sent him embarrassed, pleading glances.

Marco's leg locked with a click when he leaned his weight back on it, shaking his head in obvious relief. "Oh man, that's awesome because I've been fiddling with this new ratio in my fuel booster, and it'd be great if you could help me confirm that it's not going to blow up the ship. I've just been crossing my fingers that my equations are solid."

Boom groaned his name as she covered her face as Jun treated Marco to the full force of his scowl.

"Were you ever planning to mention that concern to, say, your captain?"

He didn't even pretend to feel bad about it, shaking his head blithely this time. "Nope. Figured you'd yell at me. I'd rather get blown up."

Ari rushed to intercept whatever Jun's scathing response might have been. "I would be happy to assist you, Mr...." He trailed off with a pointed look at Theo.

Theo slapped himself on the forehead, blaming his forgetfulness on the butterflies still fluttering through his bloodstream at the relief of having Ari with him once more. "Forgive me; I've abandoned my manners entirely. Crew, this is Dr. Aristotle Campbell and his companion, Mr. Stone. Ari, this is the Crew. Axel's the pilot, and you can just ignore everything he says—"

"Hey!"

"—This is Marco, ship engineer, and apparently, your latest admirer. And this is Boom, formidable security expert and Marco's sister. I think we should all get along famously, don't you agree?"

Boom appeared skeptical, but poor Marco might as well have had angels and hearts floating around his head.

Extending one of his awkward little bows in the general direction of the Crew, Ari said, "Charmed to make your acquaintance."

Marco rushed to leave the bridge, tripping on his organic leg as he skirted around Jun. "I'll go get you a sample, and we can check it out, okay?"

Ari didn't have time to answer before Marco was gone, humming jauntily as he hurried to the lift.

Chapter Twenty-Nine

With his brother momentarily distracted, Theo snagged Jun by one of the heavy leather straps of his holster. "Come along with me."

Jun squinted at Theo with a confused wrinkle of his forehead that reached right into Theo's chest and hurt him with how cute it was. "Why?"

Smoothing a hand across the strap, Theo threw his hair back over his shoulder. "I suppose we could do this here, if you'd rather, but I intend to finish our conversation. I'm not letting you off the hook just because you abandoned your plan to be rid of me."

When Boom snickered behind them, Jun took off down the corridor without another word, Theo in tow by the hand hooked in his strap.

The restless drumming of Theo's fingers echoed hollowly in the lift, the only sound as he organized his thoughts, wanting to be as clear and coherent as possible. It was time to be blunt. Direct. Theo's feet hurt from all this dancing around the thing that had grown between them.

Jun stood stiffly by his side, facing the door with a grim expression as if he expected it to slide open and reveal his doom.

One would think Theo had asked him to cut himself open rather than to talk about his feelings.

Though, for Jun, perhaps the two were more alike than one might suppose.

Jun led them to Theo's bunk, and Theo couldn't help but wonder if it was a strategic choice to ensure that Jun could have a place to escape to afterward. In case the room became saturated with emotion, or something.

After closing the door, Jun hovered, crossing and uncrossing his arms as he rocked back on his heels. It was as close to jittery as Theo had ever seen him, tough shell cracked open to reveal the turmoil within. "Well? I'm listening."

Theo tucked his hair behind his ears, taking a deep breath to ground himself before he started. He examined Jun's face, registering every twitch as he put up his walls and plastered over the cracks. "Do you know that the study of languages includes much that remains unspoken? Body language, facial cues, eye contact. Gestures and actions and, simply, priorities. You have been telling me how you feel all along."

It wasn't even subtle, the way Jun's eyes widened in obvious distress.

Theo rushed to reassure him of his expectations. He wouldn't ask Jun to change for the sake of Theo's ego. Jun was perfect as he was. "You're a man of few words, and I'm a man of many, so I suppose it falls to me to make the leap. Jun, I lo—"

Jun stumbled forward with the gasping sound of a man coming up for air and gripped Theo lightly by the arms. "Wait! You don't—Theo, you don't understand. I'm not safe. You won't be safe, with me. I can't ask that of you. I won't ask that of you."

Of course he wouldn't. It wasn't in his nature, annoyingly self-sacrificing as he was. Trust Jun to run away from the things he most wanted at full speed.

Theo brought a hand up to his face and traced over the lines of ink that crept up his jaw. The lines that decorated Theo's dreams. "I don't care that you're not asking, because I'm telling you. I love you, Jun. I don't expect to hear it back; I know you have bigger things on your mind. But I wanted to tell you." His heart skidded around the corner and slammed into the wall of his chest at the confession.

Dark molten eyes watched him, entire galaxies swimming in their depths as Jun tightened his grip on Theo's arms.

Swallowing against the unwelcome lump in his throat, Theo continued, "I can finish the translation elsewhere, if you truly wish for me to leave." He drew a shuddering breath as Jun's lips parted, face stricken. "As long as I remain on this side of the Verge, I can transfer the data to you over secure lines. My brother can take whatever you need aboard our ship to work on in his lab. Our assistance can be done remotely, if you are simply finished with me."

It wasn't the longest romantic entanglement of Theo's life, but it was certainly the deepest. Uprooting Jun from his heart would leave massive, tunneling scars, but he would do it. If that's what Jun wanted from him.

Theo had been a little bit selfish all his life, carefree and, sometimes, thoughtless of others. He had never offered such a personal sacrifice to anyone but his brother. But, for Jun, Theo would release the yearnings of his heart and accept the loss with grace.

For Jun, Theo could think about the needs of someone else before himself.

After a few more seconds of silence, he began to fear he would shake apart and float out into space if Jun didn't give a response. Finally, the dam burst, and Theo blurted out his thoughts, everything in him focused on Jun's troubled face. "Please say something, Jun. I'll graciously accept whatever your choice, but I can't wait in suspense a moment longer. So, please just, say something."

"Copper."

Theo drew back a bit in disbelief, wrinkling up his nose as he repeated back the word.

Jun appeared just as surprised as he was. A deep flush stole across Jun's cheeks as he did an excellent impression of a mortified goldfish before stammering out the rest. "You asked, once. About my favorite color. It's copper."

A sharp, resplendent bolt of joy struck Theo right through the center as he listened to everything Jun was saying with his face, and body, and nonsensical words. "You said it was black."

Jun wet his lips, then shook his head and fingered a strand of Theo's hair. "It's copper. I just didn't know that, yet."

It was the most romantic thing a man had ever said to Theo, and he had once gone walking with a poet who had described his toes as rosebuds.

That was, perhaps, not the best comparison, but Theo had little control over his wild thoughts. Everything was careening at double speed inside his head.

Inside his heart.

He bumped his head against Jun's hand where he gently grasped his hair, unable to contain the joy bubbling up in his slowly spreading smile. "Jun, are you asking me to stay?"

The relief that washed over Jun's face at Theo's prompting made Theo want to wrap him up in blankets and hold him close. Forever, if possible.

"Yes." Jun spoke as if he had been shoved to the end of a gangplank and faced shark-infested waters if he didn't get his words out in time.

It took discipline, but Theo just watched him expectantly, letting the silence stretch out like taffy until it was thin enough to snap, the whole time Jun's face creasing with the effort of expressing himself.

"Stay with me."

Theo held his breath, still waiting even as he rocked up on the tips of his toes, feeling like he might vibrate out of his skin.

Abruptly releasing Theo's hair, Jun shoved one of his own sleeves up past the elbow to reveal a flash of red. It was Theo's garter, tied securely around his arm. A tidal wave of fondness swept Theo away at the sight. Had Jun been wearing it ever since? Carrying it with him like a knight's token?

After teasing the knot free, Jun held the ribbon in one hand while he plunged the other into his pocket to retrieve a balled-up handkerchief with rusty stains and—

Theo's initials monogrammed on the corner.

With a shaky breath, Jun uncurled his hand to let the handkerchief fall open around a tiny wire star. He then draped the ribbon beside it.

He offered it all to Theo on his palm, the silk crushed where it had been coarsely tied and the star misshapen from handling. His voice dragged soft and slow like a hand down Theo's spine, his gaze caught so close to his there was no prying them apart. "I love you, Theo. Please stay."

In his dreams, Theo had listened for those words a thousand times over, but never—not once—had they reached his ears.

It was indescribable, the bright flash of light inside of him, the warm glow that settled in his chest. The sudden serenity, as though the ravenous, starving beast that wailed inside of him was finally put to rest.

He laughed through the tears welling up and reached out to cup Jun's face with trembling hands. "Of course. Of course I'll stay. I would love nothing better than to be with you. You have me, Jun, wherever you may go. Whatever you must do."

Jun slid his fistful of tokens into Theo's pocket and gathered him in his arms. All traces of nervousness had vanished, his embrace strong and face raw with desire. "And you have me."

Taking a firm hold of Jun's shoulders, Theo stretched up tall, lifted by hope and love and the answering emotions on Jun's face.

Would he—? Now, surely? Oh, please—

Jun's lips fell on his like a benediction.

The kiss was barely deserving of the name, composed of sharp teeth and hot breath and very little in the way of softness.

It was bliss.

Theo had always loved kissing, but there had been nothing like this before.

This was no slow, sweet gentleman's kiss; this was like being boiled alive from the inside and loving every second of it.

Jun's lips were plush and gentle, brooking no argument as he used them to coax Theo's mouth open, to let his clever tongue press inside.

He caressed the contours of Theo's lips, then traced the edge of his teeth with a rumble in his chest that made Theo weak at the knees.

Theo gave a small, pleading sound, and Jun lifted him from the ground, then strode toward the bed.

They didn't break apart even as he set him down on the mattress. Jun crawled after him, and they panted into each other's mouths rather than pausing for breath. Entirely wrapped up in each other, in the moment.

Kissing Jun was amazing.

It was so good that Theo was perfectly willing to ignore the sudden blare of a ship-wide alarm. He whined in protest when Jun sat up with a heartfelt curse.

The coms buzzed on, and Boom shouted over the sirens.

"Captain, get your ass up here! Barnes is demanding to speak with you, and we would all super appreciate it if he didn't blow the ship to smithereens."

Jun adjusted himself in his pants with a grimace before he stood and offered a hand to Theo.

He helped him up with care, his gentle attention at odds with the blaring sirens and flashing lights all around them. The lights glinted off his sardonic eyes as he arched a brow at Theo. "This is what it means to be with me. Are you sure you're ready for it?"

Theo dropped a swift kiss on Jun's swollen lips and bounded past him to the door. He grinned over his shoulder as he stepped out into the corridor beneath a halo of strobing red light.

"Adventure calls, Captain. Try to keep up."

Glossary

AUGMENTS–physical augmentations popular in the RS (Restricted Sector) including but not confined to: bionic appendages, sensory enhancements, functional tattoos that connect to the stream.

BRITANNIA–Core planet, Ari and Theo's home world.

CHIP–physical currency used both within and beyond the Verge.

CORE–the inner circle of planets protected by the Verge. Includes Britannia, Ari and Theo's home world.

DEEP DARK–slang for ungoverned open space outside of the barrier of the Verge.

DISCONNECTS–those living in the RS without augments, a small minority.

DOLLS–slaves, usually of a sexual nature, originating from Core planets and traded like collectibles within the RS.

DREI X–small planet in the Wastes of the RS.

ENFORCERS–Core military and law enforcement.

GORYEO–Core planet, Jun's birthplace.

IDENT–short for identity. An electronic payment system based on body codes such as fingerprint or retinal scan, commonly used in the Core.

MIST–recreational drug in the RS.

OUTLIER–anyone born outside of the Verge, residing in the Restricted Sector.

PATCH–language spoken in the Restricted Sector.

RAIDERS–lawless space pirates, usually found in the deep dark, sometimes part of larger Crews, or crime syndicates back in the RS. Often involved in supplying the mines with indentured servants, or running the Doll or Mist trade.

REGENERATION FLUID–aka regen. Accelerates healing, commonly used in the Core and RS, scarce resource along the Verge colonies and the deep dark.

RESTRICTED SECTOR–aka the RS. Populated planets and colonies located beyond the barrier of the Verge. They have been cut off from the Core for centuries.

SINGER–informant, Verge colonial slang.

SONIC–alternative method of cleaning without using water.

STATION–space stations, common in the RS.

STREAM–RS version of the internet, not available within the Verge.

VERGE–a physical energy barrier enclosing the Core planets and surrounding colonies. Also refers to the colonies themselves which line the inner curve of the barrier. The closer to the barrier, the fewer the resources and the lower the social standing.

VERGE COLONIES–settlements along the asteroid belt lining the interior wall of the Verge, circling the inner Core. Limited resources, similar to frontier life.

VERGE RAT–pejorative term for Verge colonists born outside of the Core.

WASTES–an area of the RS that has been ravaged by marauding Raiders and Crews.

About the Author

A.C. Thomas left the glamorous world of teaching preschool for the even more glamorous world of staying home with her toddler. Between the diaper changes and tea parties, she escapes into fantastical worlds, reading every romance available and even writing a few herself.

She devours books of every flavor—science fiction, historical, fantasy—but always with a touch of romance because she believes there is nothing more fantastical than the transformative power of love.

Email
acthomasbooks@gmail.com

Facebook
A.C. Thomas

Twitter
@acthomas_books

Website
www.acthomasbooks.com

Instagram
www.instagram.com/acthomasbooks

Tumblr
www.acthomasbooks.tumblr.com

Other NineStar books by this author

The Verge Series
Restricted

Burying the Hatchet

Coming Soon from A.C. Thomas

Shattered

The Verge, Book Three

The action continues in *Shattered*, the exciting third book in *The Verge* series. Follow Ari, Orin, Theo, and Jun as they work together, through adversity and adventure, while saving a couple of worlds in the process. Coming to you in 2022!

Also Available from NineStar Press

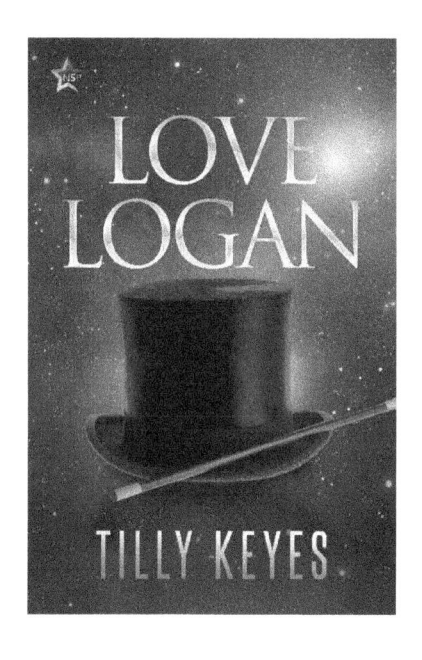

Connect with NineStar Press

www.ninestarpress.com

www.facebook.com/ninestarpress

www.facebook.com/groups/NineStarNiche

www.twitter.com/ninestarpress